PURE HEAT

A Firehawks Novel

M.L. BUCHMAN

sourcebooks
casablanca

Published by Sourcebooks Casablanca, an imprint of Sourcebooks, Inc.
P. O. Box 4410, Naperville, Illinois 60567-4410
(630) 961-3900
Fax: (630) 961-2168
www.sourcebooks.com

Printed and bound in Canada.
MBP 10 9 8 7 6 5 4 3 2 1

Dedicated to the man who led me time and again among the trees: my father.

Firehawk *n*.
A Sikorsky UH-60M Black Hawk helicopter refitted for firefighting operations.

On Earth, something is always burning!
            —NASA "Fire and Smoke" website

Every fire mentioned here, except those fought by the characters of this book, was real.

Chapter 1

STEVE "MERKS" MERCER HAMMERED DOWN THE LAST half mile into the Goonies' Hoodie One camp. The Oregon-based Mount Hood Aviation always named its operation bases that way. Hood River, Oregon—hell and gone from everything except a whole lot of wildfires.

Foo Fighters roared out of the speakers, a piece from his niece's latest mix to try and get him out of his standard eighties "too retro" rock and roll. With the convertible top open, his hair whipped in the wind a bit. Hell, today it could be pouring rain until his hair was even darker than its normal black and he wouldn't care. It felt so damn good to be roaring into a helibase for the first time in a year.

Instead of rain, the sun shone down from a sky so crystalline blue that it was hard to credit. High up, he spotted several choppers swooping down toward the camp. A pair of Bell 212 Twin Hueys and a little MD500, all painted the lurid black with red flames of Mount Hood Aviation, just like his car. He'd take that as a good omen.

He let the tail of his classic Firebird Trans Am break loose on the twisting dirt road that climbed through the dense pine woods from the town of Hood River, perched on the banks of the mighty Columbia and staring up at Mount Hood.

This was gonna be a damn fine summer.

Helibase in the Oregon woods. Nice little town at the foot of the mountain. Hood River was big enough to boast several bars and a pair of breweries. It was also a big windsurfing spot down in the Gorge, which meant the tourists would be young, fit, and primed for some fun. The promise of some serious sport for a footloose and fancy-free guy.

And fire.

He'd missed the bulk of last summer.

He hammered in the clutch, downshifted to regain control of his fishtail, and did his best to ignore the twinge in his new left knee.

Steve had spent last summer on the surgeon's table. And hated every goddamn second he'd been away from the fight. It sure hadn't helped him score much, either. "I used to be a smokejumper until I blew out my knee." Blew up his knee would more accurate since they'd barely saved the leg. Either way, the pickup line just didn't sweep 'em off their feet the way you'd like. Compare that with, "I parachute into forest fires for the fun of it." Way, way better.

And never again.

He fouled that thought into the bleachers with all the force he could muster and punched the accelerator hard.

Folks would be milling around at the camp if those choppers meant there was an active fire today. As any entrance made was worth making properly, Steve cranked the wheel and jerked up on the emergency brake as he flew into the gravel parking lot.

A dozen heads turned.

He planted a full, four-wheel drift across the lot and fired a broad spray of gravel at a battered old

blue-and-rust Jeep as he slid in
perfect parallel-parked stop. B
sucker owned the Jeep had tak
and doors. Steve had managed t
enough to land some on the seat.

He settled his wrap-around Porsche Design sunglasses solidly on the bridge of his nose and pulled on
his autographed San Francisco Giants cap. The four
winning pitchers of the 2012 World Series had signed
it. He only wore it when appearances really mattered.
Wouldn't do at all to sweat it up.

He hopped out of the car.

Okay, his brain imagined that he hopped out of
the car.

His body opened the door, and he managed to swing his
left leg out without having to cup a hand behind the knee.
Pretty good when you considered he wasn't even supposed to be driving a manual transmission yet. And he'd
"accidentally" left his cane at the roadside motel room
back in Grants Pass where he'd crashed into bed last night.

So done with that.

Now he stood, that itself the better part of a miracle,
on a helibase and felt ready to go.

He debated between tracking down a cup of coffee or
finding the base commander to check in. Then he opted
for the third choice, the radio shack. The heartbeat of
any firebase was its radio tower, and this one actually
had a tower. It looked like a very short fire watchtower.
Crisscrossed braces and a set of stairs led up to a second-
story radio shack with windows and a narrow walkway
all around the outside. All of the action would funnel
through there for both air and ground crews.

...terior wooden staircase led in switchbacks up ...shack. The staircase had a broad landing midway ...t gave him an excuse to stop and survey the scene. And rest his knee.

He could have done worse. Much worse.

Hoodie One helibase was nestled deep in the Cascade Mountains just north of Mount Hood. From here, he could see the icy cap of the eleven-thousand-foot-high dormant volcano towering above everything else in the neighborhood. A long, lenticular cloud shadowed the peak, a jaunty blemish in the otherwise perfect blue sky.

The air smelled both odd and right at the same time. The dry oak and sage smell of his native California had been replaced with wet and pine. You could smell the wet despite the hot summer sun. At least he supposed it was hot. Even in early summer, Oregon was fifteen to twenty degrees cooler than Sacramento in the spring. Sometimes the California air was so parched that it hurt to breathe, but here the air was a balm as he inhaled again.

Ah, there.

He inhaled again deeply.

Every wildfire airbase had it, the sting of aviation fuel and the tang of retardant overridden with a sheen that might be hard work and sweat. It let him know he'd come home.

The firebase had been carved into a high meadow bordered by towering conifers. Only the one dirt road climbing up the hills from the town a half-dozen miles below. A line of scrungy metal huts, a rough wooden barracks, and a mess hall that might have been left over from a summer camp for kids a couple decades back.

You certainly didn't visit firefighting bases for the luxury of it all.

You came here for the fire. And for what lay between the radio tower on which he perched and the grass-strip runway.

A couple of small fixed-wing Cessnas and a twin-prop Beech Baron were parked along the edge. They'd be used for spotter and lead planes. These planes would fly lead for each run of the big fixed-wing air tankers parked down at the Hood River airport or flying in from other states for the truly big fires.

Then there was the line of helicopters.

The 212s and the MD500 he'd spotted coming in were clearly new arrivals. Crews were pulling the big, orange Bambi Buckets from the cargo bays and running out the lines for the 212s. The MD500 had a built-in tank. Someone crawled under the belly of each of the 212s and hooked up the head of the long lead line used to carry the bucket two hundred feet below the bird and the controls to release the valve from inside the helicopter.

There must be a fire in action. Sure enough. He could see the refueling truck headed their way, and it was not moving at some leisurely pace. Not just in action, but somewhere nearby.

With a start, he realized that he wouldn't have to go trolling off base for company. He'd always been careful not to fraternize with the jump crews, because that made for a mess when it went south. But if he wasn't jumping anymore... Some very fit women would be coming into this camp as well.

He breathed the air deeply again, trying to taste just

a bit of smoke, and found it. Damn, but this was gonna be a fine summer.

———✦———

"Climb and left twenty degrees."

As the pilot turned, Carly Thomas leaned until the restraint harness dug into her shoulders so that she could see as much as possible. The front windscreen of the helicopter was sectioned off by instrument panels. She could look over them, under them, or out the side windows of her door, but she still felt like she couldn't see.

She really needed to get her head outside in the air to follow what the fire was doing. Taste it, feel the heat on her face as it climbed the ridge. Could they stop the burn, or would the conflagration jump the craggy barrier and begin its destruction of the next valley?

She needed the air. But the doors on this thing didn't open in flight, so she couldn't get her face out in the wind. In the little MD500s she could do that; they flew without the doors all the time.

This was her first flight in Mount Hood Aviation's brand-new Firehawk. It might rank as a critical addition to MHA's firefighting fleet, but she was far from liking it yet. The fire-rigged Sikorsky Black Hawk felt heavy. The MD500 could carry four people at its limit, and this bird could carry a dozen without noticing. The heavy beat of the rotors was well muffled by the radio headset, but she could feel the pulse against her body.

And she couldn't smell anything except new plastic and paint job.

When she'd suggested removing the doors, the pilot had laughed at Carly. Well, not laughed; the woman looked like she didn't laugh much. But she certainly implied that Carly could never get her to do that. Whoever she was, the pilot was new to the MHA outfit and Carly didn't appreciate the brush-off. When she'd insisted, she was told she could sit in the cargo bay, which had a great view with the doors open, but only to the sides. At least the Firehawk doors, on both sides of the craft, had a large, rounded bulge in the Plexiglas window. That allowed Carly to lean over enough to see straight down, which would help once they were dropping loads over the fire.

Carly wanted the wide view through the forward windscreen, in addition to the smoky air stinging her eyes and clogging her lungs. Well, she wasn't going to get it, so she'd better focus on what she could have. She shoved her hair aside and leaned her head into the Plexiglas bulge in the door and stared down.

At her command, the pilot lifted the Firehawk another five hundred feet and tipped them left. As they topped the last of the ridge, the vista opened before her. The morning sun shone down as if it were another peaceful day in the forests of Oregon. Everything was quiet on the yet unburned west side of the ridge. Stately conifers climbed, stacked like pillioned soldiers, rank upon rank of forest dripping with intensely flammable pitch. The mid-July sun baking the stands of bone-dry timber didn't help matters at all.

Mount Hood towered to the east, its glacier-wrapped head glared in the morning sun and looked so close she could touch it. This fire was still reported as small, but it was in a remote and inaccessible corner of the Mount Hood National Forest. MHA had no other fire calls, so the Forest Service had dropped this one into their laps to snuff before it got too big.

Carly waited to see what the pilot did when they crossed the ridgeline. Some retired Army major suddenly flying fire. This should be interesting.

"You fly much?" Major was some kind of high rank. Carly wasn't sure how high, but definitely senior officer. The woman had probably been a desk jockey who only touched a machine once a year to keep her certification.

"First time in a year."

Ka-ching, nailed that in one.

But the woman's voice had been dry. Or perhaps it was droll? Was she making some kind of joke?

"Ever flown fire?"

That almost earned Carly a laugh. "Not the way you're talking about it. Had to have a kid to do that." Her age was hard to tell. The woman had a sort of ageless blond beauty. Thirty maybe. But how had she made senior officer by that age?

"What was your last flight?"

"Oil rig." The way she said it was obviously a conversation ender so Carly let it die.

Maybe this Major had been thrown out of the Army for being hopeless. So bad that she'd even been chucked off the relatively mundane task of flying oil workers back and forth to their offshore rigs. If she was a Major and any damn good, rather than just having passed on her good looks, what was the woman doing in a Sikorsky Firehawk over a forest fire?

Though Carly had to remember that she'd often been discounted for being too pretty to know anything. Tall, slender, and bright blond hair, unlike the ex-Major's darker blond, always made guys assume she was an idiot, though even the densest ones soon learned she was way smarter, at least about fire, than all of them put together.

Carly had been up on a thousand flights over hundreds of fires. She'd seen them scorching across the hillsides from firebases since before her first toddling steps. She'd spent every summer of her life at air base camps. In her late teens, she'd gotten her red card and joined the mop-up teams—endless hours trudging through clouds of ash and charcoal seeking any stray heat or scent of smoke.

Her college summers were spent hiking the burning hills with hotshot crews, chasing the active fire up close enough that the heat was a continual prickling wash across her skin despite the Nomex suits. She'd worked her way up the ranks, and now she lived at the helibases during the fire season.

Lead spotter. Senior fire-reader for Mount Hood Aviation, the contracted flying arm of the Goonies, the Oregon wildland firefighters. The Flame Witch. She rather liked the last one. Never reacted when someone called her that behind her back, but she'd considered it more than once for a bumper sticker on her old Jeep.

At the crest of the ridge, the entire vista changed. The clean green of comfortably resting Douglas firs and larch spreading across rolling hills to the horizon was replaced by the fire giants of lore and legend. The quiet legions on the western face of Saddlebag Gap had been transformed into towering infernos, shooting flames to twice their majestic height. Eighty-foot trees had been turned into two-hundred-foot-tall blowtorches.

The pilot didn't flinch. That was a good sign. More than one rookie flyboy—or flygirl, in this case—had simply lost it and returned them to base before Carly could even get a sense of the fire. They'd land with a full load of retardant still in the belly of the aircraft.

A complete waste.

At least something like that usually happened early enough in the season that it didn't cause too much trouble. When the late-summer monster burns rolled across the Cascade and Coast Range, a lost minute could mean success or failure in the firefight, even life or death for the ground crews.

She'd only been at the helibase for a day, but there was already a rumor mill about the woman sitting in the pilot's seat. Carly didn't care. As long as the pilot didn't bank and run away, they were good. Now Carly could see the fire, and that was all that really mattered. Ground chatter on the radio had told her that the smokejumpers were fighting a losing battle against the head of the flame. Against one head. She could see that the flanking line they were trying to clear wouldn't be ready before the fire climbed up to them.

The fire had started with a wilderness camper who'd had the good sense to call it in as soon as they lost control of it. They wouldn't be so happy when the Forest Service sent them the bill to fight the fire. The entire forest was posted with the USFS's highest warning: all burning forbidden. Every pointer on every warning sign had been swung over to the far end of the "extreme danger" red zone.

This was an easy hundred-thousand-dollar blaze. If they didn't kill it fast, it would be many times that by tomorrow. One saving grace was that there were no homesteads out here to burn. When you started burning million-dollar homes perched on scenic hillsides, then costs started adding up quickly.

The fire was still just a Type III, so she could work as Incident Commander—Air on this one. She radioed Rick that she'd be coordinating directly with the Incident Commander—Ground at base. She was trained and authorized to serve as ICA on fires right up to a monstrous Type I response, but she found it incredibly distracting to set up each little aircraft run and her bosses at MHA agreed. Her skills on the big fires were best used as a Fire Behavior Analyst. As an FBAN, her job was about predicting the shifts and changes of a fire rather than the hundreds of tiny details of fighting them minute by minute.

This fire had climbed the western face of Saddlebag Gap, splitting from a single tail at the campfire into a dozen different heads, each fire front chasing up a deep-cut valley etched into the landscape, carved by ten thousand years of trickling streams.

Most of the heads were dying against a cliff wall at the upper end of their little valleys, leaving long trails of black behind them. Smoldering black tree trunks denuded of all branches and foliage were all that remained. Their shoulders were yet wrapped in the lingering smoke of dead and dying fires. They'd need heavy mop-up crews to check it all out, but there shouldn't be any real problems.

Three separate heads were still running hot, finding more fuel as they climbed to the ridge, not less. They fired showers of shining sparks upward into the climbing smoke plume that darkened the sky ahead of them.

The pilot tipped the Firehawk helicopter and headed toward the embattled smokejumper crew on the ground.

"No, wait." Carly hadn't finished understanding the fire from their vantage point five hundred feet above the ridge crest. Most Army hot-rodders thought you fought fires down between the branches. It was a relief that this one didn't, but would she get close enough when it mattered?

The pilot pulled back to a hover, and Carly could feel the woman inspect her. Rumor was that the pilot almost never spoke, except to her husband and her newborn girl. Carly could appreciate that. She tried to recall the silent woman's name but decided it wasn't important. Time enough to learn names if the new pilot lasted.

The flames climbing toward the fire crew were bad, but the crew had an escape. They could forge a path through that notch in the ridge and down the other side, ahead of the fire.

The number two head from the north was clawing up the ridge with no one to stop it yet. It radiated a malevolent, deep orange, as if saying, "I'm going this way, and just try and stop me. I dare you." The next sticks of smokejumpers would be here shortly. That's where they needed to jump.

"Base, this is ICA Thomas. How many smokies in your next load?"

"Three sticks, Carly."

"Roger, jump all six of them on the number two head. Out."

The number three head…

"That's the one." Carly pointed for the pilot. "That's the bitch. Hit her. Hit her hard."

The pilot didn't move. She was just looking toward Carly again, her face unreadable behind silver shades.

They simply hovered five hundred feet above the ridge, dancing on that margin between enshrouding smoke ahead and below, and sunlight above and behind.

Had she nerved out?

"The crew's okay for now. We'll drop more smokies on number two. Number three is going to cross the ridge and burn into the southern slope. Then we're in a whole new world of hurt."

No nod. No acknowledgment. Frozen for half a moment longer. No waver in the hover, a good trick in the jumpy gusts that heat-blasted first one way and then another above a fire. Carly now felt as if she were the target of study. As if she were the one being assessed, analyzed, and mapped instead of the fire.

"Drop in twenty seconds, chief." The pilot spoke over the intercom with absolute surety, warning the crew chief in the back to be ready on his fire-dump controls. "Fifty percent drop in three hundred feet of flow, so give me a dial setting of two for two and a half seconds. Eight-second hold and then the second half of load."

Evans Fitch, who'd been silent so far, acknowledged with a simple "Ready." That was weird because normally Evans was one of those guys who couldn't shut up.

He had flown a training run with the woman and had simply described the flight as "Serious, man. Real serious."—whatever that meant—in his atypically abbreviated speech, as if the pilot had stripped him of his voluble word supply.

Not counting Carly as spotter, there would normally

only be one person flying in the Sikorsky Firehawk, but with a newbie pilot, even one who came with helitack certification, they were overstaffing. Evans was manning the duplicate set of drop controls, which connected back to a console in the helicopter's cargo area where everyone except the pilot and copilot rode. Carly would have to decide how long they needed to have Evans at the backup controls.

The woman's numbers were wrong. The drop length was okay, but the turn couldn't happen that fast. Before Carly could protest, the helicopter dipped and turned so sharply that Carly found herself hanging on to the edges of her seat so she wouldn't be thrown against the harness. The rotors beat harder through Carly's headset as they dug into the air, thrusting the Firehawk toward the third head of the blaze.

"Winds?" the pilot asked.

Carly blinked as they dove into the smoke. Visibility alternated from a hundred yards to a hundred inches and back as they plunged toward the maelstrom. The heat in the cabin jumped ten, then twenty, degrees as they flew into the hot smoke over the fire.

"Pretty mellow, steady at fifteen from the west-northwest." She could tell by the shape of the smoke plume and the slight movement in the droopy-topped hemlocks still outside of the fire.

The pilot simply left a long enough silence to remind Carly that she wasn't stupid and had known that. Of course, any decent pilot knew how to read the winds at altitude. The woman was asking about the real-world winds, a hundred feet over the treetops. That was a whole different question. As a pretest for planning a parachute jump, the smokejumpers would spill out weighted crepe-paper streamers that would twist and curl in the thousand conflicting air currents that battered above a raging fire.

"Chaotic. Winds can microburst from forty knots to zero and back in a couple seconds, and the worst of that occurs vertically. Horizontally, the winds will carry more or less up the slope, probably about thirty knots and chaotic at the moment. The winds are better at two hundred feet, much more stable." She offered the woman an out.

"But the retardant is best at a hundred feet."

Carly considered. "In these tight canyons, yes, if you can get it in the right place." The accuracy would be better, and the tighter spread would provide heavier coverage per acre. That would be an advantage right now.

Through the next visibility break, Carly could see they were already at the hundred-foot mark and moving fast. She glanced down at the unfamiliar console, needing a moment to spot their airspeed. Damn, but they were moving fast.

The pilot returned to her silent mode, and Carly worked the numbers in her head while she held on. Dial setting of two would be about right at this speed, if the flame retardant landed in the right place.

A loud bang could be heard even over the heavy beat of the Firehawk's rotors. A tree had just gone off like a bomb. Superheated until the pitch didn't ignite, it exploded. A thousand shards of tree in every direction. But the pilot had them moving fast enough that they were in the clear on this one. Not even the bright patter of wood chips against the fuselage.

"Drop in five, four, three, two, one. Drop now. Now. Now."

Carly more felt than heard the mechanical door opening on the thousand-gallon tank of flame retardant mounted under the belly of the helicopter. Most pilots drifted higher as the load lightened. This pilot was good enough that their altitude remained steady. Even better, the pilot held the same height above the treetops as they dipped into the valley, then climbed up the other side. She'd seen pilots who tried to hold stable to elevation above sea level. They either learned fast or were thrown out of the service. It was fine in a chaparral fire, but up here in the mountains, firefighting altitudes always had to be referenced from the terrain or you could fly straight into a mountain.

Leaning into the curved side window and twisting to see what she could, Carly pictured the pattern of the red mud. With a slight arc, half of the mud landed just at the very leading edge of the fire, and half on the trees just ahead of the flames. Textbook perfect. Normally, you'd attack the flank, narrowing the fire to extinction. But here they didn't have that luxury. By the time they flanked it, the fire would be over the ridge. It was still small enough now that maybe they could just cut its throat.

She'd counted to two and half, then again felt the slight vibration through her seat as the dump hatch's hydraulics slammed shut. The Firehawk helicopter somehow went from a hundred and twenty knots in one direction to a hundred and twenty in the other.

Carly couldn't quite tell how they'd done it so abruptly, though her eyes did momentarily cross from the g-force that knocked the air out of her lungs like a punch.

Some part of her mind had continued to count seconds. At eight seconds, Evans popped the retardant hatch again even as the pilot repeated her call of "Now. Now. Now." Somehow, impossibly, they were lined back up on the fire. It had taken a hard-climbing turn to avoid slamming into the wall of the valley that they had been crossing laterally. But again, they were just above the top edge of the flames, bouncing through the rough edge of superheated air currents bolting for the skies.

Carly sat on the uphill side, making it so that she couldn't see exactly where the pilot placed the drop. That was a good sign. Beginners thought that dumping the retardant directly on a fire did something. It really didn't. Retardant had to be dropped ahead of the fire. It was a sticky, nasty goo that clung to branches and bark like heavy glue, tinted bright red so that you could see where it lay. It cooled the unburned fuel that the fire sought and trapped the oxygen-laden air away from the wood so that it couldn't burn. No oxygen, no fire.

So this second pass, if the pilot did it right, should be laid just upslope from the first pass, overlapping to allow for the different direction of flight to coat the back side of some of the unburned trees and branches that had been coated in the first pass. But mostly the second pass would be targeted on the untouched and yet unburned trees. All to create a wider swath of protected fuel.

This one drop of retardant wouldn't be enough. Carly could tell that by the rough ride of the Firehawk helicopter through the air pockets as they hammered down into the valley and back up the opposite slope.

They'd need another load right away, and probably two or three after that, to cut this head. The fire-heated wind roared up the valley too hard, too fast. Even the wide barrier laid down by the near-perfect drop wouldn't stop this beast.

But they'd sure slowed it down.

The ex-Army pilot hovered once again over the point of the ridge, turned so Carly had the best view of the fire below.

Carly keyed the radio.

"Tanker base. This is Firehawk Zero-one. Come back."

"Tanker base. Go ahead."

"Three heads. We hit north hard. You'll need two flanking loads to trap it. But first load we need water and foam on top of the crew on the south head. They're jumping the next couple sticks of smokies into middle head. Over."

"Roger that. Out."

"Out."

Even as she took her hand off the mike switch, she saw the jump plane, MHA's beautiful old DC-3 twin-engine, with the next round of smokejumpers. The plane was swinging above a high meadow not far from the middle head of fire. Two brightly colored paper streamers spilled out into the wind. They fluttered and twisted, showing a strong draft up the valley but no chaotic crosswinds. She'd seen the winds tie smokie streamers in knots while they still turned in the air. The smokies would be watching them intently to decide their best approach.

The plane turned again, and on the next pass, four jumpers spilled out, two sticks. The smokies'

rectangular parachutes popping open in a bright array
of Crayola red, white, and blues. In contrast, their heavily padded and pocketed jumpsuits were a dusky, dirty,
soot-stained yellow.

As the plane circled to drop the next stick of jumpers,
the pilot spoke, breaking Carly's reverie as she watched
the choreographed ballet of a coordinated fire attack.

"Seen enough?"

"Roger that. Let's get another load."

The nose of the chopper pulled up sharply. In some
kind of crazy compound maneuver that Carly had never
experienced before, the body of the helicopter spun on
its axis. Now they were equally abruptly nose down and
moving fast back toward the firebase. Not one wasted
moment of motion.

"Where did you learn to fly like that?"

Again that long, silent moment of assessment from
the pilot.

"Army."

"I've flown with plenty of Army jocks. They don't
fly like you. I've been up with enough of them to know
that the Army doesn't teach this."

"I flew for the 160th SOAR, Airborne. Major Emily
Beale." Then a note of deep chagrin entered her voice.
"Retired, I guess."

It was now Carly's turn to remain silent as they roared
back toward the helibase for the next load of retardant.
SOAR. The Army's secret Special Operations Aviation
Regiment. The best and scariest helicopter pilots on the
planet. Well, they certainly wouldn't need Evans as a
backup on any future flights.

"Why are you flying fire?"

"As I said, had a kid. Didn't seem fair to her if I kept flying military."

"Oh, like flying fire is so much safer."

Emily Beale again answered with silence.

Chapter 2

STEVE'S ATTENTION WAS DRAWN UPWARD BY THE HEAVY thunder of a big rotor.

He forgot about the birds gearing up in front of him. A Firehawk came pounding out of the sky. At a thousand gallons, this was a heavyweight champ among this flock of medium and lightweight-rated birds. The only Type I helitanker in MHA's fleet.

There were heavier choppers around. Columbia and some others had Vertols and Chinooks, but they were downright ungainly compared to the Firehawk. Built from a military Sikorsky Black Hawk, she was the perfect combination of force and agility. A Firehawk could deliver six times the load of the MD500 into nearly as tight a space—and do it faster.

It was a dream machine like his Trans Am. Just the sort of craft for taking a girl out cruising. Like the other planes and helicopters of MHA, the Firehawk was painted gloss black with bright red and orange flames flowing back from her nose. It was about the most evil-looking machine he'd ever seen. The California Department of Forestry painted their Firehawks a blah white and yellow. MHA's color scheme was way cooler.

The bird came in hot and fast, leaving the ground crews to scramble out of the way as it swung into the retanking slot. She had one of the Simplex Aerospace underbelly tanks rather than a dangling bucket. She could either be reloaded with a hose if she landed, or she could dip a twenty-foot-long snorkel hose into a handy lake or swimming pool and suck up a quick thousand gallons. Sweet rig. There were only a dozen or so Firehawks in existence, but their immense reliability and toughness were making them a new star in the helitack firefighting world.

The Firehawk was also one of the reasons Steve was here at Mount Hood Aviation. If you were gonna fly, you needed to fly with the best.

Steve saw the guy stumbling out of the back as the ground crew latched in the two-and-a-half-inch retardant recharge hose. The guy took a moment to collect himself before he walked quickly away, as if he had no intention of climbing back aboard. As if he never wanted to.

It would be two, at most three minutes before they were refilled and airborne again. The pilot barely bothered to slow the rotors, merely flattened them so that there was no uplift.

Steve admired the Firehawk's long lines. He wasn't chopper rated, but it would be a seriously cool next step. The doctors had given him a flat "no." His knee wouldn't take the abuse. But what did they really know? They'd also told him he probably wouldn't ever walk again and here he stood. Maybe he could coax a couple free lessons out of the pilot.

He watched the guy who'd climbed out of the back of the Firehawk head into the barracks. Nope, definitely not coming back.

Steve checked the smaller choppers. They were still finishing the layout of the lines, the crews making sure the big buckets wouldn't get twisted up in flight. The Firehawk would be next on the scene. He hadn't seen fire in a year. Hadn't eaten smoke in all that time. Hadn't felt the heat wash across his face with that brush of pain that left you wondering if you'd still have eyebrows when you got back to camp.

He hobbled back down the radio tower steps and trotted over to the chopper, doing his best to mask any limp. He also kept his head low under the spinning rotor blades. He couldn't help it, though he knew they were eight feet in the air.

Without asking, better to beg forgiveness than ask permission, he climbed into the cargo bay and grabbed a headset. They were just disconnecting the recharge hose, so his timing was right on.

"Hey. Just landed on base. Okay if I ride along?"

He could see the pilot shrug as if he didn't care. Whoever sat in the copilot seat started to turn but didn't complete the movement before they roared back aloft. Observer most likely, since he didn't think a Firehawk required two pilots.

They hadn't wasted a second on the ground. Good. He liked a sharp crew. He'd waited too many times in the fire while the pilots stopped for a cup of coffee or to whack off or who knew what, while he was the one with his ass in the flames.

He swallowed hard. That wasn't him anymore. He'd miss the fire. The challenge of racing ahead of the flames, cutting line, and battling the monster. But the doctors had told him that while he might be able to walk, the other damage around his artificial knee would never again let him tackle the ultramarathon of firefighting, of being a smokejumper.

Steve strapped in and checked out the cargo bay of the

Firehawk as they lifted. First thing that struck him was the pristine paint job. Other than a couple of footprints on the decking, this sucker was factory fresh. Downright beautiful. He sniffed the air. He couldn't quite detect the new car smell over the bite of the retardant that had just been pumped into their belly tank, but he could feel that it was there.

The cargo bay of a Firehawk had room for a dozen people if they weren't carrying four tons of fire retardant. The ceiling was only four and a half feet high, but the seats were low slung and comfortable. Two of them nestled up close behind the pilot and copilot's tall chairs. These would be for the crew chiefs when one was required. Hopefully, one of the seats would be for him.

The rest was open in case they picked up a helitack crew and all of their gear. Right above the cargo-bay doors were the heavy hooks for ropes so that the crews could rappel down into some otherwise inaccessible fiery hellhole. Neatly coiled lines hung from quick ties across the back of the bay. On either side of the cargo bay were the long doors that slid back to make the bay so easily accessible and open to the outside world.

This was real. He'd done it.

He scrubbed a hand across his face, hoping he hadn't screwed up in his decision to come here. He'd trained. He'd learned new skills. Rebuilt his knee and his life, but that didn't mean he'd done it right.

Well, too late now. He'd contracted for the summer. But he just had to see the fire. Had to remind himself why he'd put up with all of those god-awful hours of physical therapy. The unendingly brutal hours learning new skills so that he could get back to a fire.

There was enough space across the back of the copilot's seat for the control equipment he'd need. If they put him on the Hawk. Right now it sported a small console of basic tanking controls. A quick glance forward between the seats showed that the pilot had a duplicate set.

So, the guy who'd bailed at the helibase had been running the drop controls. Then they'd decided he wasn't needed. Only reason to fly the extra body was a newbie pilot. He didn't fly like a newbie. This guy was really smooth.

Something about the pilot. Steve leaned forward for a better look just as the pilot spoke.

"Ground control. Firehawk Zero-one on-site in two minutes."

Not he. She. He leaned far enough to see between the tall-backed seats. Long, dark blond hair, back in a ponytail, so he hadn't spotted it at first around the seat back. Good chin. Mirrored shades. Bulky headphones and mike boom obscured some of the view. A vest worn loose hid the rest of her shape. Not much to see, but a good start with what was visible.

"Zero-one, this is Ground. That was fast. We need a hit on us this time."

The pilot turned to face whoever perched in the copilot seat. The seat back was too tall for Steve to see the occupant or what their response was, apparently nonverbal.

He wouldn't have heard the reply anyway. Almost head on, the blond pilot was distractingly nice to look at. He quick-checked the left hand she had on the collective control and saw no ring, but she did sport a white tan line. Maybe married. Maybe recently divorced and seeking a little bit of consolation. He'd have to keep an eye on that. Yet something about his brief view of her face told him maybe not. Something about her expression said she wasn't the sort you'd want to mess with.

'Course, Steve never turned away from a challenge.

"Roger, Ground," the pilot continued. "You clear?"

Steve remembered the time he'd been on the ground and the pilot had missed the drop and hit the crew. The rust-red flame retardant had bowled most of them off their feet. The impact had hurt, and the retardant itself stung like a goddamn swarm of mosquitoes. Half of their gear stopped working. Air intakes on chain saws plugged with the crap. Portable pumps cemented so bad that you couldn't pull the starter cord well enough to start the engine. He'd since learned to duck behind a tree if the pilot looked sloppy on his run.

"We're shifted, now flanking the south side of the black so you're clear on the north."

That should be plenty safe. The fire had already burned across that area, therefore called "the black." A destitute landscape of grays and charcoal, dust and heat. Now the ground crews were scouring alongside the area already burned. There they'd be hunting and killing spot fires that were spinning off from the main blaze and seeking new fodder.

The flank of the fire's leading edge would be clear for a helitanker strike. Once they'd dropped their load, it should create a temporary buffer alongside the advancing fire. Give the crew time to rush forward and maybe cut in a firebreak to turn this beast back on itself.

"Roger. One minute out."

Looking forward to see through the windshield didn't show Steve much from his position in the back. The two people in the pilot seats had a good view, but most of what he saw was the instrument console spreading across his sight lines.

The large cargo-bay doors were still slid open. No reason to close them on a hot summer day.

He pulled off his cap and leaned his head out into the slipstream enough to see but not enough to be battered by the roaring wind.

The plume of smoke was gathering over the ridge ahead. Three primary plumes and a little stuff off to the sides fed the brown-black cloud that loomed over the ridge like an ogre's massive club.

They approached directly across the ridge, so low he wondered if their wheels were going to hit the protruding rocks.

It was like they'd tipped over the edge of the world and were plunging into hell. A hell as familiar as an old friend and as dangerous as an unexploded bomb.

Flanking the black along the south? The ground crew was nuts. They were going to get pinned.

"The way they're set," Steve called over the intercom. "They think their escape route is over the ridge." From up here he could see what they couldn't, the flames threatening to climb up behind them from the next valley over. Not an escape at all.

"He's right." Another woman. On the intercom. A woman in the copilot's seat. He'd climbed aboard a girlie bird. Nice voice, some part of him noted.

His heart ached for the team on the ground. They

needed serious help, and they needed it fast. Did either of these women have what it took to deliver?

"Ground, Zero-one."

"Ground, come back."

"Ridge behind you is a trap. Get into the black now. We're going to cut your flank."

They didn't respond.

The pilot took them up over the heat, which tried to brush Steve back into the cabin, but he leaned out farther trying to spot them. He could see the crew scrambling downslope toward the black, the only answer that mattered. A microburst slammed the chopper down toward the flames, but the pilot compensated so fast that there was little change in the altitude.

"Crew clear" sounded over the radio in a gasping breath, but he wasn't sure. It was too fast. The ground boss wouldn't have had time to count his guys yet, the way they were scattered.

The pilot swung them down over the heart of it. A couple of trees exploded when the superheated pitch simply went off. A whole line of trees toppled over right behind the crew still scrambling into the edge of the black.

"Shit!" came over the radio.

"What is it, Ground?"

"Trapped. A couple burners toppled and my leg is pinned. Getting hot. Shit! Dump. Right on me. Dump."

"We don't have you, Ground."

Steve leaned out and searched the area. This is what he'd trained for, waited for, but his equipment wasn't here yet. Not for another day.

"Kicking smoke," came Ground's strained response.

Five. Ten. Fifteen agonizing seconds they waited until the billow of brilliant green smoke from the man's marker flare finally showed among the brown-smoke and orange-flame mess down below.

"Eight o'clock, two hundred yards out," Steve called. Damn, the fire was on all sides of the guy—and close. The green smoke flare had mixed right into the brown and black generated by the fire.

The pilot was already diving on the spot.

The doors opened and the load of retardant hammered down. The guy on the ground would be lucky if he didn't drown in the stuff.

Steve scanned the cabin quickly. He found a rope and harness. A portable breather and a Pulaski tool, ax on one side, adze on the other. The tool was as new as the chopper and sharp enough to slice skin if he wasn't careful.

The rest of the crew had continued to scatter downslope. They'd be a long time getting back up the near-vertical terrain to the injured man. Several burning trees now lay scattered across their path of retreat like matchsticks.

"Get me over him!" Steve shouted into the headset.

He snapped the rope onto the ring in the ceiling, slung it through the rappelling brake on the harness, and strapped himself in.

"Wait!" one of the front-seaters called out.

"I'm safe if we do it now. I've got air and can get in on him before the fire catches its breath and overruns him." Steve ripped the headset free and pulled on the breather. His voice echoed strangely inside the face mask. It was an echo of his former life. One tug on the forehead strap and it fit like a favorite pair of shoes.

"Now!" he shouted forward, then stepped out the cargo bay door.

They were too high and still hovered over the flames.

There were times you trusted your helitack pilot, and this was going to have to be one of those. He just hoped he'd been right about her being experienced, based on watching a ten-minute flight.

Even as he slid downward, the chopper moved. He wasn't rigged for the heat. Jeans and a button-down shirt rather than a Nomex jumpsuit and fireproof underwear. But he wore good boots and had the Pulaski jammed into his harness. Would have to be good enough.

He began to fear that it wasn't, but the pilot got him clear of the flame before he slid too low and started to cook. He went from black smoke to green and almost planted his boots on the man's red-covered face.

It looked like blood. Steve hoped it was retardant. That much blood and the guy wouldn't survive to be rescued.

First he scanned the area, ready to signal for an immediate evac, but the pool of red retardant had knocked out the fire completely for twenty feet around and slowed it for another twenty beyond that.

Steve cleared the line from his rappelling brake and looked down.

The guy pointed frantically toward his foot pinned by a six-inch-thick tree limb connected to a tree trunk at least three feet across. Too big to leverage free. No digging beneath because he was on rock.

Steve shifted a few feet toward the tree and laid in with the Pulaski. He could hear the guy's hiss of pain each time Steve planted the ax. The vibrations up the tree limb must hurt like hell. He ignored the man and kept swinging. Long swings, even strokes, making each slice count, each swing kicking another large shard of wood loose.

Halfway through, he glanced up to make sure the guy was watching the fire. He was, but Steve checked anyway. The outer ring of defense was already cooking again. The flames were building.

He turned back to his chopping, resisting the urge to try and hurry. Hurry never helped in these situations. Steady and even, make every slice count.

At fifteen strokes a minute, it took him three and a half minutes to complete the chop through the limb. He kicked it aside to avoid burning his hands on the smoldering wood. Next time he'd bring gloves.

The man's white teeth looked surreal through his red-masked face, but he was smiling. It turned to a grimace when he worked his foot.

"Sprain. Don't think it's a break. Thanks. I'd sign you up, but you ain't dressed for it."

"Too late." He'd never be able to sign on again. Steve held out a hand. "Merks Mercer."

The other man took it. "Terry Thomas. But that's TJ to you."

"We need to get you out of here." Steve hauled the smokie to his feet, but it was clear he wouldn't be walking anywhere.

The flood of retardant had created a calm pool in the midst of a full-surround firestorm, but now the pool's outer ring was gone. The edges of the inner ring were starting to burn and smolder despite the heavy coating.

Steve had forgotten how damn loud fire was, especially when it was pissed at being denied its prey. It roared at them louder than a whole stadium of Giants' fans after a bad ump call. It spat embers that died in the red soil and clawed up every little branch. The flames towered above them to all sides except upslope. With TJ's ankle, that wasn't going to happen.

The heat pounded against him, Steve's cotton shirt and denim jeans offering no protection against the scorching breath of the fire though it still lay twenty feet away. For half an instant he wondered what the ignition temperature was on the two materials and which part of him would burst into flame first.

"Hell, we need to get me out of here, too." Preferably before he answered the question about the flammability of his clothes.

He and TJ both looked down at the pouch on TJ's hip. Inside lay a foil fire shelter designed for one. They both knew the statistics—one in five wildland firefighters died when the fire overran them. A foil shelter theoretically made a burnover survivable, but probably not with two inside if they even fit.

As Steve looked back up, a movement caught his eye. A line from the sky. No, two of them.

Two ropes from the helicopter. Both with clips on them. Somebody up above was thinking. He double-checked the knots, done right.

The two men exchanged glances. They were both clearly thankful that they wouldn't be spending their last moments breathing each other's air. They snapped in and flagged the chopper upward with a hand signal.

In moments they were drawn upward until they floated above the fire, which now screamed in frustration below them as it closed too late over the small circle they had so recently occupied. They were climbing through the smoke with the chopper a hundred feet above and the fire now twice that below. Dangling like puppets on a shoestring.

Steve had clipped his line to a ceiling D ring, not the winch, so they'd have no way to reel him back up.

TJ floated along as well, eight feet over and about ten feet up. He hung from a slightly shorter line tied off from the other side of the chopper.

Neither had a radio. Steve never had one, and TJ held out his with a look of disgust. The radio was saturated with bright red goo. Steve made sure his sunglasses were well seated and then gave the okay signal to the copilot he could see hanging out the door and looking down at them.

No good place to land them and climb aboard. And if somewhere under that red goo, TJ was bleeding, then time was of the essence.

The three smaller choppers showed up to attack the fire even as the Firehawk pilot turned for base. All Steve and TJ could do was hang from their ropes and enjoy the ride back, dangling from MHA's newest chopper like a pair of live rats no one wanted to touch. Five hundred feet below, the edges of the fire gave way to towering trees as they floated back toward base.

Chapter 3

THE PILOT SET THEM DOWN SWEET AS COULD BE RIGHT by the retardant tanks.

Steve managed not to collapse to the grass when he landed too much on his overworked left knee. By grabbing out to steady TJ, they managed to hang on to each other well enough to remain upright.

He and TJ took a deep breath in unison when they had their balance and their eyes were no longer crossed with the pain. A shared nod with a grimace said more than enough about that.

Then Steve called out, "Whoop! Now that's what I call flying!" Though his body was buzzing from the pounding of his shirt flapping against him in the rushing wind, he felt high as a kite and well on the way to drunk.

Dangling under a helicopter was absolutely the most beautiful way he'd ever found to fly, aside from dangling beneath a parachute. Yet another thing the docs had forbidden. They enjoyed doing that far too much, but the way his knee felt right now from the unaccustomed exercise told him that just because they were doctors didn't necessarily mean they were wrong.

He and TJ shared a single bark of laughter at just how close their escape had been, and then Steve managed to duck under TJ's arm before he fell down.

The helicopter settled not far behind them as they shed the ropes and harnesses and Steve kept TJ stabilized.

"You okay?" An angel had come from the chopper to TJ's other side.

There was no other word to describe her.

Voice soft and sweet. She was tall. A black T-shirt clung to her frame and showed her to be slender in all the right ways. Her bright-blond hair floated past her shoulders and her smile lit her entire face. Blue eyes. The bright blue of the sky.

Bright with worry she was desperately trying to hide behind that dazzling smile.

"Fine, darling. Fine. Dodged it with just a bunged-up ankle, thanks to your friend here."

"My friend?" She peered over at Steve. A look of complete distrust shadowed her face as abruptly as the sun had shone there a moment before.

Steve knew he was standing like an idiot with every bit of smooth smacked out into left field. All he could manage was a gawk. This clearly lowered her estimation of his mental abilities even as he stood there trying to tag base, any base.

She was wearing his San Francisco Giants baseball cap.

He'd dumped it on the cargo bay floor without a thought. It could have been blown out over the fire.

But she'd retrieved it and put it in the only safe place that was handy, atop her head.

He thought of asking for it back, but it looked damned cute on her. Maybe he'd ask for it later. He found it way too easy to imagine her wearing only… *Clean it up, Mercer. You don't fall for any woman that fast.* The hat was black with a flame-orange *SF*. She matched the helicopter behind her. That was all. Pretty as a picture.

"You should be on a calendar somewhere."

"Never get me to pose, especially not for you." Her comeback was immediate and near vitriolic.

Okay, it had been a dumb thing to say, even if it was true. But even her voice was amazing. He thought about asking if she sang but then thought better of it. He didn't know if his libido would survive this woman heading up a rock-and-roll band wearing, maybe, tight leather.

The angel turned her attention back to the man's foot, clearly marked by being the only part of him not coated in the sticky red retardant.

Steve noted with some chagrin that his new jeans and shirt were going to need a serious discussion with a washing machine. He'd been coated in red and soot all over.

"Let's get you over to the medic." She started guiding the trio to the main building.

"Just a sprain."

"Just an old man being luckier than he deserves."

Had he just saved the angel's father? That had possibilities. Together, they hobbled TJ toward the main building.

A guy met them as they neared the cluster of weather-beaten picnic tables for eating outside during nice weather.

"Set him down there." The man pointed at the nearest bench. "Betsy won't want him messing up the dining room until we hose him down some." His voice slow and easy.

A big guy. The kind who could bench-press the picnic table. His eyes hidden behind mirrored Ray-Bans.

"Where's Rick?" Angel was in full protective mode, interposing herself between her father and the rest of the world.

"And who are you?" Then she turned on Steve. "And you?"

Steve held out a hand, only a little red-smeared. "Steve Mercer, but everyone calls me Merks."

She ignored the hand. Left it hanging there and turned back to face the other.

"I'm your new ICA," the big guy informed her.

Steve reeled his hand back in unshaken and decided to sit down on the bench next to TJ. Clearly the man was enjoying the entire scene. He nudged an elbow into Steve's side, leaving a round, red smudge on the only clean spot on Steve's shirt.

"No, Rick is our Incident Commander—Air." Angel went toe to toe with the big guy.

Steve wasn't sure he'd be arguing with the man in the mirrored shades. He looked like a serious piece of work, lethal through and through.

"No." The guy looked like he might be enjoying this too behind that serious expression of his. "Rick is now your Incident Commander, period. With me onboard, they're expanding the region and he's overseeing both Hoodie One and Hoodie Two camps. He just took the Beech Baron plane to lead the tanker drops onto your Saddlebag Gap fire. Then he's swinging down to the camp near Crater Lake. Party to celebrate his promotion is tomorrow, if you get that fire killed by then."

"It'll be dead tonight and mopped by the end of tomorrow, if the tankers are really inbound." She managed to say it in a way that clearly implied it was none of the new ICA's doing even if he might, possibly, by pure accident, have gotten the facts right.

Damn, she was incredible. She seriously reminded

Steve of a mama bear he'd spooked in the Montana wilderness a couple years before. Closest he'd come to dying. Until last summer's fire, anyway.

"Don't even need the Firehawk anymore on this one, though it's nice we had a chance to break her in on a little fire," the ICA informed her comfortably, his big hands tucked in his jeans pockets. "MHA's air tankers are on site and will punch this one down hard."

MHA had several big airplane tankers, a converted DC-7 and a couple of BAe-146s. Hell of a hammerblow when there was space for the big jets to get in.

"Great. So now I'm saddled with some knothead ICA who thinks he knows what he's doing because he's read a year of *Fire Chief* magazine."

"I've also read the last year of *Wildfire* and get the biweekly *Wildfire Express*. Does that count? Do you want to check my subscription to the *Wildfire Today* blog? It's a good one. Glad to give you the link if you don't have it. Or do you want to see the list of sixty-four fires I flew to last year for training?"

"Sixty-four?" Steve couldn't help interjecting. That was a buttload of fires for a single season.

"I think the most interesting one was jumping with the Avialesookhrana."

"You jumped with the Russians? I hosted a couple of their guys last summer on an exchange program. They couldn't believe the equipment we had. Sacramento had just gotten their first Firehawks. I was supposed to go back this season..." Steve let the words dribble off. He'd been in his third surgery when the deadline for sign-ups had passed him by. He took a breath when Carly inspected him strangely. "...but I'm here instead."

"What did you do, ride copilot on sixty-four flights?" Carly was undaunted.

Steve had to admire the man's confidence. He remained positively cheerful behind his shades while the most beautiful woman Steve had ever seen spit venom at him. Steve raised an eyebrow at TJ, then nodded down toward the man's ankle.

TJ laughed, stopping whatever the next round might be. Fisticuffs, maybe?

"Don't suppose," the smokie offered laconically, "anyone wants to get me a beer? After that, maybe someone can tell me what I did to my goddamn ankle."

The focus shifted neatly. The ICA knelt down and began unlacing the boot.

"Do you know what—" the beautiful angel started in, still in full mama-bear mode. Damn she really was incredible, a mix of beauty and danger. She was definitely hitting deep and solid into the field of Steve's personal preferences in women. Not what he usually ran the bases with, more like the ones he sometimes admired from just a bit too far away. This time he was up close and personal.

"Just go and get me a bag of ice and a pair of crutches," the unflappable ICA told her. "Ace bandage, too. Then we can see if we need a trip to the hospital."

"And don't forget my beer," TJ called after the woman running off to get supplies.

The way she ran was heart stopping. Not some girlie trot; this was an outdoors woman on a mission. Steve's attention was drawn back by TJ's hiss of pain as the ICA slipped the boot free. Then TJ huffed out a breath of relief.

"Don't need no hospital. Just a sprain. My boy Merks here was right quick." TJ slapped him on the back, no doubt leaving a broad, red palm print.

"That was quick thinking." The pilot came up beside the ICA. Steve had been right on about her on both points: a serious looker, maybe even in his angel's league. Also clearly a force of nature; it looked as if the woman didn't even bend. And she'd slipped on a gold band with a simple diamond that indicated the tan line on her finger was honestly earned. How close she stood to the ICA told the rest of that story clearly enough.

"Quick is my trademark. Merks Mercer. Mercer, Mercury, Merks," Steve gave the origin of his nickname. Or he *was* quick, before he'd lost his knee.

"Also," the pilot looked down at him and continued with no change of tone, "if you ever jump into a fire from my chopper again without full gear, I'll have you dreaming about the day we'll let you put out anything as dangerous as a book of matches. Am I clear?"

Steve wanted to laugh, but looking at his reflection in her mirrored sunglasses, all of the blood ran out of his system. "Uh, yes, ma'am."

With no change at all in manner, just as calm as could be, she turned to her husband.

"Where's Tessa?"

Somehow, that changeless tone made her reprimand all the more painful.

"Betsy wouldn't give her up." The ICA grinned up at her, running an idle hand down the back of her leg where she stood by him while Steve tried to recover his breathing.

"She's in her cradle in the kitchen. Probably getting

hungry. Betsy found a cute hat for her. She said every baby needs a hat."

The pilot leaned in to kiss her husband soundly on the mouth, then headed off toward her daughter.

"Is she for real?" Steve whispered the question only after she was out of earshot. Even then, he waited until she was inside the building and was glad a helicopter came roaring in behind them for a refuel, though the chopper made his whisper have to be more of a shout.

The guy just smiled at him. "What do you think?"

Steve decided he'd make certain a spare Nomex suit including a fire shelter was stashed on whatever chopper he ended up in. Maybe he should pack a parachute as well, in case she chucked him out at altitude.

"Well," the ICA addressed TJ, "you, sir, aren't going to be running anywhere soon." He was watching TJ's face as he shifted the ankle back and forth. Winces and pained looks, but nothing worse than a hard grimace. "But I'd agree with your diagnosis of a sprain. We'll ice it overnight, then ship you to the doc if it isn't on the mend in the morning."

"Thanks, young man." That made the ICA smile.

"Mark Henderson." They shook hands. Then he glanced at Steve. "And you must be my stray pilot."

The angel-bright woman had returned with ice, bandages, crutches, and a six-pack of beer, the bottles already sweating with the midday heat.

"Bless you, Carly." TJ took one of the beers, knocked back a long swallow, and then rested his elbows on the table behind him. His breath hissed a bit as she knelt and wrapped the ice bag around his ankle. Then he relaxed into it and took another slug of beer.

Carly. His angel had a name that somehow was precisely her. She must have noticed his attention.

"That's Ms. Thomas to you."

Mark pulled the ice bag off for a moment and wrapped the bandage around TJ's ankle with a neatness and efficiency that spoke of much practice. Even Carly didn't fault him.

"Are you sure about—" Carly was cut off by a loud squawk from the radio dangling at Mark's hip. Mark pulled it free.

"Base here."

"This is Ground Two. We're a hundred percent contained. The tankers stopped all three heads short of the ridge and they burned out on the walls. The 212s wrung its neck and are driving in the nails right now. Hotshot crew and a bunch of red cards just arrived to help with mop-up. We'll be hanging on for the first round of dousing, which will take most of the afternoon. Then we'll let the Type IIs follow it through the night and tomorrow. Should be truly dead this time tomorrow. Tell Betsy we should be home for dinner."

"Roger that. Well done. TJ's fine, already knocking back a cold one."

TJ raised the bottle in silent salute.

"Damn it! Make sure he saves some for us. Ground Two out."

"Roger and out." Mark clicked it off.

The ICA had the decency not to flaunt his knowledge of the situation, which left Carly still as hot as one of her fires and looking for another target. Steve figured he'd best lie low for a bit until she cooled down.

He pulled a pair of beers from the six-pack that

the angel had dropped on the table and held them out to Carly and Mark. They were readily accepted. He snagged himself one and twisted off the cap.

Steve knocked back a mouthful and decided this was near perfection. A small fire quickly beaten. Busy helibase going on behind him. A new friend sitting beside him. A stunning woman settling to sit on the bench at the next picnic table over. Sitting facing them so that he could really enjoy the view.

Damn, she really was perfect. Well-worn boots attached to the longest damn legs he'd seen in a long time wrapped in jeans that showed she worked for a living. All those slipstream curves and a crystalline-blue glare that threatened to strike him out before he even got to the on-deck circle, never mind the batter's box.

The best thing about the day, though, was that he'd been in the field again.

Definitely the best part.

Knowing that his nerve had stood the test of time when it came down to it. When life was on the line, he'd managed to face the fire demon again. Hadn't even thought of it, even after months in bed and physical therapy with far too much time to wonder if he'd lost the edge or not.

That would be "not." Steve felt as if he could breathe for the first time in months, in a year. Then he looked over at the angel as she mellowed a little, as if the beer had soothed a throat gone too dry. Okay, still having his nerve was the best part of this day, but she was a damn close second.

Mark took a small taste of his beer, then stood from squatting over TJ's ankle and stretched out his legs. A bit over Steve's six feet and seriously fit. "Still not used to the fact that it's okay to take a drink."

"Why not?"

The ICA settled on the bench next to Carly. Steve almost managed not to envy him the position, but he did. Though the view was better from where he sat two whole feet farther away.

She shifted down the bench from Henderson, making it clear she wasn't done lambasting the ICA yet.

"We lived on twenty-four-hour call for months at a time. And with twenty-four hours from bottle to throttle, it didn't leave a lot of opportunity to just enjoy a beer."

"The FAA rule is eight hours between your last drink and when you can fly."

Mark tipped his bottle in acknowledgment. "Spoken like a civilian pilot."

"Are you SOAR, too?" Carly's voice changed. No note of derision now, her anger washed away with the simple question.

"Major Mark Henderson, retired, at your service." He bowed his head politely.

Steve wondered about the attitude change. Army guy. So? Tons of Army guys flew helitack when they were done with their tours.

"Then you and Emily..." She nodded toward the main building.

A beatific smile lit his features. "Oh yeah. Definitely."

Carly glanced back and forth between them and then lowered her voice. "She's kind of scary, if you don't mind me saying."

"No kidding." Steve couldn't agree more.

Henderson's smile grew. "In all the best ways."

Steve laughed because the man was just too happy. "What's SOAR?"

Carly opened her mouth, but the Major cut her off, not hard, just not interested in the topic.

"Story for another time."

Steve had been hoping to draw Carly into conversation. So with that avenue closed, he sought another opening. He leaned toward the man slouching at ease beside him.

"So, TJ, any other daughters or sons in the service?"

It was as if he'd dumped a half ton of icy, mountain-lake water on the group.

Carly scowled at him, and Steve was suddenly glad that looks couldn't kill. Then she exploded to her feet, leaving her beer behind as she headed toward the barracks.

He almost went after her. Would have, if his knee hadn't frozen up with sitting still after the hardest day in a year. Still, he'd have struggled upright but for the slight shake of TJ's head.

TJ was inspecting his beer carefully. Rolled the bottle briefly between his palms.

A quick glance at the ICA showed that Henderson didn't know what had just happened either.

TJ rolled the bottle back and forth once more.

He clambered to his feet, Steve helping him and Henderson offering him the crutches.

Having no way to carry the bottle, TJ drained it and handed the empty back to Steve before turning away. He stopped with his back turned before taking the first step.

"I don't have any kids in the service, thank God." TJ remained staring at the ground in front of him. "And I don't have the privilege of calling her mine." And then he headed off without looking back.

Steve and Henderson watched him hobble out of sight.

The ICA then rose and patted Steve's shoulder before heading over to the main building and the woman nursing a baby outside the back door with a towel over her chest and the baby's head.

Steve was left alone to await the return of the crews.

Talk about throwing a pitch in the dirt. What the hell had he just stepped in?

Chapter 4

CARLY SAT BY HER UNCLE AT DINNER.

TJ was holding court at the head of a picnic table, his foot propped up on a five-gallon plastic bucket of foam mix that had been dragged over. It was a fine evening, warm but no longer hot. Twenty or so people ranged around the half-dozen tables. The blue sky and dry air said that the arrows on the roadside fire-danger-level signs weren't going to be moved down from red anytime soon.

Betsy had served up her famous baked potato bar, being loud and flirty the whole time, a skill Carly had never acquired. She shouldn't have tromped on the new guy so hard. After all, he rappelled down to save her uncle, not reluctantly but rather demanding to be lowered immediately. That he kept looking at her as if she were some pinup girl had ticked her off, though. That and her nerves over TJ.

The potato bar selections included so many awesome toppings that it always took a while to dig down to the potato itself. Carly had gone light tonight with roasted cauliflower and a pesto salmon sauce to die for, so rich and aromatic she hadn't been able to pass it up. Still, she'd had trouble getting it to settle in her stomach. She'd brought TJ his favorite shredded steak and a fried-egg topper rather than what he should be eating. But he'd earned it tonight. Earned it for scaring her half to death.

The hotshots were still out on the site, chasing old embers and dousing smoldering areas, but the smoke-jumpers were all back. The pilots were all in, as well. The sun was setting, and Forest Service shut down all non-night-equipped flights a half hour before sunset.

All of the senior jump crew had gathered at the head table with her and TJ. Their stated intent: to harass the old man for his injury. But the relief shone bright and clear across all of their features. They were really gathered to prove to themselves he was okay. He'd been jumping since the beginning, the first one signed on to MHA. He'd helped to form the Goonies. Ever since her father—

Carly doused that thought, hard, before it could start to burn yet again.

"We're gonna have to change your para-cargo, TJ."

"Why's that?" He aimed a smile down the table at Chutes McGee, their loadmaster. He was responsible for what was in each cargo load parachuted down to the smokejumpers once they were on site, making the nickname fairly obvious. Pumps, hose, food, tents, and sleeping bags for the long fires. All of the Goonies' para-cargo passed through Chutes's gnarled hands.

"Next dump, I'm gonna load in a wheelchair so you can get up and down the ridge safe."

"Still faster than you, Chutes, even with the crutches."

Laughter circulated around the table. It was good laughter and Carly did her best to join in. Chutes had been an all-state cross-country runner when he was in college and still ran in the woods every morning they weren't attacking a fire.

Uncle TJ and Chutes were the two senior guys.

Chutes on the wrong side of fifty to be loading and humping pallets and parachutes all season, and TJ was on the wrong side of forty to be smokejumping, even if he kept acting as if he was on the right side of thirty.

Someone else was razzing TJ about not knowing smokejumping from tree-jumping, and when the hell was he going to get halfway decent at either one?

TJ patted her leg out of sight below the table as he leaned over to whisper to her, "It was just a tree, honey. Caught by a bad fall. I'd have gotten out. Maybe not so well if your young man hadn't come along, but I'm fine."

She took his hand and held it tightly, feeling the heavy calluses. Squeezing it hard to prove to herself he really was okay here beside her.

"Hold it!" The words registered. "My young what?"

TJ nodded casually across the way. "That love-struck mooncalf who can't stop staring at you. Or maybe it's me. I'm pretty damned good-looking for my age, you know. Women keep telling me so."

"As long as those women are all named Aunt Margaret, we'll be okay."

TJ squeezed her hand and faced down the table, raising his voice back to normal without releasing his grip. "Well, all of you had gone tree-jumping down the hill. Knew you were too lazy to climb back to me, so I just waited for my buddy Merks over there."

Everyone turned to look at the new guy.

Carly couldn't stop herself from turning with the others. Handsome. Not gorgeous, like that new Incident Commander—Air Major Henderson, retired, who she still had to straighten out. But more handsome, as if he'd traveled a hard road yet still found some bright lights. A really good smile there, despite suddenly being the center of attention. For all of it, he didn't appear to be playing games. A friendly wave that engaged and welcomed. Almost as if he'd become everyone's best friend all of a sudden.

And in a way he had. He'd rescued TJ and now been thanked for that act in front of all. Some might be angry that they hadn't been there. Angry at themselves for not being right there, for not having TJ's back. His fire partner, Akbar, had thought TJ was just a yard or two behind him until the falling tree had cut him off with a wall of fire.

In the end, all that mattered was the moment when TJ and Steve had both been lifted clear of the flames, waving to the cheering crew below.

Then she saw Mercer's gaze shift to where she and TJ sat, and his face shuttered like a hard-doused fire. He looked down, but not fast enough to hide a sour grimace. One that didn't appear to be assuaged by a hard slug of beer or a fierce stab of his fork into dinner. A stab that drew nothing to his mouth but empty air. He didn't pay any more attention to his food or even try again with his fork. Whatever he was paying attention to, it wasn't his food.

And, at least at the moment, it wasn't her.

If it was just them, she'd go and ask, even though he was a newbie. But her uncle's hand and her weak knees at his close call were enough to stop her.

—⁂—

Steve's knee hurt like hell.

He half wished he still had the damn cane. Then he'd

look like the cripple he really was. For a moment there, one brief moment, he'd been part of the crew. Backslaps and raised beer salutes from other tables.

Then he'd looked at TJ. Twenty years older than Steve and almost three decades of fighting fire. People here worshipped him. Chutes, the jumpers at the next table, and the pilots and maintenance crew who shared Steve's table. All of them affirming that's what a man should be.

And there, shining beside TJ like a golden light, a woman he didn't know, but who sure as hell wouldn't want a cripple. And the doctors had assured him he'd always be just that. Too much tissue loss, too many staples and screws and plates. "At least you kept the leg," they kept telling him. About the only good point, and he'd had to fight with them about that even as they were putting him under.

As soon as he tactfully could, he withdrew. Steve dumped the rest of his dinner in the garbage and tried not to limp as he delivered the tray to the kitchen cleanup bucket, then headed around the end of the kitchen building.

Pretty damned morose, Merks—he tipped the beer bottle up to check it in the fading evening light—*especially on half a beer*. He'd never really started the first one that afternoon. It had long gone warm and flat before he'd left the table to find his quarters and move in. A duffel bag shoved onto a shelf in a room made cramped by a pair of bunk beds, cramped even without anyone else in the room. He hadn't met his bunkmates yet; they must still be out on the fire. Another damned reminder of where he wasn't.

He dumped his beer on the ground and tossed the

bottle into recycling as he passed it. A casual glance showed that though he was in plain view, no one was watching him, no one except Carly. Her face was turned just a little more than necessary if she was merely talking to Chutes, the loadmaster.

Gods, it used to be so easy. A woman who looked like that… That wasn't even it. A woman so convinced of her own abilities that she'd face down someone like Henderson. That was the kind of a woman he would have just walked up to, maybe even spent some time getting to know rather than just targeting her. Back when he was a whole man. Back when he could walk.

Steve got around the corner and out of sight walking tall and easy.

Then he let go of his control. The left knee buckled, and he collapsed. His back slammed against the back of the building, then he slid downward until his butt landed hard on the ground. All he could do was lie there and massage the screaming muscles and stare up at the mountain. The only places the sun still hit were the shining glaciers atop Mount Hood. A beacon in the evening light.

If the thing were a goddamn beacon, shouldn't it be guiding him somewhere?

Chapter 5

THE NEXT MORNING, THE TRUCK WITH STEVE'S GEAR showed up right after breakfast. A breakfast where he'd carefully sat with his back to the angel. The truck was the smallest field version SkyHi made, assembled on the frame of a small apartment-sized moving truck, a twelve-foot-long box, and a low, ten-foot trailer on the hitch. The trailer consisted of a hitch, two wheels, and a small catapult launch for the drones. The whole thing didn't look all that different from a snowmobile on a trailer with just a few more jacks and features.

The truck itself was the most basic rig, but with dualies on the back. All of the gear inside the truck's cargo bay couldn't weigh more than a couple hundred pounds, so the dual tires on the drive axle would allow him better traction if he ever had to haul up a logging road. That was nice.

It was painted jet black. The manufacturer's bright yellow SkyHi logo and, below it, the red-and-orange flame-licked MHA logo of Mount Hood Aviation made it look sharp and dangerous. He liked that. On top of a good night's sleep that had eased his muscles, the sight of that truck did a good job of clearing out last night's attitude.

Steve had the delivery guy bring the rig past the parking lot, slip it between the buildings, and park it just beyond the parachute loft. On the blank side of the farthest building of the camp. Good for clearance is what he'd tell everyone, and it was.

Also, it maximized his privacy once people got used to him. He was in a mood to have a minimum of witnesses watching him limp around all summer.

"Need a hand setting up?" The driver tossed Steve the keys as he climbed out of the cab.

"No thanks. I've got it." Steve had to prove he was still good for some damn thing. As soon as he said it, he knew he'd be sorry. His knee was better, but it still throbbed from yesterday's overuse and wouldn't be getting any better from all the labor needed to set up his gear. The work wasn't stressful, but it would keep him on his feet for much of the day.

He considered calling the driver back. Then the angel wandered over, and he couldn't take back his words in front of Carly.

The guy waved and climbed into a yellow-logoed black SUV that had followed him into camp. He could have had two helpers. Crap. In moments they were gone and he was left holding the keys. Literally.

"Pilot."

Steve turned to see Carly standing close beside him, looking at the logo on the truck. Her arms crossed over her chest. Not aggressively clasped, just comfortable being a little closed off from those around her. Looking as good as she did, it was easy to understand why that might be her default at-bat stance.

Her profile figure was perfectly outlined in a black T-shirt, which he now knew said "MHA Goonies" across the back in large red letters. And she still wore his baseball cap. Her long ponytail of hair, so light it was almost the color of the sun, pulled through the back loop. No way was he going to ask for his hat back.

"You said you were a pilot, but you didn't say what kind."

"Actually ICA Henderson said I was." And what idiot part of him had decided that the way to charm a woman was to correct her on trivia that didn't matter? The idiot part of him that gave up last night because there just wasn't a chance. *Turn it around, Mercer. At least be civil.*

"But, yes, I'm a pilot. A drone pilot." Didn't sound the least bit sexy, no matter how he said it. Helicopter pilot would have been cool, wildfire helitack pilot even better, but even if his injury compensation had covered the stiff costs of chopper pilot training, which it hadn't, the docs had insisted his new knee couldn't take the constant strain that the pedals would require anyway.

He'd doubted them until last night. After lying against a building until long after sunset because he couldn't even face the pain of standing up again, maybe he'd believe them a little. Of course, he'd already proved them wrong by standing and walking on his own two legs. That had also been a never-again, so screw them.

So now he flew SkyHi surveillance drones. They looked like the model airplanes he used to fly around the backyard as a kid, but on steroids. Instead of weighing a couple pounds, having a two-foot wingspan, and costing about thirty bucks, the drone weighed fifty pounds, had a ten-foot wingspan, and cost about a hundred thousand. But it was a long damn way from walking a fire.

"What can this do that I can't?" Carly wasn't looking

at him but continued to focus her attention on the truck. Maybe it wasn't him she was crossing her arms at.

"Hard to answer, because I don't know what you can do." With any other woman, that would have come out smooth and easy, a flirty, teasing pickup line.

With Carly Thomas, it came out of his mouth a bit awkwardly and as a strictly factual statement, which made it sound even worse.

Her glare shifted from the truck to him, showing that she'd picked up the connotation even if he hadn't managed to give voice to it.

He shrugged it off and moved toward the truck. He did have a purpose here. He did have a way to join the firefight, at least peripherally.

"It can see in infrared, would have found TJ faster than I did. It also can remain on-site while other craft can't. The drone can stay aloft for twenty hours without refueling. We could have seen that the ground crew was headed the wrong way and warned them just that much sooner that the ridge behind them was a false retreat. It can…"

"Whoa. I get the idea already."

Okay, he had been sounding a bit defensive, but it was all he had left. Flying a drone. Pathetic.

He unlocked the padlock on the truck's rear door. Pulling up sharply on the handle, he nearly dislocated his shoulder when the door didn't move. He must be more frustrated than he'd thought and shook out the hand that he'd scraped up on the unmoving handle. He tugged again, more gingerly, but it didn't budge in the slightest.

A quick inspection revealed a keypad on the side

of the truck. They'd never told him about a key code. But he did have his user-level password that was registered in the SkyHi system. He tried that, rather than having to look stupid and call support just to open the damned door.

The door rolled upward on quiet electric motors. They'd programmed the truck just for him. That was unusual. It hadn't been that way on any of the training vehicles.

Carly moved to stand beside him as the truck's contents were revealed. One side was a long service bench where he could perform all except the most advanced maintenance. These drones were almost completely modular. If a part broke, all he had to do was insert a spare and send the original back to the factory for service. A clear space on the bench at the end closest to the door allowed for setup of a flight control console.

On the other side, a tall rack of cases was revealed row by row as the door rose. Two shelves for the birds in heavy, gray plastic boxes a foot high, two feet wide, and about six feet long. Two smaller cases fit together on the next shelf; they'd have the command consoles. The antenna rig on the next. Just what he'd expected.

What he didn't expect were the two large black cases at the top of the stack. The birds and gear were always packed in gray.

Except once. His last day at SkyHi for training, he'd seen black-encased birds.

He stepped up on the low bed and turned on the light inside the cargo bay to be sure. They were definitely black, not merely shadowed by the early morning light. He inspected them more closely. A glance at the codes

stenciled on the side stopped him cold. Then, as casually as he could, he reached for the straps holding the
antenna rig.

Steve started to loosen the shipping strap. Carly
climbed up and undid the other one. As they carried
the antenna out into the light, he glanced back up at the
black boxes. They were definitely there.

After his training at SkyHi had finished. After they'd
certified him in both flight and maintenance of the birds.
After he'd received formal notice that MHA was hir-
ing him for the fire season and he'd done all of their
damned paperwork on top of SkyHi's own serious stack
of forms, one of the techs had taken him aside.

Together, Steve and Carly made fast work of unfolding the antenna and hooking the sections together. Part
of him paid attention as they attached the base to the
socket on the outside front corner of the truck's box. He
threaded the cable from the omnidirectional antenna at
the top, down through the clips on the pole, and plugged
it into the socket by the truck's passenger door. With the
base attached, they tipped the antenna into place. Carly
kept it stable while he seated it properly and secured the
mounts up the front corner of the truck's box.

Now he was glad that he'd dismissed the help from
the SkyHi techs. Carly was not only much easier on the
eyes, but clearly good mechanically as well, bracing the
antenna just right and double-checking the mounts he'd
tightened down. Never hurt to have a second set of eyes
on things.

The other part of him thought back to that tech on
his last day at SkyHi's compound. A man he'd never
met through the months of residence there had pulled

him aside after breakfast. The guy had led Steve into a different building.

There he'd been trained on a different kind of bird. A drone in a black box.

At the time, he'd thought it a pretty serious breach of security. The guy had acted as if he were just showing off a cool toy. But was Steve authorized to know about this thing? Sure, they'd done some serious background checks on him. But a version of these drones was also used in the military, so he'd guessed that their tight security made sense. Even if he was just going to fly them over fires.

The black-box birds were different. These were the military's version of the drones. It had creeped him out even to see them, never mind receive twelve hours of training on the enhancements. He'd have to call SkyHi and find out what sort of a screwup had delivered two military drones to a forest fire helibase. What if it wasn't a mistake? He shook his head. That didn't make any sense.

Some mechanics teasing each other out on the airfield brought his attention back to the otherwise quiet morning.

Steve finished anchoring the antenna mounting and then moved to start setting up the trailer.

Knowing his curiosity was going to get the better of him anyway, Steve decided he'd peek in the black boxes before calling SkyHi. Though one thing for certain, he was going to be alone when he opened them.

"What's wrong with your leg?" Carly startled him with her question.

Stupid. When he wasn't paying attention, he favored it more than was really needed anymore. The consequence of remembered pain. Time to bite the bullet. And usually people didn't have the guts to ask how he'd crippled himself. They'd just give him a look of pity and step wide on the sidewalk as if a limp and a cane had made him so ungainly that he needed a six-foot-wide corridor to navigate in.

"My knee." Why in the hell did he keep correcting her? Especially since it really was most of his leg, his knee had just been the worst part of a bad scene. "Tore it up last summer jumping the Crystal Peak fire." He started unfolding the catcher arm on the trailer.

"You're a smokejumper?"

"Past tense." It came out as a growl. Damn it. Maybe he should just shut up.

He unlatched the first ten-foot section of pole from the side of the trailer and held it in place while Carly bolted it to the next section in silence. He was starting to recognize that she did that. She thought about things a lot. Saw things, things that others didn't. He began to wonder just how rare it was that he'd gotten past her defenses by asking if she was TJ's daughter. Pretty damned rare would be his guess.

He pulled the wrenches out of his back pocket. He hadn't even remembered grabbing them while he was in the truck. Training paid off, made some motions automatic, even though he'd been distracted by the extra drones in the black boxes.

She tightened the bolts nicely. Really good hands. Strong, but with that impossibly feminine slenderness. Long, strong fingers. Like she'd been born to play the guitar or something. Again, he started to picture her in some rock and roll... no, country band. She'd be the quiet, total knockout of a bass player. Not the showman, or rather showgirl, that got all the attention as he'd been imagining yesterday. Even in an all-girls' country band, she'd be the one he'd be watching.

They finished assembling the drone's retrieval tower in silence, thirty feet of pipe upward and an arm sticking out ten feet to the side. He cranked it up into position until it towered three stories above them.

Just stay focused on the job.

That was going to be his best bet.

By the way she looked at him yesterday, Carly had already made it clear that any headway he'd made rescuing TJ had been totally offset by his question about her family.

Chapter 6

CARLY LOOKED UP AT THE FRAGILE RIG SHE'D JUST helped assemble. A tall pole with a sideways extension sticking out of the top and a couple of thin guy wires for support. From the tip of the extension, a rope dangled down. Steve—"Merks" was just silly, though the nickname did kind of fit him when he'd rappelled out of the helicopter to save TJ's life—moved with a speed borne of confidence as he set up the equipment. Not just born of practice, but of innate skill. She'd bet that whatever he did, he'd do it well.

"What does this do?" He clearly wasn't going to talk about his leg and how he'd injured it. And she didn't want to talk about how scared she'd been by TJ's accident and how chaotic her emotions had been all yesterday. She'd come out to help him this morning as an apology for the total shit she'd been to him yesterday, newbie or not. Apparently not.

She hadn't pinned him as a smokie, though she should have. Only a smokie would have jumped the fire in a light shirt and jeans to rescue TJ. Only a first-class smokejumper would be so driven to overachieve.

Steve attached a couple of heavy shock cords to the lower end of the rope and attached those to the trailer, drawing the rope taut.

"It's how I land the drone. I fly it into the rope. The rope slides along the wing and gets caught on the wingtip. Sort of snags it out of the sky."

"And if you miss?"

Steve stood up from finishing the attachment on the trailer. He aimed his ridiculous smile at her. She'd thought it ridiculous the first time she'd seen it. It started on the left side of his face, a quirk of the corner of his lips, then a sideways slide that would have been a leer on most men's faces, but his dark eyes joined in and softened it.

"I never miss."

"Yeah, right." What else could she say to a line like that?

"If I ever did, I'd fly it around and come back at it again. In an emergency, I could aim for a clump of bushes or a field of corn, maybe. But then I'd have a lot of repair work to do and MHA wouldn't appreciate the spare-parts bill."

She looked up at the rope again and tried to ignore how he looked at her. She'd long since learned that guys couldn't stop looking at her and that it meant absolutely nothing.

But somehow with Steve it was different. She had a nasty feeling that he didn't just look at her, but that he saw her. How had he known to ask that one question last night? Her one and only weak spot, and it was the first thing he'd arrowed in on. Okay, one of two spots, but she couldn't even bear to name the other.

Subject change. Time for a subject change.

"How long until you fly one?" She focused back on the stack of plastic cases in the back of the truck.

"Couple hours." He didn't move to start. Carly could feel him standing behind her and a little to the side. Could feel those dark eyes watching her. She didn't need to turn to see him clearly. Her mind's eye had captured him the way it captured the terrain of every fire and almost never captured a guy.

Tall and lean. Fit. Damned fit, as you'd expect from a former smokie, all nicely accented in his midnight blue T-shirt and worn jeans. He wore a smokejumper's heavy boots; they all did. On her feet they looked heavy and clunky. On him, they just made him appear strong, powerful despite the limp. Clearly a sore subject. Well, she'd proven yesterday that she had her own sore spots.

She liked that he'd let her help and that he hadn't used it as an invitation to push at her. Or to chat her up. Or brush against her. Or... She'd had enough guys see her as a target that it was a pleasure not to be treated like one.

"You need a hand with the rest of it?" She turned to find that indeed he had been staring at her. But there was no guilty turn away. No abrupt shift of the eyes upward. He'd been looking at her profile, not her butt, with no downward drift of eyes now that she faced him. He simply looked at her as if considering the question.

Was it part of some passive-aggressive trick he'd worked out to woo the ladies? No, she decided after waiting a beat. It felt clear and honest. Which simply made it all the more powerful.

Well, her first dating rule of no rookies didn't apply, not if he used to jump fire. Her second rule of never dating a smokie usually completed her protection, but in Steve's case it was null and void because while he had been a smokejumper, his limp made it clear he wouldn't be, at least not this summer.

She'd need to come up with a third rule, and come up with it soon, because she had no defenses against nice guys.

"Nothing hard. I'm okay if you need to tackle something else. Appreciate your help on the antenna and catcher. Those are a pain to do on your own."

Again, he'd made it her option. Clearly not turning something into make-work to keep her close, but not closing the door either. Leaving it up to her about what to do. Leaving it for her to decide if TJ was full of it about Steve's attraction to her.

She'd just decided to stay and help when she spotted the Beech Baron turning final in the landing pattern for the runway. Rick. She still had to find out why Rick was no longer ICA and who this Henderson guy was. SOAR or not, why the hell was he ICA on fires?

"Uh, I need to catch up with him." She waved at the small twin-engine settling to a perfect landing on the grass strip.

Disappointment clouded Steve's features but he covered it quickly. Which was sweet of him on both counts.

"Well, your help is welcome, anytime."

She turned and headed off. A quick glance back showed that he was still watching her, and that crazy smile had slid sideways across his face. He stood a little hipshot, favoring his left leg. His near-black hair just long enough to be tousled by the morning breeze. And those dark eyes watching her. Not her butt, like most men. Watching her.

Carly did her best to turn her look into a glare.

Steve appeared unfazed. "You make a picture, angel. A damn fine picture."

Angel? Sure. Whatever. She turned and walked to the line where Rick was taxiing the Baron into place.

Angel.

The way he said it, with a voice gone smooth and an extra half octave deeper than his normal speaking voice, she could like that even better than "Flame Witch." Clearly, Merks Mercer was used to mowing down the ladies.

The problem was, she could feel it working on her all too well. And she didn't find herself complaining much.

Chapter 7

STEVE SET UP THE COMMAND CONSOLE AT THE END OF the workbench in the back of the truck. Then he tackled the launcher on the trailer, doing all the boring stuff first. He knew he'd draw a crowd as soon as he unpacked the drone.

He pulled out the bottom gray case and had the first drone assembled in about fifteen minutes. They'd painted it the black and flame red of MHA, which looked pretty damn cool. He ran a hand over the paint job, so smooth it felt like water. They always said if you were going to do something, why not make it the very best. He'd liked that about SkyHi.

Fifteen minutes was longer than he really needed by about ten minutes, but he wanted to be dead perfect on this one. Also to make sure his training was really anchored into place in his head when he didn't have a SkyHi instructor to hawkeye his every move.

Sure enough, in that fifteen-minute span, his audience grew from the occasional curious passerby to at least half of the base personnel. About twenty stood in a loose circle a dozen paces back from the truck and trailer.

He assembled the drone directly on the rail of the trailer's catapult launcher, a narrow steel rail ten feet long that angled up into the sky. The drone's sleek body was as big around as his thigh and short enough that he could easily touch both the nose and the three-bladed rear propeller at the same time.

The lower side of the nose was made of clear plastic. From above, he inserted the standard dual-mode camera, normal and infrared light. The camera was little bigger than a high-end digital and included a steerable mount so that he could remain focused on one point for several seconds as he flew by or longer if he circled. Into the mid-bay he snapped the flight control and radio circuit boards, neither much bigger than his open palm.

While he had the middle open, Steve attached the pair of slender swept-back wings, each as long as the drone itself. Then added the bent wingtips with the catcher hooks so that he could land it. Everything slipped together perfectly.

Fully assembled, the drone weighed just fifty pounds, including the two gallons of gas that would keep it aloft for the next twenty hours, if needed. Once he fired off the engine, he'd release the motorized catapult. In just seconds she'd be flying along at a sweet ninety miles per hour.

The console at the end of the bench was already powered up. He flipped on the bird's electronics. All of the radio links to the main console showed good, so he was ready to go. Fire off the bird, step into the truck, and sit down at the console. Then he'd be flying.

He tried to scan the crowd surreptitiously.

Angel was back, along with an older guy he didn't recognize, maybe the Incident Commander Rick Dobson. Henderson stood with his wife; she cradled a baby and leaned against him.

"Kid looks ready to go." Steve admired the tiny hard

hat atop the baby's head. It was knit of bright yellow yarn, with a tiny pink flame for an emblem on the front of it.

"I think four months is a little young to be fighting fire." Emily's voice was dry. Was she humorless or teasing? The woman was damned hard to read.

"Not a bit. Right, Tessa?" Mark leaned down and made a funny face at the kid, who cooed in response. "See, she agrees with me, honey."

Emily patted her husband's cheek, as if in sympathy for being such a charming idiot.

Cute. The three of them were really cute together. Steve wondered what the angel's kid would look like when she had one. It was easy to picture her with one, maybe two.

He caught where his mind had gone and stamped that ember out quick. Since when had he thought kids were cute or he'd ever want one?

Dobson, the family trio, and his angel crowded up close.

"It looks like a toy." Carly tapped the drone's nose in a friendly manner.

"I've read all the report." The IC had a strong baritone voice, one clearly used to commanding a fire. "Supposed to help, but I never actually saw one up close or flew a fire with one. I'm trusting you on this, Henderson."

The ICA stood easy, his thumbs caught in his jeans pockets, his eyes behind his standard Ray-Bans. "Oh, these birds can do some interesting things. Up until now, the few drones used on firefights were flown by NASA as a courtesy. MHA is the first time that they've been released to a private outfit. So they sent along their best." He nodded toward Steve.

Or at least it would look that way to anyone other than Steve. To Steve it looked as if Henderson were actually acknowledging the equipment racks in the truck over Steve's right shoulder.

Steve half turned before he stopped himself from looking again at the black boxes. When he turned back to Henderson, the man smiled blandly as if of course he'd been just acknowledging Steve. No way could Steve ask him, "What the hell?" in front of this crowd.

About twenty people had gathered round. He recognized Chutes, the loadmaster, and Betsy, the camp cook. Two of the 212 pilots who he'd shared a dinner table with last night showed up, though he'd missed their names, Tom and Jim maybe? Andy and Bruce? He'd met too many people too fast. Mickey and Bruce, that was it.

TJ came swinging up on his crutches.

Steve pulled out a small folding stepladder that made an okay seat and set it down for him.

"How's the ankle?"

Angel came up from behind to help TJ as he settled onto the ladder with a nod of thanks. "Still swollen like a son of a bitch, but pain's down to about half. Got yourself an audience today, kid."

The man's broad wink made it clear who he thought mattered to Steve in the impromptu crowd.

Yep. The guy had him down cold. Angel remained close behind TJ. Steve tried not to look up at her. Didn't do him any damn good; he looked anyway.

She rolled her eyes at TJ's back, knowing exactly what her uncle had done, even if she couldn't see it, but she rested one of those fine hands on TJ's shoulders.

Focus, dude. Focus.

Steve went through the full preflight. Not that he hadn't already checked everything, but he was too damned aware of the effects of a screwup. These folks were all pros and he was the outsider. He'd been jumping for Sacramento smokies and on a fire in southern California when it all went bad. They didn't know him from Adam.

He again checked the launcher, thirty degree up angle, aimed down the side of the runway. He didn't want any trees or other surprises, like an aircraft suddenly entering the flight pattern, to screw things up.

He keyed his handheld radio on the control frequency to chat with the tower.

"Tower, this is SkyHi flight"—he checked the number on the drone's vertical tail fin—"November-three-five-seven-sierra-hotel requesting clearance for launch. Over."

"Roger, SkyHi. Let's see what she can do, Merks. Pattern is clear. Winds out of the west at ten. N357SH cleared for flight."

That's exactly what the gear mounted on the antenna was telling him as well.

"Thanks, Zach." One of the guys from his dinner table last night.

"All clear," he called to the crowd, though it was fairly pointless. Everyone had left a lot of space around the launcher. Far more than necessary. Steve hit the power switch on the launcher and started the drone's engine. He slapped the off switch.

"What's wrong?" someone called out. It felt like the beginning of a heckle.

"Sounds odd. Just take a second to check it out." He moved in to inspect the engine. He started with the foot-long, three-blade propeller, which looked just fine. He leaned in to check out the spinner cover, ignoring his own reflection in the chrome-bright cone at the center of the props, and wiggled it. Nothing loose there.

Then he spotted the problem. He blinked and looked again. That wasn't right. He stepped over to the gray case he'd slid back on the lowest shelf in the truck after pulling out the drone. He read the code descriptions stenciled on the side of the case.

"H.E." Hush engine. They'd given him the quieted engine option, a pretty damned expensive option. Why would they do that? You didn't need to be quiet near a forest fire; you needed earplugs. Then he glanced up at the two black cases atop the rack that he still hadn't opened. Something odd was going on here, but now was not the time. Maybe they sent him the wrong truck. No, it had opened to his code and the birds had been MHA-logoed.

"So, we gonna see some flyin' today, boy?"

"Sure, TJ. Sure. Just hold on to your seat."

"Shoulda brought a Barcalounger. Be a damn sight more comfortable than this here ladder you gave me."

"Wouldn't need a seat if you knew how to avoid fall-ing trees." It was a low blow, but it got a good round of laughter from everyone, including TJ. Everyone except Carly. Damn, he'd offended her again. It wasn't as if he was bragging about saving TJ. He'd just...

Let it drop.

Focus.

Steve returned to the launcher and hit the power

switch again. The engine purred to life. For a hush engine modification, it sounded exactly right. That's what had bothered him. You could talk over the noise of an H.E. even when it sat on the catapult. You had to shout to be heard over a standard engine.

He hit the release on the catapult launch, and the bird was gone. At three g's acceleration on the track, it jumped to flight speed in just over a second. Flying ninety miles per hour, it was simply gone. Little noise, especially with the quiet engine, and no fuss. Nothing in its wake except the mild smell of engine exhaust.

Just gone.

There was a universal exclamation followed by excited talking, not that he'd done anything yet. But the drama of it was pretty slick and he never tired of it.

He climbed up the back step of the truck and sat at the console. He left the drone on auto-climb for the moment. Locater and altimeter were good. Just crossing fifteen hundred feet above ground level. Ground here was at twenty-five hundred feet, so at fifteen hundred AGL, that put the bird crossing four thousand ASL, above sea level.

The only thing around here that the bird couldn't fly over was Mount Hood. The drone capped at ten thousand feet. Better performance if he stayed below eight thousand with the hush engine. Mount Hood punched through eleven thousand.

The dual camera was giving him a clear feed. He swung once over the airfield and felt that surreal bit of vertigo when he spotted the truck and the figure sitting in the back. It was always odd to watch himself on the screen through the drone's eye view.

He also spotted the shot of bright blond hair about to climb into the truck behind him.

"Hi, Angel."

"Have you got eyes in the back of your head?"

He rolled back the observation stream on the side screen, like the best TiVo ever. Everything recorded and instantly available. The active view still rolled on the center console. The flight data showed as a broad sidebar displaying temperature, airspeed, speed over the ground, and altitude.

He paused the side frame and rolled the trackball to zoom in. Blond ponytail pulled through the back of his black SF Giants hat. Had she forgotten it was his? How odd was it that she'd kept it? He could imagine her pulling it on, probably the easiest way to keep it safe in the helicopter's cargo bay where he'd dropped it. But that she kept wearing it? He really didn't know what to make of that.

"You get that much resolution?"

He circled the bird overhead again, this time rolling in the 36x zoom on their location. It was tricky. At that level of zoom, the field of view was so much narrower that it was hard to manually aim at exactly the right spot at ninety miles per hour.

A quick glance at the readout for the truck, and he keyed in the exact GPS coordinates for the truck. The camera focused tightly on the antenna. He offset the view about fifteen feet to the west and was rewarded with a fine view of Carly's backside. The sunlight playing shadows down her back and over her hips. Her hair a golden flash down past her shoulders. The deep red "MHA Goonies" lettering easily readable across the back of the shirt.

"Damn," was Carly's only low-voiced comment. He set the bird to circle and the camera to auto-track.

Carly's sunlit back remained screen center, slowly rotating as the drone circled. Her face showed on the screen as she turned to look up into the sky.

"That's creepy."

He could almost see enough detail to watch her lips move as she spoke. A little too far aloft for that. But he noted the time mark on the recording so he could come back to the moment when she stared up into the sky, his hat shielding her eyes from the sun that now lit her so brilliantly from the front. That upturned face surrounded by the glow of bright hair, as near a real angel as he'd ever seen.

Voyeur. Okay, maybe a bit.

He heard a bark of laughter as a figure on crutches came up in front of Carly on the screen. TJ. On screen, Steve could see that TJ wasn't looking at Carly, but rather into the truck. At Steve's console image of Carly's face searching the sky.

Steve released the lock on the drone's camera and zoomed back to view the whole helibase. All of the choppers were on the ground, and the planes too. The base had three small lead-spotter planes and the bigger jump plane for the smokies.

And he very carefully didn't look over his shoulder at TJ.

"Can we see the fire from yesterday?" By the tone of her voice, Carly hadn't seen his screen capture of her, which was a damn good thing.

It only took about ten minutes to fly there; the first real fire of the season had been unusually close. One of the reasons they'd been able to respond and douse it so quickly.

The other reason they'd been called was how remote it had been from any reasonable fire road. It had taken the ground assets hours to get in there. Fires had a bad habit of forming at the most awkward and distant of places.

And half the time all of the country's limited air assets were tied up somewhere else. The United States had about three hundred smokies and roughly sixty thousand wildfires a year. Most of them were too small or were readily accessible from the ground, making the high cost of smokies and air attack uncalled for. But the remote and the big Type I fires were still a hard squeeze to staff.

The black came as a shock on the console's screens. The view had been of the undulating green of the Mount Hood National Forest. The burnout zone looked as if someone had taken scissors and clipped away all of the color from a whole section of mountainside, leaving behind only smoky grays and blacks.

Steve flipped to infrared. A dozen dots appeared along the edges of the black. He sure could have used this yesterday when they were trying to find TJ. The dots were the heat signatures of a red-card crew working to douse any smolders. All of the Type I crews had been pulled already, the smokies last night and the hotshots this morning. Now it was up to the Type II crews to spend another day or so mopping up and making sure the fire was truly dead.

He zoomed in on them and flipped back to standard light. They were digging over the soil along the edges with McLeod fire rakes to unearth any hidden embers.

Back to infrared, he circled the fire's perimeter.

He keyed his radio. "Tower, this is N357SH. Over."

"Go ahead, 357."

"Tell the ground crew they've got a hot spot at…" He read off the GPS coordinates that the system reported. The spot, still pouring out heat easily visible in the infrared, showed far brighter on his screen than the surrounding mountainside. A lot of heat there. He flipped to the normal-light camera. The area appeared to just be another section of the black. Far enough in from the edge that it probably wouldn't reignite anything, but always better safe than sorry.

He circled until he saw a couple of the ground crew wander over. On the third whack with the McLeod rake, they had a pretty intense flare-up. Buried embers that had their heat insulated by the overlying layers. Protected that way, the banked fire might have just built and generated more heat until it reached flashover.

The crew had arrived prepared, dragging an inch-and-a-half line in with them from the small pump feeding off a handy stream. They had the whole area doused and raked over fairly quickly, then moved back to the flanking patrol. He flew over the rest of the site, carefully quartering back and forth, but found nothing else threatening.

~~~

Steve jumped when Carly rested her hand on his shoulder.

He'd grown intense and quiet while he worked at flying the drone, like her father had always done. When Hamilton "The Ham" Thomas focused on something, he was worlds away. He often didn't hear a question, sometimes the first several times.

"Nicely done."

"Uh, thanks." Steve went back to watching the drone's flight, but Carly didn't remove her hand.

She liked the feel of his shoulder, liked the sense of connection. Liked the warmth and strength she could feel beneath the skin, as well. Even the minute moves he made as he shifted a hand across the trackball and clicked in a new command transmitted up his shoulder. Strong muscles, workout muscles, rippled beneath her fingertips. He didn't have the bulk of some of the smokies, but he wasn't a lanky and lean geek either. His shoulders fit him.

She glanced aside at a shadow across the truck's deck.

TJ was looking up at her. No joking smile. No tease. A soft smile simply acknowledged where her hand rested. That it rested at all. He knew what a big step it was for her, even if she hadn't until this instant.

She pulled her hand back and saw some of the light go out of TJ's eyes.

Carly climbed down and wrapped her arms around him, laying her head on his shoulder. She felt him shift one of the crutches to his other hand behind her and then wrap a strong arm around her. Smokie strong, as he'd always been since her first memories of him. He held her tight.

She closed her eyes as he kissed her on top of the head.

"Baby steps, darling. Baby steps."

She nodded against his shoulder, knowing he'd feel the gesture.

Linc had only been dead for a year. One short year since her fiancé had died in the fire, like her father ten years before, but not like him.

She'd just have to give herself more time.
And more distance from Steve Mercer.

Chapter 8

STEVE'S AUDIENCE HAD DRIFTED OFF IN THE COUPLE hours he'd spent searching the black. At first there'd been a slow but constant stream of observers, watching the black rolling across the screen as the drone crisscrossed the area. They had a ton of questions, but few jokes. That was a good sign; it meant they were interested and a little surprised. Heckling would come later, once they were more comfortable with him and the technology. They were impressed enough to have to think about it.

He remembered the first time he'd watched the feed on a console as a drone flew a Colorado fire. It had simply been an overwhelming amount of information.

As a lead smokie—as a former lead smokejumper, he corrected himself and tried to ignore the bitter taste of it—he could work as command on smaller fires, up to Type III, like the fire they'd flown yesterday. He could also lead strike teams in the truly big Type II or I fires. He'd done so countless times, with far less information than the drone provided.

By the time he was bringing the drone back over the rolling green hills, almost everyone had wandered away. These were firefighters and what excited them was a new view of fire, not of a bunch of green trees that were doing just fine. His stomach informed him it was lunchtime as well. Food and no fire, no reason for them to stay.

By the time he was landing, he had an audience of just three. TJ perched once again on his stepladder, Carly sitting on the truck's rear bumper holding TJ's hand, and Henderson. The ICA slouched against the back corner of the truck. He was wholly inscrutable, watching the sky through those mirrored shades as if he had nothing on his mind. Steve would bet that the ICA was observing Steve's every action and reaction. He had to agree with Carly's initial assessment—who the hell was this guy?

Steve considered warning them he'd be landing the bird shortly. With its speed, small size, and quiet engine, you wouldn't see it coming. One moment it wouldn't be there, and the next moment the drone would be snagged in the landing rig.

He double-checked, but no one was near the spindly tower rising up from the trailer, so he kept his mouth shut. The first time he'd seen one land, he couldn't believe that a half-inch rope dangling from a tower light enough to waver in the breeze could possibly be strong enough to land the bird, but SkyHi had assured him that they'd never had one fail.

He lined the drone up clean, double-checked the alignment of its glide path, and cut the engine by remote. He was used to hearing its arrival by the time he shut the engine off, but with the hush engine mod, the casual conversation of this three-person audience was sufficient to mask even that noise.

Totally silent now, the drone glided neatly toward the dangling rope.

It always happened too fast. With a trained flick of the wrist, so deeply ingrained by repetition that it was totally automatic, he made sure he dead-centered the bird into the vertical rope. One moment in gliding flight, the next...

He glanced out at the trailer in time to see the drone snag two-thirds of the way up the line, maybe six inches left of the main body. The rope slid along the leading edge of the tapered wing and caught in the hook at the end of the wingtip. The drone whirled a couple of times around the rope, but the shock cords took all of the energy out of the drone's flight. It dangled twenty feet in the air.

A small round of applause broke out as he climbed down, careful of his knee. Carly helped him as he lowered the rope. She grabbed the drone by one wing as he took the other.

"Watch the engine exhaust. It'll be pretty hot."

She nodded and held the drone right to keep from adding any strain on the airframe. Not that you could do much. They were tough little birds. Still, her care and awareness of the mechanical stresses only added to the attraction. Hell of a woman.

He could feel the surge through his body as he took the bird and set it on the maintenance stand. He felt good from the flight. It had been an easy one, but the adrenaline was riding pretty high after a perfect first flight in front of an audience. It was a beautiful morning and the crisp air of the high Cascades filled his lungs. His blood was flowing hot. Absolute home run first time out on his own.

And there she was, leaning over the drone. So close he could smell the sweet scent of soap and skin. Feel the lightest brush of blown hair across his cheek. When she looked up, their mouths were only a few inches apart.

It was just them. No one else. He couldn't see, hear, or smell anyone except Carly "Angel" Thomas, the Flame Witch of the high mountains.

He closed the distance and kissed her. For a second, perhaps two, all he could do was marvel at the taste of her, as if she were a perfect flower blooming fresh with the summer heat.

Steve leaned in to take more, but a hand locked around his throat.

For a shockingly long second, he could feel his windpipe being choked by strong fingers and see the heat flare up in her eyes. Even as he struggled for air, Carly's hand heaved him back.

His knee buckled as he fell backward.

He landed hard on the grass, unable to twist and catch himself.

The wind slammed out of him. He winced his eyes closed. By the time he managed to reopen them, all he saw of Carly was her back as she headed away. Fast. Her ponytail bouncing with the fury of her stride.

All the buzz of the flight was gone, burned off by the searing anger on Carly's features and choked off by her strong grip. He swallowed. It would hurt to talk for a while.

His head spun as he raked in air.

Steve shook his head to clear it.

TJ stood there on his crutches looking down at him. Might have been pity, might have been disgust. "Dumb as a thumb, kid." Then turned and swung away. Disgust. His one friend in the camp pissed as well.

Before his breath was back enough to stand, Steve was alone. Except for Henderson. He still leaned, unmoving, against the back corner of the truck as if he were a tree that had been planted there. Then the ICA uprooted and stepped over to reach down a hand.

With the assistance, Steve stumbled to his feet, then stepped over and sat down hard on the bumper of the truck.

Henderson dropped down beside him. He dug a couple of water bottles out of the box under the workbench and handed one over.

"She got you by the throat."

"You got that right." Steve croaked out as he rubbed at his windpipe and winced. It was going to hurt for days. He opened the water and tried a careful swallow. Serious ouch.

"That too." Henderson sat there as if just enjoying the summer breeze.

It took Steve a moment to see that Henderson had meant it both ways.

"When?" The ICA was once again observing the distant sky.

When what? Oh. When had Carly gotten Steve by the figurative throat? When not?

"First damn moment I saw her." It had been, too. When the angel walked up beside her uncle right after Steve had rescued him.

Henderson nodded slowly. Savored his water as if it were a fine wine.

"Want some advice?"

Steve offered a shrug. "Hard to know that beforehand, isn't it?"

Henderson merely inspected him through his mirrored Ray-Bans.

"If she really got you that deep, don't let go."

"What the hell?" Steve turned to face the man. "Not as if it matters. I only met her yesterday. But that's advice? She's never going to frickin' speak to me again."

Henderson got a dreamy expression that softened his hard features. He smiled. Steve had the feeling that the man didn't smile all that often. A slight quirk of amusement, sure. But not an outright grin that softened the man's whole demeanor. Though Steve had seen it yesterday. What had been happening?

Carly had been asking Henderson about his wife.

"Nope." Henderson knocked back another large swallow that Steve wouldn't risk with the condition of his throat. "She won't speak to you by choice. That's why you can't back off. If you let her, she'll slip through your fingers and be gone."

"Voice of experience?"

Henderson finished off his water and chucked the empty bottle back in the box.

"You've met my wife?"

"Not really." Steve had never spoken directly to the pretty blond who flew the helicopter yesterday. The one who had the baby cooing happily away on her hip and had scared the hell out of him.

"First time I kissed her, Emma planted my face into a mess-hall table on an aircraft carrier. I had to follow the woman halfway around the planet to get a second one."

Steve tried to imagine a woman half Henderson's size slamming him down and couldn't do it. Then he pictured the woman who had flown a Firehawk and threatened to end Steve's career if he ever broke safety rules again, and maybe he could picture it.

"Trust me, Merks." Henderson turned those shades directly at Steve, offering twinned reflections of his doubt. "Don't let go. Not for one damn second. Risk of mission failure is way too high."

Mission failure? Right, the guy was some kind of ex-military. Maybe he just thought that way, woman as a tactical problem. Henderson's expression, momentarily domineering and more than a little bit scary, lightened abruptly.

"So, shall we see what's in the black cases?"

Steve tried to hide his shock. No one should know the difference. Carly hadn't thought the black cases were of any significance. What did Henderson know?

"Who are you again?"

Henderson pushed to his feet and again dragged Steve to his with the ease of great strength.

"Your ICA, Incident Commander—Air. The man who wants to see the special birds he ordered for you."

Steve clamped down on his next comment. Still he didn't step into the truck. If Steve was right, there was some serious shit in those boxes. Not the sort of thing you opened around just anyone. Not even the ICA.

Henderson smiled at him. "Good. I like a cautious man. Check your delivery sheet."

"I did."

"And?" Henderson looked downright amused.

"They're not on there."

"Look again."

Steve climbed into the truck and pulled out the delivery manifest he'd tossed into a drawer.

One truck.

Launch and capture trailer.

Antenna.

Two birds, with hush engine mod. He saw the H.E. modification code on the manifest now that he was looking for it.

Two control stations, ground and helicopter mount. He'd missed that the first time, too. He'd seen the console code on the box and invoice had matched and just thought it was backup for the rig in the truck. He hadn't given it another thought or read it carefully enough. The second console case must hold the setup to install in the back of a helicopter, so he and the drones could travel to the fires. That was so sweet. He'd have to get that rigged before the next fire.

Two "special delivery items" to ICA Henderson care of MHA. With no part numbers or other codes. They must be the black-case birds.

He looked up at the Incident Commander—Air.

"Can I see some ID?"

Henderson didn't even flinch. He pulled out his wallet, flipped it open, and handed it over. The first ID was an NIC, a military national identity card. The photo matched the man in front of him. Height and description matched as well. U.S. Army Special Operations Aviation Regiment (Airborne) 160th. Rank: Major (retired). Last name definitely Henderson.

It looked real enough. Matched his driver license exposed on the other flap.

Steve recognized the edge of an MHA picture ID and slid that out as well. Steve checked it carefully, including the magnetic strip down the back. What did MHA do that needed card-swipe technology? Steve's own ID certainly didn't have that.

Back on the NIC, Steve spotted a security clearance level so high that he wasn't even sure what it meant, just that it was way above his own meager clearance that let him fly the drones.

"The 160th?" He handed the wallet back.

"The 160th SOAR(A) flies Special Forces helicopters." Henderson tucked the wallet away, then hooked his thumbs in his jeans pockets but made no move to step into the truck. He was clearly stating this was Steve's territory and he wouldn't enter without permission. Damned decent of him.

"And what is that to me?"

"Apparently nothing." Henderson shrugged. "That's how we generally prefer it. You've heard of DEVGRU, SEAL Team Six?"

"Sure, the antiterrorism guys who took out bin Laden."

"SEAL Team Six doesn't own any helicopters." He left it as a simple statement.

It only took a moment for Steve to put it together. The SEALs had ridden helicopters into the terrorists' inner compound. That meant someone else... Had the guy in front of him been flying one of those helicopters? If so, what the hell was he doing here in the Cascade wilderness?

"Uh..." Steve hoped he hadn't said anything too stupid. "I'm not sure if I should be shaking your hand in thanks. And I'll bet you can't tell me if I should be or not."

One easy way to handle it. He held out his hand.

"Thanks for your service."

Henderson took his hand and shook it back.

"You're welcome."

There was no need to ask on either side. It simply meant that this ICA was one of the best helicopter pilots on the planet. The Army would only send the very best on such a mission. And his wife flew as well, also with SOAR, Carly had said. That meant... what?

That meant that Steve was in way over his head.

He decided his summer had just gotten a whole lot more interesting and that maybe he should take Henderson's advice about Carly. It had definitely sounded like the voice of experience.

Chapter 9

"PARTY FOR RICK AT THE DOGHOUSE INN!" THE CALL sounded over the camp's loudspeakers. "Tonight is predicted clear and calm. No thunderstorms expected, so tomorrow should be quiet in the fire front. We all know how well that works. So, two-drink limit tonight if you're on the active list, one if you're driving. Someone please make sure TJ has a designated driver."

Carly laughed with those near her. A beat late, but she laughed. TJ never drank past a second beer, not even when he'd had the excuse of previous injuries. And with his leg bunged up, he couldn't drive at all.

She really needed to get off base. A burger and a brew down at the Doghouse sounded like it was exactly what the doctor ordered. Some way to unstring the tension that had left her perched on a high-wire since the moment she'd heard TJ curse on the radio.

She opened the cupboard that served as her closet. Jeans and a T-shirt? No. She was going to rub Steve "Mercury" Mercer's face in it a bit. She went for open sandals, a pair of tight capris, a blue silk blouse that matched her eyes, and a light leather vest of chocolate brown.

She considered a pink ribbon or a blue scrunchie to hold her hair, but opted for his hat instead. She'd caught him eyeing it. Four signatures on the brim in silvery indelible marker that showed nicely on the black. No idea whose they were, but she'd bet he wanted it back.

Well, he'd have to ask.

And she'd have to be in the mood.

Right at the moment, she wasn't. She didn't like being kissed in front of others. And she sure as hell didn't like being kissed without permission.

But for that stunned moment of surprise, his lips strong on hers... Well, she always told the truth to the girl in the mirror, even if it was tarnished and not much bigger than her face.

So, truth be told, for that one stunned moment, she'd lost herself in the sensation of it. The warmth and connection rooting her to the soil. It was the first time that had happened in far too long, and it was absolutely the last time it was going to happen with Steve Mercer.

She pulled on the black hat with the orange SF. Maybe she wouldn't give it back, even if he did find the nerve to ask. SF? Some San Francisco team.

She'd bet he'd go nuts if she asked him which one.

"What are you grinning at, gorgeous?"

Carly wanted to tuck a hand in her uncle's arm as they walked side by side to the helibase parking lot, but the swing of his crutches would make that an ankle-buster of a choice.

"It's a beautiful evening and nothing is burning."

"That we know about," he corrected just as her father always had.

"That we know about," she conceded with a soft smile at the shared ritual.

They arrived at her Jeep. Her seats and floor were covered with... gravel. A quick look around showed the long slide marks ending at the tires of an absolutely cherry classic black Trans Am parked beside hers. A seriously gorgeous muscle car with a bright red-and-orange Firebird rampant on the hood.

And not just a little gravel. It was as if whatever jerk drove the Firebird had thrown up whole shovelfuls. She could feel the heat rising.

Carly scooped up a fistful of the gravel off the driver's seat. It was hot from the sun beating down on her black seat. She was just about to sling it at the Trans Am when a shout stopped her.

"Hey, whoa. No hurting my precious baby."

Steven "Merks" Mercer. Of course he drove a muscle car.

He moved to stand between her and his car.

"What about my 'precious baby'?" She waved her clenched handful of gravel toward her Jeep.

"That old thing. You couldn't hurt it if you set it…" He clamped his jaw shut, clearly realizing the mistake he'd just made. Too late.

She could hear TJ laughing quietly as he cleared off his seat and climbed in on the passenger side. Carly ignored his laugh and continued to glare at Mercer.

"You couldn't hurt my Jeep if you set it… what?" she prompted him.

He hemmed and hawed, but didn't answer.

"Set it…" She leaned in close, as close as they'd been the moment before he kissed her over the top of the drone. "On fire, perhaps?"

He grimaced, then nodded.

"Yeah, sorry. Wasn't thinking."

"You know what I'm thinking?" She made her

voice breathy as she leaned even closer, their noses almost brushing.

"Uh, no."

"I'm thinking." She wet her lips with the tip of her tongue and saw his eyes widen. "That you're right. It wasn't your car's fault. I shouldn't hurt it."

"Uh, thanks."

"No worries." Then, keeping her gaze matched up with his, she grabbed his belt, hooking his underwear as she did so, pulled it toward her, and dumped in her fistful of hot, sharp gravel. She let the waistband go with an elastic snap.

As he started to jump and hop about, she climbed up into her Jeep. TJ had cleared off her seat as well.

She fired up the engine and shifted into reverse.

Steve was trying to shake the burning hot gravel away from his precious self. He'd loosened his belt and shoved a hand in his underwear to scoop out what he could. He was definitely dancing now, his boots crunching on the gravel as he shook first one leg, then the other.

"You do move pretty quick when you need to, don't you... Merks?" she shouted at him over the sound of her revving engine.

She let out a whoop, then popped the clutch, spraying him with a long stream of gravel and dirt that sent him stumbling back. She slammed into first and roared out of the lot.

Chapter 10

STEVE WAS LATE ARRIVING AT THE DOGHOUSE IN downtown Hood River. A shower and clean shirt had been necessary. Keeping the same underwear and dusty pants and boots was a symbolic thumbing of his nose at Carly. Not that she'd be paying him any mind.

The camp had been empty by the time he was ready, and there'd been no one to ask where the place was. He'd had to circle up and down the streets to find the bar. Thankfully, the pretty center of the tourist part of town was only about four by six blocks and the Doghouse Inn had a good sign.

As he'd been circling, he'd also spotted Carly's battered, dark blue Jeep. Gravel littered the paved street on either side of the front seats where she'd obviously cleared out the floor. It was nose-in parking and no one on her driver side.

Excellent!

He pulled in so tight she'd either have to climb through his car or her own. He hesitated for a moment, then checked that the street was dry. It was. So if she did climb through his car, at least the boot prints wouldn't be muddy. The joke was worth the risk of dusty prints across his black leather.

Steve surveyed the crowd from the bar's door. He was glad to see that the name of the Doghouse was ironic. As a matter of fact, this was exactly the sort of place he liked, even if he was in the proverbial dog-house himself.

Rather than being low, dark, and smelling vaguely of wet fur, it had a warm and cozy feel. Soft lighting revealed a long wooden bar that ran down one side of the room, ending in a small, open kitchen. The bar sported a collection of stools and spaces to stand. It was a bar you could walk up to and lean on while ordering a beer without having to shove and reach between a pair of hipsters with their carefully torn T-shirts, designer beer, and just-released-generation smartphones.

Wooden tables were scattered about, just a little too closely. The kind of spacing that might be tougher on a waitress but made it easy for a conversation to start at one table and flow to the next. Friendly.

The wall art was doghouses. Hundreds, maybe thousands of pictures and drawings. Some black-and-white newsprint, some drawn right on the dark wood, and a ton of photos.

The place had clearly been around long enough that visitors had sent back pictures. And they'd been doing it for a while. The wall was covered with photos and posters of all shapes and sizes. They were layered and overlapping in many places. There were regular doghouses, some with the mutt, some without. Bright pink princess ones, dark and brooding ones for your friendly neighborhood mastiff, a massive Bavarian one of dark woodwork over white sporting a little gray schnauzer napping across the threshold.

The grand centerpiece was a large painting, right on the dark wooden wall, of Snoopy in full World War I flying ace gear. He leaned forward in attack mode, hands fisted around an imaginary wheel, the wind in his scarf, and a line of bullet holes down the side of his doghouse, courtesy of his archrival, the Red Baron. The painting dominated the room.

Steve could spend hours just looking at all the pictures that literally went from floor to ceiling and covered posts and doors, but he got less than ten seconds. Chutes waved him over to the crowded bar.

"What's your poison, Merks?"

"Guinness."

"Traitor."

Steve looked down the long row of taps and didn't recognize any of them.

"Northwest microbrews are all you get at the Doghouse. Now get with the program." Chutes cuffed him on the shoulder with a bonhomie that had gone out of style while Chutes was probably still in diapers.

"Okay, how about a stout?"

Chutes turned to the bartender, a cute redhead in her early twenties. "Need a stout here, Amy. Give him a pint of the Walking Man. You'll like this." Chutes's last comment sounded more like an order than a prediction.

Steve shrugged and dug into the plate of nachos sitting on the bar. Order was big enough to gag a horse, maybe even a firefighter. Big portions. Meant he'd definitely be trying a burger tonight. He bet they'd never even heard of a wimpy quarter-pound patty here.

"So, Chutes, what the hell is your real name?"

Chutes laughed and dug out some beans and guacamole with his chip. "Damned if I remember. Ham, Carly's pop, tagged me with that about a lifetime ago. Ham named me Chutes the first day we joined. I mispacked my parachute the first time I ever did one. Ham was like that, but it was a mistake I never made again. Haven't had a failed load in thirty years. That was even before my wife came along. She always called me Chutes, too."

Did everything here lead back to Carly and her dad? "Called?"

Chutes nodded, "Lost her last year. She died easy, went out pretty fast. Tumor one day, gone a month later."

Steve nodded before eating more of Chutes's nachos in sympathy. He could hear the hurt, but also the softening of the pain.

"Didn't realize it had been a whole year."

Chutes was clearly remarking to himself, so Steve looked back at the pictures to give the man his space.

The mirror behind the bar was tilted enough to offer a view of the restaurant tables behind them though the surface had been mostly covered with doghouse photos taped on the glass.

Between a picture of a miniature dachshund puppy sleeping in a tipped-over beer mug and one of a massive Great Pyrenees sleeping in a wine barrel with the end knocked off, he caught a reflected flash of bright-blond hair in a bit of exposed mirror.

Carly sat across the room, directly behind him. Leaning forward to talk to someone blocked by a picture of a husky, this one looking out of an igloo, a cheap plastic one underneath a palm tree. Still sporting that husky smile despite the lolling tongue.

Shit. How was he supposed to know it was her Jeep when he'd slid in? Just another way to screw up on his first day with the Goonies. Now he at least had a chance to ask about the second way he'd screwed up.

"What happened to her dad? He leave or something?"
He accepted the stout and handed over a five, waved
for the cute bartender to keep the change. Kind of place
you wanted to end up on their good side. She slapped a
quarter on the bar with disdain. Whoops. He set a couple
of ones on top of the quarter and pushed them back. She
took the ones with a smile that didn't quite offer to rip
his throat out before moving down the bar.

She left the quarter on the scarred wood to glare at
him after she'd moved on.

Then he spotted the tip jar by the register, well
down the bar. He took the quarter and flicked it. It
backboarded off a surprised-looking Chihuahua peer-
ing out of a fur-lined milk crate and went in the jar with
a bright "Plink!"

The bar girl eyed the jar and then traced the flight
back to him. He offered a smile. She repaid him with a
negligent shrug and turned back, but not in time to hide
her grin.

He took a swallow to clear the last of the parking-lot
dust from his throat.

Chutes didn't even give him a "nice shot." Instead,
he was clearly still considering Steve's question about
Carly's dad bugging out.

"Or something." Chutes was studying his beer.

Steve sniffed the pint. Took another taste. Swirled it
around in his mouth for a bit. He held the mug up to the
glass of the front door, the only bright light in the whole
place as the setting sun drove straight in. Deep red tint
in the mug.

"Cherry stout. I could get used to this."

Chutes had gone all quiet, which snagged Steve's

attention because he'd gone too quiet for such a noisy, happy bar. A quick glance at the mirror showed Carly smiling at someone, but still practically shimmering with that focused energy she seemed to bring to everything.

"What 'something'?"

Chutes fooled around with his napkin for a bit on the bar top. Someone had dumped some coins in an old jukebox in the corner. The Flatt and Scruggs version of "Salty Dog" joined the general noise of the bar.

"You know Carly's third-generation firefighter." Chutes leaned in so that he could keep his voice down.

"I'm new here. I don't know shit. I just stepped in some of it yesterday and know I didn't come out smelling very clean." He looked down and raised his foot as if checking the soles.

"Not like now. Now you smell all purty."

"It's just soap, Chutes. Gimme a break."

"Okay." Chutes nodded to himself. "Okay. Ham Thomas, TJ, and me, we were the first smokies to sign up with Mount Hood. Two young bucks fresh outta high school and I was fresh out of college."

"Bet you cut a swath." Chutes had gone from handsome to rugged, but you could see that the handsome had been there.

Chutes smiled. "We all did. None like old Hamilton, though. Maureen Bukowski. She was amazing. Carly looks just like her, but with her dad's eyes." Then the light went out of Chute's eyes. "She was dead and buried before Carly was five. So, Ham brought his kid onto the firebases and she never left."

"What happened to him?" Steve wished he hadn't asked. Hadn't started the conversation. He didn't look at Chutes, just watched the little square of mirror and the head of shining hair. He swallowed some beer but didn't taste it.

"Were you in by 2004?"

No need to ask "in" where, in the wildland firefight. "Summer jobs. Didn't start hotshotting until '06."

"College boy. She'll like that."

Steve glanced over at Chutes.

"Not blind, Merks. She likes you."

Steve rubbed his throat. It still hurt a little. "She likes me fine as long as I'm far away."

"Let you kiss her. That's more than most get without a black eye." Chutes squinted his eyes and inspected Steve's face. "You're not wearing makeup, are you?"

"Oh, for crying out loud..."

Chutes laughed, then made a point of clearing his throat overdramatically as if it really hurt. Steve was fairly sure neither Chutes nor anyone else had been there for that. Clearly, like all helibases, Hoodie One was not a place to keep a secret.

"Anyway, you know about Tanker 130?"

Every wildland firefighter did. A massive Hercules C-130 tanker, old and tired with decades of service, had started a retardant drop and then its wings had simply folded up and fallen off. Metal fatigue. The crew never stood a chance as the plane augered in. The loss of that and a PB4Y barely a month later had caused the Forestry Service to retire almost all of the large tanker planes in 2004. Officially, the firefighting capacity was to be backfilled by heavy helicopters. But the heavies, like the Firehawk version of the Black Hawk helicopter, were only just now coming into play a decade later.

"He got caught in the gap?"

Chutes nodded.

The gap in air power had pushed the burden of the firefight even more than usual onto the smokejumpers for a couple of very hard years. That gap had just begun to ease off when Steve first signed on in 2006, but it was a long way from closed. New planes and choppers were damned expensive.

"I don't know quite how Carly is holding it together. TJ's, uh, accident... we'll just call it that. His accident was almost a replay of her father's death except no choppers were on site that time. Another smokie died trying to get to Ham, and two were injured bad enough to never come back. And they'd have had to cut off his leg rather than the tree limb; he caught the whole trunk. No way to get a shelter on him even if they could have reached him."

Steve glanced back at that tiny space of mirror. Carly was looking right at him. Their gazes held for a long moment. He could see the truth across her features. The fear and terror she somehow held at bay. Could see just how strong a woman she really was. He'd probably be curled up in a corner with a bottle if he'd had to sit helpless in the sky and watch it all unfold.

As the music switched over to Aerosmith wailing out "Sick As a Dog," he raised his mug shoulder high in a toast to her sitting behind his back.

She raised hers in return, met his gaze a moment longer, then turned away.

Carly didn't know if she wanted to be close to or far away from Steve Mercer. The whole evening at the

Doghouse, she'd been hanging at the table with TJ and Aunt Margaret. Everyone seemed to have dropped by the table at some point, with the other three chairs a constant rotation of smokies, base folks, and pilots. Chutes had wandered over for a while, but he'd been uncharacteristically quiet. By the way he kept looking at her sidelong, he was clearly thinking about her father's death as much as she was.

Emily Beale came by with her baby. Carly got to hold Tessa. The sleeping infant, only four months old, made a tiny, comfortable bundle. Carly had held a lot of babies over the years, but Tessa did something to her, made her smile even more than normal. Her tiny face was a mirror of her beautiful mother.

"He did good." Emily was leaning back, sipping her iced tea, and watching Carly, her voice just carrying over "Gonna Buy Me a Dog" by The Monkees.

Carly wished she needed to ask who the pilot was referring to, but she didn't.

Steve had been maintaining a low profile all evening. He'd left the bar after a while, doing his best not to limp when he was waved over to Henderson's table. She could imagine the chopper pilots seated there grilling him about flying the drone. He'd looked good, at ease. Every now and then she caught him looking at her. And a couple of times he'd caught her looking at him.

"He did." With barely a hesitation, he'd rappelled right into the heart of an inferno to rescue someone he'd never met. Sure, it's what firefighters did. But she hadn't known that about him yet, which only made it all the more dramatic.

"I'd thought he was some jerk hooking a free

helicopter ride. Then, poof, he's a fire-jumping superman." Carly glanced at TJ, who sat to her other side, but he, Aunt Margaret, and Chutes were laughing over some old story.

"So, what's the holdup?"

Carly laughed. "You mean other than him only being on base for less than twenty-four hours so far?"

"Other than that." Emily's smile indicated that somehow she knew there was a whole tanker-load of reasons other than short acquaintance. Carly wasn't going near any relationship. She fooled around with some onion rings she didn't want. Took a bite of one, even though it had long gone cold.

She knew what her reasons were for avoiding a relationship with Steve Mercer or anyone else. She wasn't ready to face that pain. Not by a long shot.

"So what was SOAR like?"

Emily nodded politely at the subject change, but Carly knew she hadn't dodged the bullet for long.

Carly looked down at the baby in her arms. The blue eyes were open and looking right at her as if to say, "I've got my shit together. What's your problem?"

Chapter 11

THE ALARM CAME IN WHILE STEVE LAY ON HIS BACK beneath the Firehawk. He anchored the last clip for the mobile rig's antenna into place. He'd already done a drone flight from the console he'd set up in the Firehawk's cargo bay. He'd wanted to verify all systems were functional before he finished anchoring all the wires and consoles in place. It had worked just fine, and now the install was done.

He walked one last time around the Firehawk to make sure it was a clean install. The new antenna was clamped to the underside of the tail boom. The wire led around the edge of the retardant tank until it reached the tank control lines. He'd ducked it through the same fuselage penetration and up into the twin-screen console.

The keyboard and trackball controls were embedded on a shelf mounted to the back of the copilot's seat. If this were a military bird, he'd be in the port-side gunner's spot, on the left side of the chopper's cargo bay directly behind Carly's high-backed seat. From there he could look out the side opening, a hole about three feet tall and half that wide. He could see most of what was below even with his hands still on the controls. He also took up only the smallest corner of the cargo bay, which meant if they ever had to switch over to helitack, he wouldn't be in the way.

The console itself was a hardened rig, so it could be

exposed to ash and smoke without damage. They could keep the cargo bay doors open as long as they didn't get directly in the heavy smoke. Hell, the rig was tough enough, he could probably drop a bucket of retardant on it and the thing would still work.

Steve gave everything a sharp tug to make sure it was well anchored before heading to where the crews were gathering around the foot of the helibase's two-story radio tower.

Last night at the Doghouse, Henderson had made it clear this was Steve's first priority, to get the drone's mobile control up and running on his wife's Firehawk. The ICA himself had helped him carry the console and tool cases over from the truck right after breakfast.

No sign of Carly this morning.

Last night he'd changed his mind and made sure he'd left before Carly and TJ did. He'd backed his car out carefully to make sure he didn't scrape up against the Jeep. No question whose paint job would lose if he did so. His gloss-black Trans Am Firebird versus her rusted blue Jeep? No contest. He decided it wasn't his best idea, teasing her right now.

Once he was clear, he'd looked up. There she was. A shining beacon in his headlights, softened by the back-light of a solitary streetlight. Just standing there. Hands tucked in pockets. Hair loose about her face, spilling down over her shoulders. The thin leather vest open at the front. At first he'd thought it was a shield, but rather it invited you to admire the body within all the more.

No, that wasn't right either. She'd dressed specifi-cally to make him crazy, and it had totally worked. He hadn't been able to look away from her all evening, no matter how many times she'd caught him staring. He'd known her for one day, and if he didn't get his hands on her, he just might break down and cry.

Her expression was quiet. Clearly she'd seen that he'd parked her in tight and had watched him pull clear. But that wasn't it.

She was thinking really deep thoughts. He wondered if they were good or bad. He couldn't tell last night.

Now, in the late-morning light of the Hoodie One camp, he wondered why he hadn't asked. Why hadn't he at least been civil enough to wish her a good evening? Instead, he'd merely raised a hand through the sunroof to wave. A wave that hadn't been returned, though he'd seen her eyes track the gesture. She'd seen it, but not responded.

He supposed there was his answer. So, he'd simply driven away. In the rearview mirror, it looked as if she was still standing there under the streetlight when the road turned out of sight.

As the final few stragglers arrived around the radio tower, he saw her Jeep come screaming into the parking lot. Clearly she'd gotten the page while already on her way here. Carly wiped the wheel like a pro and cranked the Jeep into a space, the gravel protesting as she slammed on the brakes. Even before the engine had fully stopped, she was running across the parking lot and between the buildings.

She arrived beside him just as Henderson climbed to the stair landing from which Steve had first surveyed the base two days ago.

"Morning." Steve tested the waters.

"Morning." Her nod bright and sharp. Her smile radiant.

Awash in the power of it, Steve rather hoped it was meant for him.

She rubbed her hands together. "We've got us a fire. Know anything?"

Since Henderson was probably seconds from speaking, the question hardly made sense unless you were really that psyched about fighting the next fire. And if that's what was driving her, then all that slap of power from a happy angel, well, it wasn't meant for him.

Steve just waved a hand upward, not really trusting himself to speak.

"We've got a hot one." Henderson placed both hands on the railing and looked down at them. "Any of you fight the Springs Fire in central Idaho?"

A couple of hands went up, just some smokies.

"We're headed about thirty miles west of the Springs Fire, and you know what the terrain is like. You Goonies here at Hoodie One are the closest outfit that isn't already involved with some other mess. For smokies in the DC-3, Garden Valley, Idaho, is about an hour-and-a-half flight. Choppers, you're in the two- and three-hour range. Garden Valley has a grass-strip airport with a helipad—make that a handy patch of dirt—at the east end.

"There's no retardant on site, tanks but they're dry. The restock order was somehow missed. The nearest trucks are five hours out. Limited fuel is on-site, though more fuel is"—Henderson glanced at his watch—"already en route from Boise. So, we'll be running foam mix and dipping water out of the Payette River. You have fifteen minutes until I want everyone airborne. Updates in the air. Merks, hang back for a sec. Rest of you, get gone."

Henderson had rattled the whole thing off in practically

a single breath that carried easily over the crowd. No wasted time. Exactly what they needed to know, no more, no less. They didn't know if they would be on flatlands or pitched terrain, though the groans of the few who'd fought the Springs Fire said it wasn't good. That they were bringing in more aviation fuel meant they'd be there for a while, which told them both that the fire wasn't small and that you'd need your personal gear. Perfectly efficient.

Except for Steve, left standing still while everyone else sprinted away. Chutes had already fired off the forklift and headed for the preloaded pallets of gear to move them into the jump planes. Others sprinted for their quarters to grab their gear. The smokies went straight to the loft for their jumpsuits and parachutes. That was all the personal gear that they'd be needing.

Carly rested her hand on Steve's shoulder a second, gave it a squeeze, and then bolted off.

Right. It was a three-hour chopper flight. Six hours by drone. A drone could only spend twenty hours in the air. That meant he'd spend more time in transit than flying. And he didn't have the satellite rig, never mind the FAA clearance, for long-distance control anyway. Grounded.

She'd seen that immediately, offered a moment of sympathy, then run. Smart, beautiful, thoughtful.

Crap!

He appreciated the thought even as his anger built. His first big fire, and he was being left out because he was just the drone guy. If he hadn't gone and busted himself up... He should be gearing up with the smok—

Henderson grabbed his arm and started leading him across the base.

"How fast can you prep the trailer?"

"For what?" Steve blinked.

"Airlift." Henderson was no longer the mellow but efficient guy Steve had shared burgers with last night. He'd turned into a no-nonsense ICA, a fastball pitcher, and would clearly mow down anything or anyone in his way.

Steve did the math as they hustled around the last of the buildings. "Ten minutes."

"You have five."

"I'll need help. Good help."

"Carly," Henderson shouted and waved.

Carly came running over, a small backpack across her shoulders. A leather case of charts and probably her computer in one hand.

"Help Merks. You've already worked with his gear. You have four and a half minutes." Henderson was gone before Carly came to a full stop.

Neither of them hesitated. That had been trained out of both of them early on. Whatever had been in last night's look and this morning's greeting didn't matter at the moment.

Steve keyed open the truck as Carly freed the lower end of the drone landing rope. They collapsed the tower and strapped it to the side of the trailer in perfect synchronicity. He'd reach out a hand only to have the wrench slap into it. When Carly tipped the last section into place, he'd already cleared the straps so they weren't trapped between sections.

A rotor downdraft from above almost buffeted him to his knees. He'd been too focused to hear it coming.

A large hook and lifting harness landed in the grass beside them. He didn't need to glance up to know Emily Beale hovered the massive Firehawk a hundred feet over his head. He took the right side and Carly the left, clipping the harness onto the trailer's four lifting rings.

The chopper battered them as Beale landed close alongside.

In moments he and Carly had the two gray-case drones loaded into the Firehawk's cargo bay. He had to strap them to the top of four pallets of white five-gallon buckets. Six hundred or so gallons of foam mix. Chutes had been busy with his forklift. Add the mix at a ratio of one to a hundred with water, and it was the best thing for firefighting short of retardant. It looked like an impossible amount, but Steve knew it would disappear far too fast if the fire was a big one.

He grabbed the spare tool kit from under the bench and hit the lock button on the truck. Per regulation, he waited while it rolled down, then reinserted the padlock. "Locks keep honest people honest." Even though it served no real purpose, the padlock would keep ninety percent of people from even trying to open the door. The truck's real security system was far more robust.

He reached the chopper just as Carly finished loading her gear. His own gear was all the way over in the barracks. Did he have time to run for it?

Henderson showed up at his elbow and practically shoved him aboard.

Guess not.

Then Henderson tossed a duffel at him that he caught easily enough. It was Steve's.

The ICA leaned in and shouted to his wife loud enough to be heard over the rotor noise.

"Betsy has Tessa. The three of us will be in the Beech Baron. We'll be on-site before you get there. Fly safe."

A bit of sign language flickered between them. ASL, American Sign Language. Steve could tell that much. But not a simple "I love you" sign. Which was about his limit. And "shoes." He'd had a girlfriend who'd taught him that sign so she could tell him when it was time for a present without having to say so. It had been cute at first, then irritating, then… She hadn't actually lasted all that long. He only added about a half-dozen pair to her collection. Considering her closet, he wondered just how many previous men had been suckered into thinking it was cute and for just how long.

Steve tossed his duffel behind the rearmost pallet; it would be fine there. He belted into the chair in front of his console, just behind Carly. He left enough give in the harness to let him lean out the window as they took off. He watched the lifting wire attached to his trailer slowly unwinding as they lifted it upward.

"Twenty feet more slack," he called over the intercom.

"Ten feet. Lines all clear."

The chopper eased upward more slowly.

"Taut. Lines look good." The harness wires hadn't caught or snagged anything on the trailer. That was about a fifty-fifty proposition that SkyHi still had to address with some factory redesign. Henderson had waited long enough to make sure they had the load clean, and then he'd gone off with a ground-eating stride that didn't look fast but was.

"Load off the ground. Ten feet. Still good."

Then the chopper tipped its nose down and bolted like a hound to the hunt as it continued climbing. The trailer weighed about five hundred pounds, a twentieth of this bird's lifting capacity. The foam mix took it to sixty percent of the Firehawk's maximum load, which still left her plenty of power for raw speed.

Ready for battle, the Firehawk roared east toward the fire.

Chapter 12

CARLY PLUGGED IN HER LAPTOP AND LATCHED IT ONTO the support arm rigged above her knees. If for some reason she ever had to grab the cyclic control, they'd have serious problems.

First, the laptop mount sat directly above the joystick and blocked much of her view of the control panel. Second, the Firehawk was about ten times more complex than any other helicopter she'd ever ridden in before.

A pair of display screens faced her, each surrounded by a dozen buttons that changed the screen's function. A half-cajillion other small switches and controls ranged down the center console that separated her from Emily.

The cyclic joystick and the head of the collective control on the left side of her seat were showered with more buttons for radio and retardant-release controls.

She had a chopper license and kept it current to fly a 212 or the little MD500. She'd earned her ticket in case the pilot had a heart attack or something, but the Firehawk came from a whole other world. She might as well tackle a space shuttle. It wasn't the flying she cared about anyway.

She pulled up the terrain maps on her laptop and the latest weather information.

If only she knew where the—

"Forty-four-point-two-one by minus-one-fifteen-point-eight-five." Henderson's voice came over the radio, reading out the GPS coordinates as if he'd been reading her mind. "Officially the Scott Mountain Fire, though it's still a couple miles from there and we're going to keep it that way. Class D and growing. Probably Class E by the time we arrive. Zero containment. Type II now and we're going to keep it that way. Control out."

"Shit." Merks voice sounded low over the headset. "How did it get so big before they called us?" A Type II meant multiple days, base camps, and a whole mess of resources and command structure.

"What are Class D and E?" Beale looked grumpy, though it wasn't reflected in her voice. She struck Carly as a woman who hated not knowing everything. They'd get along just fine on that trait.

"Your husband reads too much." Steve spoke while Carly was keying in the longitude and latitude coordinates Henderson had just fed her. "It becomes Class E when more than three hundred acres are burned or on fire, about a half square mile. Class F starts at a thousand acres. It's on the books that way, but what we care about is Type I, II, or III. Because of the late report, I'm guessing that it's on steep and remote terrain, which increases the type."

Carly had to remember that Steve was an experienced smokie, despite the hotdogger persona he wore so comfortably.

Beale sounded a bit less grouchy. "He does read too much. I spent a couple weeks training at Brainerd Heli and a couple more in Los Angeles County Fire Department. They both talked only about type."

Carly glanced over at Beale and could see she would enjoy finding the right way to rub her husband's nose in it.

Carly keyed the radio. "Hey, ICA Rookie!"

"Come back." Henderson sounded very grouchy, but his wife was smiling as she pushed the Firehawk east. The slightest nod indicated that Carly was precisely on track.

"Type first. Class, we don't really care; they don't even call us unless it's big. Or damn close like the little one we just did. We get all we need from Type II."

"Roger." It was practically a growl and would have every Hoodie in the loop laughing.

Beale was smiling, which was all Carly cared about.

Carly tapped into the chopper's broadband ground link with her laptop. Pulled up the mapping software. "I can confirm steep. Steep and remote. All between four and six thousand feet up. Ground support is going to be lousy. The nearest fire road is a nasty twister and ends about two miles away. Can this thing airlift a bulldozer?"

"Let's see." Emily appeared to be inspecting the sky for an answer. "Your average D9 Teddy Bear—"

"Teddy Bear?" Steve's laugh engaged Carly's own.

"Yes," Emily continued without the slightest change of tone. "Your average armored and militarized D9 Teddy Bear bulldozer made by Cat. It will knock down your typical concrete-walled home without even slowing down much. Israelis used them a lot when they didn't like a Palestine settlement. They weigh in at about sixty tons, and I expect the armor is in the range of ten tons. So, that's fifty tons of dozer and I can lift about five tons. And I can't even do that at six thousand feet. Not enough air. Even a little D4 weighs in at about twice my capacity."

That sobered up the mood of the aircraft. This Firehawk

was the new powerhouse of the MHA fleet. Its arrival had made Carly feel as if they could fight anything, but the problem was not so simple.

"Now, if you had a CH-47 Chinook," Emily continued, as if all of the technical information had turned her downright gregarious, "you could cart around a D4 dozer just fine, even to those altitudes."

There was a loud click over the intercom as she keyed the radio mike. "Honey?"

"Here, babe." Henderson's voice came clear, sounding as if he were mostly over his grouch.

"Anybody local have a Chinook or a Skycrane? Carly says the roads are too remote. We need a way to get some Cat D4s on-site."

"Roger, babe. I'll get to work on it. Well done. ICA, out."

Carly looked over at Emily. The woman had just given her all of the credit for the idea without a second thought. Any male pilot Carly had ever flown with would have taken the credit himself even for something that was completely her idea. Was that the nature of the woman beside her? Or was it the nature of decent people?

Which would Steve do?

He'd given her a lot to consider over the last two days.

His unhesitating jump into the fire. The ease with which they worked together. It was as if whenever they were working, the fake, irritating Steve faded away and the decent version appeared in his place.

Nor had she missed his change of attitude last night. Allowing her some personal space. Then changing his mind about parking her in. And it couldn't have been to preserve his precious upholstery, he was clearly smart enough to have included that in his original planning. She sure as hell would have gone looking for a mud puddle before walking across it. Actually, she might even have gone to the corner store and bought a bottle of water to create one if none were available.

He was clearly interested in her. She'd caught sight of the image on his screen during the drone's first flight, a still shot of her face in the sunlight looking up at the drone. And she'd let him kiss her. Though it was hard to admit, she'd wanted him to. That had been almost as much of a shock as the kiss itself.

Okay, honestly, his kiss had sent too many bad memories rushing to the surface, leaving her sick and dizzy between one heartbeat and the next.

Yet he hadn't pursued her through the bar like most other males on the scent. He'd actually been conspicuously decent, not even coming to TJ's table except for a brief moment when she'd gone to the bathroom.

But that wasn't what had set her on her heels last night. Steve wasn't what had made her reactions so befuddled that she didn't even think to wave good night until his taillights turned out of sight.

It was Emily's comments to her. Carly had thought that she was facing her past. But now she wondered if she was avoiding her memories.

There was also something different about Steve. It wasn't that he made her laugh, even when he didn't intend to. Nor was it the image of him dancing with hot gravel in his underwear, though even the memory still made her smile.

It was that Steve had stirred up embers she'd thought

fully doused and suppressed. The loss of Linc had left her in the black and she'd been fine that way. But her heart had been sneaky, a slow smolder that still lurked beneath the surface.

Right up to the moment Steve had looked at her for the first time and gasped out under his breath, "An angel."

Chapter 13

THE REPORTS CONTINUED COMING IN. SLOW AT FIRST, but ramping up when the smokies and then Henderson reached the site almost simultaneously. The ICA began radioing back observer reports.

"Heavy to severe. Fully active, surface and crown fire. Solid Type II." Steve heard the return of the carefully measured humor he'd learned to appreciate in the man. "Estimate five hundred acres. Class F by the time choppers arrive."

"If you," Beale ground out over the radio of their racing Firehawk, "are flying over a fire with our daughter, you're a dead man."

It was certainly a voice Steve would never want to be on the receiving end of, even if he weren't at fault.

Henderson was a very brave man and responded in a light voice. "We're at ten thousand feet and circling a mile to the side, honey. No worries. Jump teams are in and moving to flank north and south. Winds steady at thirty-five knots, too chaotic over the fire. They had to jump well outside the zone. They're just getting to the fire edge now."

Steve ached in empathy for these guys. They'd have parachuted down to open ground a thousand feet or more from the fire. Then, in heavy gear with pumps and tools and hoses, they'd trekked over steep terrain before they could even start the firefight.

When the Firehawk reached the airstrip east of
Garden Valley, they were in the bottom of a steep-sided
valley. Henderson's Baron landed on the grass strip
even as Beale hovered and landed the trailer well clear
of the helibase on a flat spot just above the banks of a
lazy bend in the Payette River.

She hovered low enough for Steve to jump out. He
looked at the gap to ground and tried not to think about
his knee.

Carly spoke over the headset, "Can you set us fully
down? Make it easier to unload as well."

Bless the woman.

After Beale set it down, Steve stepped down and slid
the drone cases and the tool kit free.

Carly climbed out, ducked under the chopper, and
unclipped the harness from the lifting hook. A quick
gesture and Beale was back in the sky, moving upslope
to the helibase before resettling.

Together he and Carly cleared the harness and
prepped the trailer. Getting the drone-catcher rig aloft
only took a few minutes. And this time he didn't take
his time assembling the bird. As fast as Carly read off
the checklist, Steve attached the pieces of the first bird.
He locked the two drones' cases to the wheels of the
trailer, so at least they couldn't be stolen without taking
the whole thing back aloft.

The radio on Carly's belt squawked.

"This is Henderson. Is the drone up?"

"How soon until the Firehawk is ready?" Steve asked
without looking up from fueling the bird.

Carly relayed the question over her radio.

"Now."

Steve capped the tank, set the auto-flight, and fired the engine, which whined to life, caught, and steadied. He fired the catapult and launched the drone into the sky. He watched it long enough to make sure it had stabilized in a lazy circle a thousand feet overhead, waiting for his next command.

Together he and Carly ran toward the chopper. He felt like a foolish teenager playing a game of tag for two. Chasing Carly, just two steps ahead, alive with the energy, the joy, the passion for what she did radiating from the very core of her being. He wanted to grab her and throw her to the soft summer grass along the slow, winding river and fall down beside her. Instead he limp-raced toward the chopper, not able to gain on her head start.

Henderson met them there. "Okay, you two are my eyes in the sky. Carly, do that magic that Rick tells me you do. Merks, make me proud."

Then he pulled Carly aside.

Under the pretense of double-checking his cabling installation, Steve shuffled close enough to overhear.

"Rick and the Hoodie Two crew are tied up on a massive chaparral fire in Nevada. You're our only Type I Incident Commander qualified. I'm Type I for air and TJ is Type I for ground. So we'll be taking the load off you as much as we can, but this is your fire. I know you prefer to focus on air tactics and strategy, but the nearest wildfire Type I Incident Commander who isn't in another mess at the moment is at least six hours away. Can you run it?"

Carly shrugged. "Sure."

Henderson stuck out a hand. "Rick said I could count on you. It's good to know."

They shook hard on it once. Then, with a shared nod, they turned toward their next tasks, Carly mounting up and Henderson striding off toward the 212s that were just arriving.

Steve's respect for the man just kept growing. It wasn't your average guy who would admit to a younger woman that she was more qualified than he was to do the job. Steve began booting up the console to take control of his drone.

A fuel truck was winding up its hose from where it had been filling the Firehawk's tanks. The squeaky whine of the rusted take-up reel overlapping the idling diesel engine. The old truck at this normally quiet strip was an equal mix of rust and red.

While Steve and Carly had been setting up the trailer, someone had unloaded the three tons of foam mix. Steve looked to the side and saw it stacked. No forklift in sight at Garden Valley airstrip. Someone had moved it all by hand. He was glad it wasn't him.

A dozen buckets remained aboard.

"You know how to set these?" Carly glanced into the cargo bay.

Steve looked at the two plastic hoses, each already plugged into two separate five-gallon buckets, ripe with the sweet, soapy smell of foam mix. You pulled the center plug on a fresh bucket, rammed in the two hoses, and engaged the clips. You'd have ten gallons of mix that would foam up the thousand gallons of water in the Firehawk's belly tank. It would cover way more territory than the water alone. Move the hoses to fresh buckets every time you refilled. Six drops, then they'd have to circle back for more foam. They'd probably need fuel every dozen drops, so the numbers worked well.

"Yeah, I got it." It would take him about thirty seconds for each changeover, and the drone would just cruise along on autopilot. In FAA airspace, it wasn't yet legal to leave a drone in unattended flight except in very tightly controlled situations. Level flight at a predesignated altitude set by an ICA was one of those.

"Good." Carly nodded her thanks for his taking the extra duty. "It saves me having to put an extra body aboard and losing another thirty or forty gallons of capacity in load offset."

The little MD500, the slowest but most agile of MHA's helicopters, showed up and began its descent as Steve and Carly climbed aboard the Firehawk. The MD500's rotors made a high, whippy sound in comparison to the heavier 212s idling their turbines while getting their Bambi Buckets attached.

Beale began cranking the Firehawk's engines, adding their high-pitched whine to the racket that rolled over to a heavy beat.

The fuel truck roared to life and raced over to service the new arrival.

A deep, diesel-engine groan rose in the background, and Steve could see a couple of flatbed trailers arrive pulling bulldozers with heavy-duty cages around the driver's seat. That meant Henderson had found a really big chopper somewhere. It should be arriving soon.

Beale called the "tower," a fancy word for Mike and TJ with a pair of walkie-talkies and a couple of folding lawn chairs set midfield. She had the Firehawk aloft before Steve even had his headset fully on. Rather than belting into his seat, he slipped on a harness and clipped the couple-meter-long lead line to a ceiling D ring. Now he could move around the cargo bay to service the foam buckets if needed without being able to fall out of the helicopter, or not fall very far.

Steve got the console powered up, and as soon as he had a radio link with the drone, he sent it winging toward the fire.

Beale struck out over the Payette River and descended slowly over a lazy curve of blue water. Not much room. Trees towered on both banks, and the Payette was barely a hundred feet wide here. The rotor disc was over fifty feet wide. It was a tight squeeze, and he held his breath until Beale had the chopper slid into place.

The other choppers would have an easier time with the tight fit. They dangled buckets eight feet in diameter at the end of two-hundred-foot lines. The Firehawk dangled a twenty-foot-long suction hose to fill its belly tank.

Steve leaned out to watch. The big, fat, five-inch hose lowered from the Firehawk's tank.

"Snorkel wet," he called as it entered the water.

The onboard pump kicked to life, sending heavy vibrations buzzing through the deck plates and up his legs. Twenty seconds later and a thousand gallons heavier, they clawed aloft, Beale retracting the snorkel as she went.

As soon as they climbed out of the valley, there was no question of where to go. The gray-brown plume blossomed in the northern sky like a fist.

"The wind," he said over the headset without even realizing it.

"The wind," Carly agreed. That's why it had spread so fast.

The tower of smoke was leaning well to the east. A westerly was pushing the fire—and pushing it hard. He leaned as far forward between the seats as he could until he was almost beside Carly. He looked up through the front windshield. At about twenty thousand feet, the plume was sheared off.

"Jet stream." The upper air currents were ripping off the top of the smoke and carrying it east in a long cloud.

Steve shifted back to his console.

"Damn." The drone was arriving at the fire, affording Steve his first good view of it. The beginning of the black was still smoldering and the leading edge was a mile beyond it. This sucker was still spreading fast.

"What? Can I see?" Carly was trying to do the impossible and turn far enough in her harness to somehow see the display mounted on the back of her seat.

Steve pulled out a tablet display, tapped it on, initiated the link, and handed it forward. Now it would emulate what he was seeing.

"Turn left and zoom out."

She'd assessed the view and the nature of the fire before she even had a solid grasp on the display.

He re-aimed the drone's camera.

"There… See? Now pan right again. Okay, straight ahead and up." There was a pause before Carly continued. "That's it."

"What's it?"

"Look here." She tried to hold the tablet where he could see it and point at the same time.

"Just circle it with your finger. I'll see it on my screen."

She drew three quick circles that faded even as she finished. But he didn't need to see more.

"Triple strike."

"What's a triple strike?" Beale cut in.

"This isn't one fire—" Steve started.

"—It's three," Carly finished. "Three lightning strikes on three adjacent ridges. Must have been a heck of show."

"Does that change how we fight the fire?"

"Yes, it lets me know how the fire is moving. Steve, can you circle higher?"

He'd already clicked onto the "tower" frequency and gotten clearance from Mike to do just that. He sent the drone spiraling upward as he zoomed out for a wider view. They were still five miles out in their helicopter, about two more minutes of flight time, when he got high enough to see the full fire.

"Can you overlay a terrain map?"

Steve tapped in the contour lines. "Damn, that's rough terrain."

"Smokies earning their pay today."

"Spoken like an air jock." His statement had more edge than he'd intended. Steve had humped hills like this. It was no fun at all.

He had the system run a quick heat-area analysis. He'd had a chat with a programmer back at SkyHi. The woman had written him an auto-trace feature that outlined the boundary where there was a twenty degree or more difference in the infrared values. The algorithm traced a line, checked the scale of the view, and reported the engaged acreage.

Steve keyed the ICA's frequency. "It's official, sports fans. We're now a Class F, twelve hundred acres."

"Roger that," was Henderson's dry reply. "ICA aloft. On-site in ten minutes."

"Where do we hit it?" Beale's voice indicated she wasn't going to be wasting any more time teasing her husband.

"Right here, full load." Carly traced a line that showed up on Steve's screen, then held the tablet out for Beale to see.

Steve tried to puzzle it out. That wouldn't have been his first call. Not even close. He'd have hit the line in front of the ground team to cool them off a bit.

The Firehawk was already on the run for the foam drop by the time he figured it out. They had foam, not retardant. It was better at suppressing fire than blocking it. The terrain map showed a ridge hidden under the treetops. If they could keep the fire from crossing over, it would give the smokies a chance to cut a firebreak along the ridge.

He flipped to infrared and zoomed in. Sure enough, there they were, but how did she know?

He switched back to normal vision and saw the first tree going over, the first of many that would be cut down to make a gap in the forest that, hopefully, the fire couldn't jump. Of all the windblown trees spread over the climbing hills, she'd seen that tree, its lone top moving differently than the others because the smokies were busy cutting it down.

She was brilliant.

He swallowed hard and wondered—if Carly had been his spotter in the air at Crystal Peak last summer, would his knee still be whole?

Chapter 14

SEVEN HOURS.

Carly threw herself down on the grassy bank between the drone's launch trailer and the smooth-flowing Payette. Her body thrummed with exhaustion as if she'd been fighting the fire on the ground. Three hours in transit and seven hours over the fire until the sunset had shut down flight operations. Forest Service prohibited air-attack from thirty minutes before sunset until thirty after dawn.

There were exceptions—the Firehawk and one of MHA's tankers were night rated. The problem was that the personnel contracts called for ten hours consecutive downtime for pilot and machine out of every twenty-four hours. A one-flight call at midnight would delay the next morning's attack until after 10:00 a.m. So, if there were no emergencies, they were done for the night, which in midsummer was about ten hours anyway.

But for the last seven hours, every twelve and a half minutes they'd been back with another thousand gallons of water and foam. Except for five-minute stops at the airstrip every dozen runs for refueling and getting more foam, they hadn't stopped at all. Thirty-two runs on adrenaline and energy bars. Thirty-two thousand gallons from the Firehawk alone. That amounted to a couple of nice backyard swimming pools worth of water.

Carly could sure use one of those now. Of course she was so tired, she'd probably drown in a kiddie pool.

Her mind chewed over the firefight. She could picture where every single run had fallen. If they could have kept going, she could have seen how best to overlap the next twenty drops to slow the fire and turn it to help out the ground teams still sweating it out there in the dark.

The two big airplane tankers running retardant out of Boise could deliver twice the amount, but their round trip, including landing and refill, made it so that they barely equaled what the Firehawk had delivered. The three smaller choppers had done what they could, but they were slower each trip. Besides, even combined, they carried little more than half of the Hawk's load. Though they were great for killing spot fires that tried to jump into untouched woods.

If she had the energy, she'd go and pat the chopper on the nose.

No way. Maybe she'd just sleep right here.

She heard the rustle of someone coming toward her through the knee-high grass. Then she smelled him, or rather what he was carrying.

"Food!"

"Two burgers, fries, slaw, an apple, and some chocolate."

"Oh God, Steve, I'm all yours." She didn't even feel too stupid for saying it. Her body was that hungry. She sat up. "What are you going to eat?"

He handed her one plate stocked exactly as promised as he sat down with an identical one.

"Two burgers of my very own?" She tried to look at him all moony-eyed. It must have worked because he almost dumped his own plate in his lap. She looked down at hers to hide her smile in the fading light.

"You were amazing." Steve's voice was awkward, a little rough.

"No, it was your drone imaging." She took a big bite and talked around it. "Can you imagine how maddening it usually is for me to see the fire for only a minute at a time? And then while my flight is getting the next load, I can't see where anyone else is hitting it, never mind being able to direct them."

She knew she was practically babbling with the high charge of adrenaline, all she had left going for her, but it was too strong to stop.

She crammed down some fries, only warm but still crunchy. She was so hungry that she wouldn't complain if they were cold and soggy.

"We got in an extra run every hour with the Firehawk because of you. Because I could see what I had to see before we got on-station, with just a quick double-check as we did the drop. And with the drone, I could help Henderson direct all the other drops even when I wasn't there. It's better than the view from the ICA's spotter because you can be wherever I need you. We kicked ass up there." She held up a hand palm out and he high-fived it. "Damn, we were good."

Steve was quiet, looking north, watching the ridge that blocked their view of a fire fifteen miles away. He looked awfully good, silhouetted against the softening red of the sky. All quiet like that.

It brought a quiet to her too. Quiet enough that the hyperawareness that had been coursing up her nerves settled into the background. At length she could hear the river running close beside them. Could hear the last of the crows and a few jays settling in for the night, nesting among the trees across the water. The last rattles of the helibase while the ground crews prepped the base for tomorrow's attack. Each chopper would get a full servicing.

The retardant trucks had arrived and loaded the big tanks at the airfield. Which was good; they'd burned through most of the foam they'd brought with them. It was time to switch over the Firehawk and at least one of the Huey 212s to the gooey red retardant.

They'd be ready to start protecting unburned fuels by morning. Water and foam were about fighting fire directly. Retardant was about spreading on the trees that hadn't yet burned to help rebuff the fire by sealing the fuel away from the air.

"Twenty percent." Steve's voice was little more than a whisper. They had it twenty percent contained.

A good start for a half day. Today was more about slowing it down and not just letting the flames run rampant. Tomorrow they'd begin corralling the beast. Of course, that didn't take into account any wind shift during the night, or how hard the smokies and the three D4 bulldozers they'd airlifted in could hold the line.

Steve's face was little more than a silhouette now against the dusky pink sky. From here, down in the Payette Valley, the fire and its massive plume were invisible. Down river, the sky had been painted a brilliant pink, descending even now to a dusky orange reflected off the river.

Carly somehow knew what Steve was thinking. She noted that he wasn't sitting cross-legged, but rather with his left leg stretched out straight before him like it hurt too much to bend. But that wasn't where his attention lay, despite the palm he rubbed along the sore muscles. He was facing north toward the tall ridge, thinking of the fire. That he should be there. She'd bet her next paycheck that he felt guilty about not being the one up on that burning ridge chasing the smoke, cutting the next firebreak.

Carly rested a hand on his good thigh and leaned in to kiss him.

He startled, returned abruptly from his thoughts, and then settled into the kiss. With a plate in one hand and a half-eaten burger in the other, he could only lean in. Their only contact was her hand on his right thigh and their lips. It was a kiss as gentle as the night. He tasted of mustard and ketchup. He tasted of fire smoke. And, someone save her, he tasted so damned good.

She felt him set aside his plate and she started to pull back. She didn't want to be caught and held; she'd just wanted the kiss.

"Oh no, you don't." His voice sounded rough and barely louder than the water. But rather than cupping her neck or clamping his fist in her hair, he slid his fingertips soft as a wisp of smoke along the back of her jawline by her ear, creating just enough pressure to ask her to stay.

She held there on that teetering edge, but couldn't.

She couldn't.

"I'm sorry," she whispered and pulled away.

He let her go.

The light was gone by now. Carly could tell that he was looking at her, trying to read her. But despite the dark, she couldn't meet his gaze. She stared down at her plate. Groped for a french fry and chewed without tasting it.

They ate in silence past the arrival of the first stars. Past the last of the palest pink bleeding out of the west. There was a glow of some work lights from the camp, but they were not enough to block the sky, which filled with a wash of crystalline stars.

She set aside her plate and shivered slightly. Between her racing thoughts and the exhaustion, a chill shook her again despite the warm night. There was nothing left in her.

Unseen hands wrapped a blanket around her as she sat.

"You were thinking…"

"Hoping. Yeah, I'll admit I was." Steve shifted beside her, lay back, and gently pulled her down beside him.

He left the choice up to her. At the last moment she shifted so that she lay inside the curl of his arm and her head came to rest on his shoulder. He arranged a second blanket over both of them.

Carly let herself settle into his warmth and looked up at the night sky.

"Cassiopeia."

She could feel his voice rumble up through his chest. "What? Where?"

An arm shadowed the stars and pointed. "The big W there in the sky, like a kid's drawing of a throne from the side. Only her throne shows, not the great and rather vain queen Cassiopeia herself. And see there, the great empty square in the sky and the two lines of stars trailing off to the northwest?"

She nodded, knowing he'd feel it where her head rested on his shoulder. She kept her arms tucked between them, her fingers interlaced beneath her chin.

"The square is the winged horse Pegasus and the trailing stars are the queen's daughter Andromeda climbing upon the horse's back to be rescued."

"Rescued?"

He nodded and she tried to ignore how much she was enjoying the vibrations of his voice through his chest. She shouldn't feel relaxed here or safe, but she did. She tentatively slid an arm onto his chest.

"The queen boasted she was more beautiful than the sea nymphs. Being a bit vain themselves, the nymphs unleashed a monster that could only be assuaged by Cassiopeia and her husband Cepheus chaining their daughter to the sea-cliff rocks to be consumed."

"That doesn't sound right."

"Chap by the name of Perseus agreed with you. That's him there, that bent triangle."

She didn't particularly follow the sky; rather she followed the flexing of his muscles where her arm draped over his chest. It was easy to miss his chest. His dark eyes and magnetic smile dazzled, his self-conscious limp distracted. But his chest was really something wonderful. He might drive a muscle car, but he clearly had worked hard to keep his smokie conditioning despite his injury. The arm curled against her back, the hand resting lightly on her hip. They too spoke of a man who worked himself hard.

"So Perseus saved the girl."

Carly had lost the thread of the story. "He saved the girl?"

"He did. The poor monster didn't get to eat the girl. Worse, Perseus showed the head of the Medusa to him, and the sorry beast turned to stone and sank. When the gods put him in the sky, they banished him down below the ecliptic. He's still stuck there, down below the horizon for half of the night."

"Sounds as if you're on the monster's side."

"Always felt sorry for him from the first time Dad told me the story."

Carly wondered about the king and queen who had chained his daughter to a great rock. She was a wildland firefighter. It's what she did. She stayed in the air rather than jumping into the fire like her father or TJ. Or on the ground like her grandfather, at least until the emphysema had gotten him. She liked who she was. But each fire she flew was as dangerous as being faced by a fiery monster from the depths.

Her mother, dead and gone when Carly was still in kindergarten, couldn't stand the life of a smokejumper's wife. Carly might not remember much about her, but she remembered that. Her father dead now too. They might as well be among the stars.

And Steve had rescued TJ, rather than the fair maiden, which didn't fit the tale at all, unless it did.

She meant to ask him how it might, but fell asleep instead and dreamed of Steve waving a banner high on the cliffs of ancient Greece.

His was the only banner cheering for the monster.

But even in her dreams, Carly wondered where that left the maiden.

Chapter 15

CARLY WOKE ALONE IN THE PREDAWN LIGHT.

She hadn't slept outdoors in a long time, not since she used to go camping with her father. Linc had never been one for camping.

A sharp "Whoosh!" drew her attention upward.

The drone shot low above her, out over the river, then climbed rapidly.

She jerked upright. Both blankets had been wrapped close about her. Dew spangled her face and hair. The warm night was now gone to cool morning.

The spot beside her was clear of dew as well. Steve must have woken a little earlier to launch the drone, but not enough for any dew to form.

They'd slept together, just slept. She rarely slept a whole night through anymore. And never during a fire. She'd just wake up in the middle of the night with her mind churning over the fire's variables.

Steve had given her a gift of sleep.

And more, but she couldn't put the right word to it. At least not yet. It was all muddled in last night's dreams of monsters and maidens, daughters and flying horses.

She watched the drone circle upward, finally high enough to catch the first ray of sunlight where it shone like a star. Then it turned tail, arrowing toward the fire, and was gone.

Time to get moving.

She grabbed the blankets and trotted up the hill.

Steve was perched in the back of the Firehawk, intent over the console. TJ and Henderson were close behind him. Steve was so intent on the screen that he didn't look up or perhaps even notice when she arrived.

She carefully dropped the blankets behind a foam bucket, then slipped an arm around TJ's waist and watched as the drone climbed up over the fire.

"Looks like they made some headway last night. See, here." Steve zoomed in on the northwest flank. The firebreak had held and been extended, well past where she'd expected.

"What are the winds?" she asked. Something didn't look right.

Steve startled for a moment and shot her a quick glance even as he tapped for the information.

He fully turned toward her, but she saw the numbers and swore.

His smile, half-formed, was wiped from his face as he turned back to the screen.

Last night's winds had eased from the west-southwest. A calm night had let the ground crews do some serious rock and roll. But though the morning winds were near calm, they were out of the north. If it held as a northerly when the day's winds picked up, the firefighters were in deep trouble.

After just a moment, Steve was twisting the drone around and zooming as far ahead as he could to focus on the southwest flank.

"Damn!" they cursed in unison.

Emily came walking up with a cup of coffee and a plate of food.

"How fast can we be aloft?" Carly cut off her greeting.

Emily didn't even blink at the abrupt transition. Rock steady.

"Long enough for you to eat this if you're fast." Emily shoved the plate toward Carly and climbed into the chopper.

"Retardant. We need retardant for this. Foam won't do it."

TJ called over to the tank line, and Evans immediately began rolling out a two-and-a-half-inch hose.

Henderson walked around the outside of the helicopter, removing engine covers and checking fuel tanks for any water that might have condensed overnight.

Carly managed to cram down the English muffin and egg sandwich while Steve circled the perimeter of the fire once more.

She tossed the paper plate in the trash bag and climbed aboard. The moment the radio was up, she was calling for status on the Boise tankers. One aloft, the other ten minutes behind.

By the time the Firehawk's engine was humming, Carly could see the small choppers cycling up.

"Tank full. Hose clear. Preflight good," Henderson shouted.

He made a quick hand sign, to which his wife nodded, and they were aloft. "My heart flies with you." It made Carly's heart melt when Beale flashed back, "Mine with you." Carly had learned American Sign Language as a high-school class project, gotten her father to help her, and they'd kept it up for a couple of years. Until he died.

Carly turned away and checked her watch as Henderson slammed the door shut and latched it.

By U.S. Forest Service code, it was literally the first minute they were allowed aloft, thirty minutes after sunrise. The fact that the Garden Valley airport was deep in a shadowed valley and wouldn't see the sun for hours didn't matter.

The cup of coffee swung in a gimbal on her door. She could really use it but didn't have time right now.

"Steve, where are the crews?"

He handed the tablet forward to her.

Even as she looked, he marked the tiny dots of body heat. A twenty-man hotshot crew was scattered down the flanks of the black, working their way along the edges of the burnout to make sure no smolders or spot fires were flaring up. They and the smokies had clearly worked through the night and truly reinforced their line. They'd saved the ridge.

But the shift in wind, now confirmed from stations up in Canada, was bringing trouble—and bringing it fast.

Calling in tankers wouldn't be enough. The D4s could work their way over, but they'd have heavy going. It would be hours before the dozers were in place, if they could cross the terrain at all.

"I need the smokies to move and move fast."

"Hold it." Steve cut her off over the intercom even as she reached for the radio transmit button.

Each second itched at her. The display on the tablet swung and zoomed for almost half a minute.

Steve was looking at something, but she couldn't discern the pattern to his hopscotching, zigzag views.

She bit her lip in impatience, easing off only when the pain felt hazardously close to drawing blood.

"No way," Steve insisted. "No way can they move

that far that fast. Not doubling back through the black and definitely not over the head of the fire. The terrain is too rough, especially now with how exhausted they must be. They worked straight through the night to hold that line. They're going to be knackered."

"I don't have much ch—"

Steve cut her off. "Beale. Let's dump this load, then switch over to helitack. Carly, warn the crews we're coming to get them and need a space."

Even as the Firehawk crested the ridge and Steve saw the fire come into direct view, Carly was on the radio. She pointed out the line for Beale to follow for the drop while she was informing Henderson of the change in tactics.

Steve could hear Henderson on the radio to TJ right away, and then he started shifting the tanker drop patterns.

Carly kept a dead-even voice as she tweaked Henderson's plan a little west, confirmed the clearing size with the ground boss, and asked Steve for a view ahead on the drone.

She constantly amazed him. Not the woman in a man's job thing. He was fairly sure he wasn't shallow enough for that. Carly simply stood head and shoulders above any other incident commander he'd ever worked with. She was just that damn good at her job.

She was jumping frequencies fast enough to make his head spin and directing different flights to coordinates so fast he couldn't keep them straight.

Steve began tying lines onto the ceiling D rings of the cargo bay, setting up the descending lines to either side for the smokies they'd be picking up shortly.

With the hum of the motors through the deck, he could feel the helicopter dance more lightly as it shed half its weight in six, long-drawn seconds of retardant drop. Steve hung on as they peeled off toward where the smokies were gathering their gear.

He looked east out the cargo bay door. If the fire crossed the next valley, the flames would find a dozen directions to expand, rather than being pinched off for lack of fuel as Carly had originally planned.

The first tanker roared in right behind them, but it wouldn't be enough.

Not by a long shot.

The wind would be picking up in the next hour or so. It would be blasting up the narrowing valley and driving the fire like a blowtorch into an expansive territory. The area was listed on their databases as unburned in thirty years. That meant the forest floor would be covered with dead branches and dying trees. The whole side of Scott Mountain would go up like a single torch. Probably more like a bomb. Home run for the fire gods, a shutout for the home team.

Even as they moved in over the smokies, the crew felled two more trees. They'd cleared an area just big enough for the Firehawk. Branches that were sticking up from the fallen trunks were trimmed even as the Firehawk descended, cut so that the spinning rotor blades wouldn't catch them.

Steve could tell they were a good crew, had trained hard together. They'd probably slept only two or three of the last twenty-four hours, passed out in place on some burned-out hillside in full fire gear. Despite that, they had the landing site prepped by the time Beale brought the chopper in on five minutes' notice. That was tight work, a good team.

In a Firehawk, smoke was an occasional thing; a cloud passed through, heating and flavoring the air for a moment before you blew past and circled once more in the clear. Anything heavy was distant. Far away.

But the smokies were immersed in it. They began piling in, dragging aboard the scents of char and ash. Their yellow Nomex jumpsuits coated half-black with it. Pulaskis with notched edges from where they'd caught a rock. Wooden handles worn shiny by long use. Those with fiberglass handles had black carbon etched into every tiny mar on their surface.

Steve began tossing fresh water bottles to the smokies before even the first was settled. A dozen guys piled in with all their gear.

The scent of the fire was a slap to the face, like aftershave, so familiar it was almost home. The extra sweetness of burned sap smoke, the bitter edge of sweat and exhaustion.

Steve wished, from the core of his being, that he was still one of them. That his suit stank. That the insulating long johns under the fire-resistant clothes under the fire suit itched like murder. That his parachute was a weight on his back that he'd been carting over rock and tree for a full day. His PG bag half-empty because he'd kept pulling energy bars and occasionally an MRE out of his personal gear. Each Meal-Ready-to-Eat was a pound off the pouch but one meal closer to being hungry.

He pulled out a plastic bin and the guys started digging in. Reloading on trail mix and water. On MREs and chocolate bars.

"Two minutes," the ground chief replacing TJ shouted over the rotor noise. "They're dropping us back in. They tell me there's a wind coming. The good news, we're in a notch and just have to cut off a few hundred yards of fire travel. The bad news is we're going to need a two-hundred-foot break at a minimum. They can't move the dozers for another three hours; the heavy lifters are tied up in Utah at the moment. So it's up to the Hoodies. You guys ready." It wasn't a question.

Anyone who wasn't chewing shouted their agreement. The ones whose mouths were full pounded their boots or the butt of their Pulaski on the steel deck. The chopper rang with the noise.

Steve got the attention of the crew chief and directed him to the screen.

He zoomed back and showed the guy the wide-area view. He superimposed the wind shift since last night.

"Oh shit." The guy saw it.

"We're dropping you here." Steve zoomed in. "Your back door is here if the fire gets to you too fast. Over the ridge, then book your asses southwest. It's counter-intuitive, but the wind will be driving the fire away from you."

"Roger that."

Beale slid to a hover.

The nearest big clearing was way too far away. All she'd found for them was a hole between a couple of seventy-foot trees.

The guys started slipping the ropes through the rappelling brakes hanging from the front of their harnesses. As soon as the chopper stopped, they kicked the lines free and started sliding to the ground, tree branches slapping at them as the wind from the rotor wash beat down upon them. The guys didn't even wait for one teammate to fully descend before the next one started down. With a rope out each cargo bay door, the cabin was empty in under a minute.

"We're clear," ground control called up.

It looked like a bomb had gone off in their pristine chopper. Smoke smudges, garbage overflowing the plastic bag hanging on the side, mud coating the deck and the lower parts of the walls. A couple of scars in the paint from a stray Pulaski.

Steve began pulling up and coiling the ropes. He pictured the leader squatting on the ground so recently trampled flat with everyone's landing, sketching a strategy in the dirt.

They were fighting fire while Steve was flying around a damn toy plane. He really was turning into a typical air attack twit. He hadn't even asked the guy's name.

Chapter 16

THAT EVENING, CARLY DIDN'T SEE STEVE AT THE drone site or the rigged-up chow line at midfield along the Garden Valley runway. She told herself she wasn't searching for him, even as the setting sun roared down the valley and cast her shadow all the way back to where the helicopters perched at the far east end of the airport.

She'd probably be better off if she didn't find him. If she just took her sleeping bag and curled up somewhere on her own, she'd be better off. She'd just go for a walk along the river before crashing out.

Sure, Thomas. Just pretend you aren't going where you're going.

I'm just taking these blankets rather than my cozy, one-person sleeping bag in case I feel like sleeping outdoors again.

Uh-huh.

No, honest.

Right, Thomas. The woman in the mirror had never been very forgiving, even when there wasn't a mirror around.

The winding watercourse led her invariably upriver to "their" spot. She didn't want to have someone in her life. She didn't want to have a "spot" with someone. But somehow she did. Somehow they did.

And, of course, she'd completely avoided it when she'd checked the drone trailer. She'd been only a few dozen paces from the bank of the Payette. But she'd set out to prove something, though she'd be damned if she knew what, by looking for Steve everywhere except where she knew he'd be. And he was.

He sat as he had the night before, his left leg stretched before him. His arms wrapped around his right leg and his chin on his knee. Right at the top of the riverbank, looking out over the slow-flowing water.

"The lonely beast banished from the northern sky?"

He just shrugged and kept staring across the water, though there was nothing to see but the far bank a hundred feet off. Even in the failing light she could see that he hadn't washed or even eaten. His hands were still dirty, his face darkened by smoke. The fire had fought hard, and they'd done almost as much helitack as they had working as an air tanker.

His clothes were soot covered as well. They, too, didn't match the man she'd decided was awfully fastidious, showering to clear off a bit of parking lot and gravel dust. It seemed a strange trait in a smokie, or even a former smokie.

"Guess I should have returned the favor and brought some dinner."

His nonresponse finally had her squatting down to look at him more closely.

"You okay?"

That shrug was the last answer she needed.

"Talk to me, Merks." It was the first time she'd called him that, but somehow it fit him at this moment.

She saw the gesture start.

"If you shrug again, I'm gonna smack you a good one. And I'm just the woman who'll do it."

"Then I won't." His voice was tight, rough, even dangerous.

She stood and half considered leaving him there. It wasn't as if she wanted to get closer to the man.

"You're a mess, Merks."

"Yeah, I figured that much out myself. Thanks for your help. I'm fine."

She headed upslope, back toward the helibase. The sun was gone now, the heavens gone dark, dark blue.

She stopped and looked back at the lonely figure by the riverbank. And above his head, the first star shone in the night sky. Steve could probably tell her what it was. It was so bright that it pretty much had to be a planet. Nothing else shone in the sky yet but that lone glittering bit of brightness.

She wanted to ask, but not when he was in this mood.

But it wasn't her mood. They'd trapped the fire at the notch, working the flanks hard to force it to die against the massive firebreak backed up with tons of retardant. They'd have it killed by tomorrow if there were no more overnight surprises.

Carly didn't want to celebrate, that could hex things, but she wanted someone to share the triumph of the day with. Someone who understood the fire and understood what it took to beat it into submission. Few enough knew what it took to face a fire day after day and drive it back into the sky where it lived until the lightning drove it down again.

She headed back down to him, but he must have heard her coming.

"I said I'm fine." A true growl this time.

That did it.

"So am I," Carly told him. She dropped the blankets. Then, with a quick squat and shove on her part, Steve was sliding down the bank, hollering as he hit the water.

"Shit!" His head popped above the surface. "Goddamn, this is cold." He started clawing up the grassy bank.

"Get back in until you're clean. Nothing worse than a dirty, stinking grouch." Carly moved above him and shoved down against the top of his head. Even as his feet went out from under him, he reached and snagged her wrist.

She didn't even have time to cry out before she plunged into the water half on top of him.

She surfaced and spit a mouthful of water in his face. "It's not that cold, you wimp."

"The woman is a goddamn polar bear."

It was cold, though not bitter. But she sure wasn't going to admit even that. She ducked underwater to pull off her sneakers and chucked them up on the bank.

To prove her point, she moved out into the chest-deep current and swam lazily upstream, just fast enough to counteract the current so that she stayed in place.

Steve sloshed to the bank and pulled off his boots. He rinsed them free of mud and tossed them up onto the grass.

"C'mon, tough guy. Let's go for a swim."

He stepped into the current, reached out a long arm, and shoved down hard on her back, submerging her completely on a squawk that nearly made her inhale river water.

She stayed under, made a lucky guess, and got a hand around each of his ankles. A quick bracing of her feet on the sandy bottom and she jerked up, flipping him over backwards.

Carly was laughing when he surfaced.

He got a hand behind her neck. A big, powerful hand.

She took a deep breath, knowing she was going under and couldn't do anything about it.

In the last of the light she could see his face.

Not playful.

Not laughing.

Wild. Half-mad.

For an instant, she was afraid as his hand tightened around the back of her neck. Then he dragged her against him with all the force of a hard parachute landing, when you open late and smack hard against the earth.

His mouth was on hers. Hard, taking, greedy.

For perhaps ten beats of her heart, he ravaged her so fiercely that she couldn't think. Her mind wouldn't function.

No one had ever overwhelmed her senses with sheer power. All she could manage was to wrap herself around him and hang on.

Then she was free. Practically thrown backward into the current.

He stood chest deep in the water, cursing.

"I'm sorry!" The words wrenched out of him. "God, I'm so sorry. Just get away from me, Carly. Leave now!"

She didn't move. Couldn't. Not when she could see the pain etched across his features.

"Go!" he practically screamed into her face, like a wild animal trapped in the fire, unable to escape, knowing it was doomed.

He hung his head, panting. Gasping for breath he couldn't find. His chest heaving aside small waves of river water.

Carly had only seen such pain once, no, twice before.

When it was her own face in the mirror. When her father died, and when Linc…

Both times she'd been helpless. This time she could act.

She rested her palm against the center of his chest, the soaked T-shirt in no way stopping the heat pouring off him.

A step apart, they were connected by a pain most didn't understand because they'd never been there.

She didn't shush his gasps. Didn't lie and tell him it would be okay or that it would hurt less someday. All she did was leave her hand over his heart as the last of the light faded from the surface of the river, bled from the sky itself.

A kiss. She didn't consciously move forward, wasn't aware she had until their lips touched and she tasted the salt. Tears, unseen in the twilight, trickled down his face. She kissed his cheeks, his salted eyes, his forehead.

Then she curled much as she had last night. Her cheek on his shoulder, this time her arms wrapped tight around him as the cold river slid quietly around them.

Slowly, so slowly she could have counted the minutes before he moved, his hands came around her. Not to her waist, nor tracing her hips or cupping her breasts. He simply wrapped his arms around her and held her tight to him, so tight she had trouble breathing.

The shivers that shook him had nothing to do with the cold water that flowed about them. The convulsions rooted from somewhere deep inside and jarred him against her, until all she could do was hold on until they eased.

When at long last he was still and his breath almost

normal, he moved his hands to her shoulders. Offered to push her away, let her free. A silent "thank you" by the gesture of a slight squeeze.

In answer, she kept her arms around him.

This time when he kissed her, the need was no less, but it didn't ravage. It didn't ignite or burn with its heat. Instead it smoldered deep and strong. A slow burn that could last for days.

That almost made her forget they'd been standing still in cold water.

Steve swept her up in his arms and carried her from the water.

As he went to set her in the tall grass, he almost dropped her.

"Goddamn it!"

She could feel him shift as his bad leg lost traction. Could feel the anger come back into his shoulders.

"Real romantic there, flyboy." She tried to make it a joke.

He started to say something as he set her on the grass, but she cut him off.

"And if you apologize, you're going back in the water. Now kiss me again."

He knelt between her legs and leaned down toward her.

As he did, he swore again and then collapsed to his left, landing hard on her leg, rolling off to end up flat on his back.

She put a hand over his mouth before he could speak or curse again.

Carly replaced her hand with her lips and slowly stretched out on him. Body to body from their lips to their toes.

Did she want this?

God, the man's kiss could make her feel drunk all on its own.

Last night she hadn't. Last night the specter of the past had loomed large before her, blocking the sight of the man who had held her close while she slept.

She moved to his neck and breathed him in. Smoke and fire. Heat and pine. He smelled of the forest in all its forms.

Tonight. Tonight was a world away. Tonight she did know what she wanted.

She sat upright, straddling him, feeling his arousal through their wet jeans.

Somewhere she'd found certainty.

Would she regret it in the morning? Maybe. But the morning was a whole world away as well.

Knowing she was invisible in the dark, she unbuttoned her shirt.

Steve lay on his back in the grass above the river and marveled at the feel of Carly's trim waist. He slid his hands under her soaked shirt to discover the true lines of her perfect shape, even though it was covered in goose-bumped skin.

The same hands that he'd used to grab her, to very nearly hurt her. He'd attacked her like some mad beast.

And what had she offered in return?

He could still feel the outline of her fingers over his heart. Who was this Flame Witch? He'd heard the nickname, but never thought she'd cast a spell over him.

And how could he want her so much? Plenty of

women had turned his head over the years, just never for long. They were fun, and he did his damnedest to be fun for them too. It had always been easy to turn away and look elsewhere when it grew dull and boring. Or she got too clingy. Or…

Steve wanted Carly Thomas; he needed her. Like no woman he'd ever needed in his life. If that wasn't a scary proposition, he didn't know what was.

He dug his fingertips into those lower back muscles that he'd been dying to touch, caress, learn. He slid his hands a little way under her tight waistband, hips that even da Vinci never would have thought up.

She leaned in and kissed him on the lips, then shifted upward. A soft hand on his cheek guided his mouth to her bare breast. Already aroused, he took her as gently as his desperate need allowed.

Carly cupped the back of his neck and pulled him against her hard, holding him there until his control let go and he drank her in, until he could feel her very being curling up somewhere inside his chest and her moans filled his ears.

He'd been embarrassed that he'd dropped her, that he couldn't kneel over her, that his knee was too weak to leave him a whole man.

And still she offered herself up to him.

He placed his lips between those perfect breasts and kissed her there. Kissed her hard. Kissed her as if he really meant it.

The odd thing was, he did.

Chapter 17

THEY WASHED IN THE RIVER. GIGGLING LIKE CHILDREN. Carly hadn't laughed that high, girly laugh since… ever. Her girly laugh had probably died with her mother when she was still in kindergarten. Carly Thomas had been the only child in her class in Hood River Elementary who didn't have a mother, no matter who the other kid's moms might actually be shacked up with. Her friends had a lot of odd family arrangements, some three families deep on both sides, but at least they all had mothers.

But she also hadn't had a man ever help her out of soaking wet jeans on a grassy bank by a soft-flowing river. Coax her until she knelt over him, his hands cupping her behind, the both of them naked in the silver light of the crescent moon.

Having no protection, he had pulled her up his body and taken her with his mouth until her body burned and flared. Until the very last bit of fire in her was wholly quenched and she lay sprawled atop him, exhausted, spent.

Steve wrapped the blankets about her before pulling on wet clothes, now cold with river water and the cooling night.

She slapped his ass as he set off toward camp to get them dry clothes. Yet another first.

Sated, alone, Carly watched the night sky, trying to find the story Steve had told her last night. The vain queen and the sad king she could find. But the beautiful daughter lost upon the rocks and the noble hero evaded her.

Steve returned so quietly, she barely heard him set fresh clothes down beside her. A mere shadow against the stars as he undressed and slid between the blankets with her.

"Anyone see you?"

He pulled her tight until she lay as much on him as on the blanket.

"No one's awake. TJ is asleep in his chair, the radio to ground control beside him. I wrapped a blanket around him."

She kissed his cheek.

"You're a good man, Steve Mercer. How did that happen?"

"Damned if I know. It's certainly not what I set out to be." He gazed up at the stars with one hand tucked behind his head, the other wrapped around her shoulders.

"What did you set out to be?"

"A mad letch. A defiler of beautiful women near and far." He slid a hand suggestively over her breast, but he kissed her so gently on the eyes that she could barely feel the pressure of his lips. As soft as the night.

"No, really."

"My friends wanted to fly—rockets, Air Force jets, jumbo airliners. I just wanted to be a firefighter. Ever since…" His voice drifted away.

"Ever since?"

"Another story. Another time." She could see his silhouette against the stars.

"Steve," she warned him.

"Not tonight, please. You don't want me blubbering all over you a second time." But he didn't look toward her, simply remained staring up at the heavens. Maybe that's where he found comfort, looking up at the stories in the sky.

She stroked his cheek, granting him permission.

In response he kissed her so slowly, so deeply that she had no answer but to lose herself in the rhythm of their lovemaking.

While getting their clothes, he'd also scared up some protection. She wasn't going to ask where.

This time when she straddled him and took him deep inside, her world turned and didn't stop. Dizzy with the powerful rush, she worked him deeper and deeper until he filled her soul.

She couldn't be feeling this.

Couldn't allow it.

But there was no way she was going to stop it either.

Just before they both came, she heard him whisper, "An angel in the stars."

Chapter 18

"QUIET MORNING."

Carly blinked her eyes open to see Emily standing above her in the predawn light. The woman stood casually, a few feet to the side, and looking out over the river. There was an odd smile on her lips. Almost sad. No. But perhaps nostalgic. As if her words belonged in another place, another time.

The man Carly lay curled against remained sound asleep, a self-satisfied smile revealed in the soft glow of a new day. No traces of last night's pain creased his face.

"Men always look so innocent when they're asleep." Emily's smile was soft, shared. "Don't be too long waking him up. Mark will want the drone on-site soon."

Emily turned to walk back toward the camp as Carly did her best not to blush. "Once Mark wakes up and gets that same smile off his face, that is."

And she was gone.

Carly wanted to linger over Steve's body. Trace light fingers through his dark hair. Follow the outlines of his workout-strong chest. Maybe see that bad leg he was so ashamed of. To think about how he'd made her feel.

But time was wasting.

With a few strokes, she aroused Steve's body before he completely awoke. She sheathed him and drove herself down upon him.

His eyes snapped open with a single "Whoosh!" of air bursting out of his lungs. It didn't take him but a moment to get with the program. He might be a deep sleeper, but he woke up plenty quickly with the right motivation.

He wrapped his hands around her hips and stopped her for a moment. An agonizingly long, wide-eyed moment. She could feel the heat on her skin follow his gaze as he inspected her from her face, down over her chest, and right down to where their bodies were connected in a tangle of curling hair, his dark, hers so light.

"Now that's an amazing sight." Then he pulled her down and kissed her. Kissed her right through any fears of what it might be like to wake up together the morning after.

Chapter 19

THE FLIGHT BACK TO HOOD RIVER LEFT CARLY feeling disjointed. Uncertain.

The Hoodies had beaten this one and, other than some minor cuts and burns, come out clean. Exhausted but clean.

It had taken most of the third day, but they'd finally been able to turn the fire over to a Type II Incident Management Team. There would still be flare-ups and spot fires, but the winds had held steady. The heart of the fire, cornered by retardant drops, had died for sheer lack of fuel against the triple fire breaks cut by the smokies and hotshots.

Carly and Steve had found a few moments during the day when it was just the two of them—while flying the drone over the scene before it was time to retrieve the smokies, after retrieving the drone, and collapsing the trailer in preparation for the flight back to Hood River helibase.

Steve had remained quiet. Reticent.

Not a word about the sex.

She didn't expect a profession of love, but she hadn't expected him to avoid holding hands in public. She'd always liked holding hands, that feeling of connectedness. Carly had missed that.

With Steve, there was not even a gentle brush of fingertips on shoulder in passing. Nothing. He barely met her eyes.

He'd avoided her questions, no matter how gently she started them, about why he'd been so upset last night. Even the question about why he'd always wanted to be a firefighter went by the wayside.

She watched the landscape rolling by beneath the Firehawk. The twisting river valleys looked as snarled up as her innards felt. The flats from Boise, the dry brown hills and clustered trees of the Umatilla National Forest, the dry gullies and patchwork fields in eastern Oregon, and finally the familiar, heavy green of Mount Hood.

For the entire flight the intercom had been silent. She could feel Beale looking over at her a few times, but she refused to turn and meet the woman's questioning gaze.

How could so much connection, so much sharing as she and Steve had done last night be gone like a single match doused with a full load of retardant?

She didn't help him land the trailer or unload his equipment. Instead, she rode the helicopter to its pad once he cleared the lift harness.

She clambered into her Jeep, and seeing that Aunt Margaret had driven up to meet Uncle TJ, Carly left fast and drove to Hood River. Down to the small house that was listed in no phone book. Up a small dirt road that had no name. The cabin she and Linc had built together in the woods back when he'd still been alive to share a dream.

Off call for at least forty-eight hours, Carly shoved her phone in the charger, crawled under the covers, and tried not to cry herself to sleep.

Steve got the drone trailer back up. Fifty-fifty chance that the next inning of the fire season would be in their range, and he'd rather be ready.

He missed Carly's help. She made things easy. Alone, he couldn't get the pieces to mate, only realizing after twenty minutes' struggle that he had the middle of the mast flipped backward, by which time, he'd cross-threaded a bolt that had to be sheared off. Barked a knuckle bloody in the process.

He'd been… Damn! He didn't even know what.

He'd been through a couple too many innings in that last twenty-four hours, that's what had happened. He'd been such a train wreck last night. Steve Mercer, an emotional train wreck. That was a changeup pitch, if there ever was one.

So what if he had dark moments now and then? He'd made it through with no drugs. No antidepressants. No painkillers after they took him off the heavy, post-surgery stuff. Toughing it out had been brutal, but he'd pulled it off.

Dark moments still blindsided him, like this morning when they'd been getting dressed. He'd still been naively dazzled by an angel's beauty as she slid impossibly long legs into the off-the-rack jeans of someone who worked for a living. They'd looked fantastic on her, made her more real than some tailored, slim-leg, designer crap.

He was naively dazzled until he saw where she was looking.

His left leg.

He'd looked down, somehow expecting it to be whole each time he did. Each time it was a surprise that his leg would never be normal again. And he'd worked the right leg hard to compensate for being a cripple, which only increased the contrast.

A third of the muscle from lower calf to upper thigh was simply not there. A long scar ran up the side of his leg from ankle to hip, still a broad weal despite the six months since the last surgery. He'd have that scar for life.

The doctors had argued that there wasn't enough muscle tissue left for the leg to be saved, and he'd fought them every inch of the way. No metal or plastic prosthetics for him. He'd refused to sign the form allowing them to cut it off, even if they thought they had to while he was under.

Cripples didn't fight forest fires, no matter how many times the hospital's physical therapist had insisted on always using the word "challenged." If one more person told him he'd be walking-challenged or activity-challenged or...

"Looking sour, Merks."

Steve sat down on the rear bumper of the truck as Henderson came up to him.

"The damn antenna didn't want to go together."

Henderson didn't even bother to look up at where it now shifted gently back and forth in the morning breeze. He simply parked himself on the bumper beside Steve.

"That would make you pissed, but you've been eating lemons."

Steve grunted in response. Yeah. Probably.

They sat together in silence for a while. Henderson all relaxed, looking up at the blue sky as if it were a marvel.

Crap. He was allowed to be in a goddamn foul mood if he felt like it. Wasn't he?

"We've got a couple days' dark, supposedly. Rest and recoup and all that. What are you going to do?"

Damned if he knew. He'd been here less than a week and spent most of that time on fires. He sucked on the still bleeding knuckle. He really needed a Band-Aid, but that would require climbing back into the truck again, which would only remind him about his knee and... screw it. It had almost stopped bleeding now anyway. Almost.

Henderson looked at him for a long moment. "C'mon."

"What?"

Henderson stood and headed for the parking lot. "Just lock the damned truck and come on."

Chapter 20

THE DOGHOUSE WAS PACKED.

Cars on the street had windsurf boards on roof racks. Kids from all over had come to take on the Gorge, which offered some of the best winds in America. Yet another reminder of what Steve couldn't do.

It would help if more of them were kids. But there were a lot of guys and gals who either were out to prove something or maybe, just maybe, were actually good. Plenty of them older than Steve.

Like a cluster of misfits almost lost in the hipster windsurf crowd, a group of the Hoodies huddled around a six-top table near the Snoopy doghouse. They shoved a couple chairs together at one end as he and Henderson squeezed in.

Chutes was sitting across from them, next to Evans, the "mud" geek in charge of the retardant supply and the bucket rigs for the choppers. Mickey, who flew one of the 212s; his mechanic, Jackson; and Betsy, who ran the base kitchen. A couple of guys Steve didn't know yet, including the current ground leader and his assistant.

"Akbar the Great." Chutes introduced the small Indian man with the call sign of Ground Two.

When Steve had met him in the chopper, he hadn't realized the man's size or his skin coloring. Between the heavy gear and all the smoke stain, neither had been visible, nor relevant. Over the preceding three days it had become clear that while TJ was missed, MHA put top men on the ground.

"And Two-Tall Tim, 'cause he's as tall as any two of us strung together and three of Akbar." One of the most interesting-looking men Steve had ever seen. Even sitting, the slender Eurasian towered over the rest of them, at least six-six, maybe more. Steve decided that the man looked both exotic and almost alarmingly handsome. Paired with Akbar the Great, whose head didn't even reach Tim's shoulder while they were seated, they were clearly different species or from different planets.

Handshakes all around, careful not to place an elbow in someone's beer.

The waitress dropped off a couple more glasses and a fresh pitcher of beer. Steve poured. A nice, hoppy wheat beer. That brightened his outlook on the day.

The conversation drifted back and forth over the Scott Mountain Fire for a bit. Every time a group of windsurfers got a little too loud at a nearby table, the Hoodies raised their voices just enough so that they couldn't be ignored. Then they set to talking about parachutes and helitack and "jumping fire" and the story of the burning tree, the one that almost got Akbar as well as TJ, got bigger and closer every time.

You could see some of the windsurfer girls and their awesomely fit bodies leaning closer and closer to the Hoodies' table. Evans, Akbar the Great, Mickey, and Two-Tall Tim were dishing it out and the girls were eating it up. These guys could clear the room of women if they wanted to.

Steve knew the ploy well. He actually found himself

not joining in, which surprised him as much as anything in this long, dreadful day.

Henderson was happily married, apparently happily enough that he didn't even flirt on the side.

The ICA noticed Steve's attention. "She'd kill me if I even looked. You have no idea how lethal the woman is." Then he smiled like the happiest man on earth.

Chutes wasn't playing either. At first Steve thought it was age, but then he noticed how close Chutes was sitting to Betsy. Maybe after a year alone, he was finally open to other opportunities. Steve wondered if Betsy noticed or if she just thought it was old friends sharing a meal.

The waitress broke it up when she came to get orders. Steve opted for the fish and chips.

Then Henderson leaned in.

"We've got a problem here."

Steve could feel the whole mood of the table shift. Suddenly the ICA was sitting there, or maybe it was the military Major. He'd shifted the mood and taken command of the whole table with five words. How the hell did Henderson do that?

"The problem is, you've got a couple of Hood River newbies here." He nodded to include Steve. "And a bit of clear time. What the hell can we do?"

Everyone relaxed, having thought for a moment they were suddenly going to be ordered back to base to re-pack all the chutes.

"Hiking." "Surf the gorge." "Killer waterfalls." "Portland's just an hour away. Best bookstore on—"

"No. No. No. And no." Henderson cut them off. "I

can see that I'm going to have to talk to Rick when he flies back in. You guys are thinking way too small. Who here fishes?"

Chutes, Akbar, and Betsy.

"Fishing?" Steve's soft aside echoed the others around the table.

Henderson just winked at him as he replied to the group, "Now we're talking. The sport of kings."

"Thought that was horse racing." "No polo." "Golf." "Golf isn't a sport." "Might be for a king." "Bowling," someone tossed out. "That's not a sport. In Canada it's hockey, but they don't have any kings." "Commonwealth country, they have a queen, or at least they borrow her now and again."

"It's fishing, folks." Henderson spoke over the others, once again with that command voice of his. "Trust me on that. And what do we have a bunch of, just lying around when we're not fighting fires?"

"Parachutes." "Fire hoses." "Smokies." That got a laugh. "TJ." That got a bigger laugh.

"Helicopters," Steve said.

Henderson slapped him hard on the shoulder, clamping him in place with a hand that could crush a full-grown ox.

"Helicopters," Henderson smiled. "Now, who knows where we're going?"

"Oh," Betsy said in her throaty voice. "I definitely know the spot." She elbowed Chutes in the ribs.

She'd definitely noticed who was paying attention to her.

―⁂―

Steve considered begging off after the meal. He and Henderson were heading over to the big pickup that the ICA drove.

Steve didn't want to go guy camping and prove that he had no earthly idea how to fish.

He wanted…

Now that was interesting. He wasn't sure what he wanted. He didn't want to go fooling around with the drones. He didn't want to just "hang out with the guys." He'd passed on going trolling for girls when he decided to leave the table.

Tim, Akbar, and Mickey had already enticed two brunettes and a trio of blonds over to their table with renewed stories of firefighting and flying helicopters.

What Steve wanted was…

It finally clicked. What he wanted was to see Carly. He'd been oversensitive about his damned leg. Knew he'd pissed her off. She'd been in his arms last night and felt so good, so right. That's what he wanted. He'd have to apologize, which was against his normal practices, but she deserved that much.

"You know…" He considered how to break it to the ICA. He didn't want to tick off Henderson, not after he'd been so decent these last few days.

"We'll need poles, waders, tents, and a couple Pulaskis for chopping firewood." Henderson spoke over Steve's next thought as if he were merely continuing the conversation at the table.

"I was thinking…" Steve tried again with no better luck.

"Ice coolers, too. Do you know if TJ fishes? Bet he does. Strikes me as a sensible sort of man. Let's go see if we can roust the guy, or at least boost his gear."

"Uh…" Maybe Steve would be better off if he just went with the flow.

"Besides…" Henderson waited to finish his sentence until they'd both climbed into the front seats of his pickup's crew cab. He waited a long moment in silence.

"Besides, I know his niece loves to fish."

Henderson started the pickup with the roar and rattle of its big diesel engine.

As far as Steve knew, TJ only had the one niece.

"Count me in."

Henderson merely smiled as he headed them toward TJ's.

"Knew I could."

Chapter 21

CARLY SAT WAY IN THE BACK OF THE FIREHAWK AND
wondered how in blazes Emily had talked her into coming. They had another twenty minutes roaring through
the skies until they reached the Rogue River, up in the
heart of the Umpqua National Forest.

One moment she'd been mostly asleep under the covers at six in the evening, in the privacy of her own cabin.
The next she'd been holding a cheerfully burbling Tessa
in her arms while Emily and Aunt Margaret were getting
out her fishing gear, sleeping bag, and tent, and folding
some clothes into a knapsack. Her cabin was small—
bedroom, kitchen and a small great room. So they didn't
have far to go to find everything.

Now she was wedged between TJ's ice chests and
Betsy's cooking gear. Henderson and Emily were fly-
ing; Emily had her daughter. Carly hadn't realized the
ICA also flew choppers, though it made sense. Two
SOAR pilot majors. Bet they had some stories to tell.

Aunt Margaret and TJ, along with Chutes and Betsy,
were having a gay old time sitting on a couple of jump
seats installed in the middle of the cargo bay. Akbar the
Great and a cute windsurfer blond named Tori, who was
a good foot taller than he was, were perched on the tents
and sleeping bags discussing ancient Greek dramas, as
far as Carly could tell.

And Merks bloody Mercer sat up in his little control

seat and pretended he wasn't massaging his leg. He
was also pretending that they weren't sitting like two
boxers who'd retreated to their opposite corners of the
roaring aircraft.

She covered her eyes with her palms.

He'd tried to be nice when she showed up in Margaret
and Emily's tow, still carrying Tessa. That was the one
thing that made sure she couldn't bolt, having someone else's baby in her arms. Had that been intentional?
Margaret sat with her back toward Carly. Emily was invisible up in Carly's spotter seat in the copilot position.
Maybe Carly didn't want to know just how thoroughly
she was being manipulated.

Steve had tried to be nice.

"I'm sorry for… you know."

Yeah, she knew. For making her feel like shit.

She'd liked his body. Enjoyed it. Liked the way it
felt against hers and the way it made her feel. She'd also
been surprised at how good he made her feel. A whole
part of her had been closed off for the year since Linc's
death, a part she'd somehow forgotten.

And in the light of the morning she could see what
she'd also felt in the night, the damage to his leg.

The rest of him was so tan, it made his leg a stark,
pale contrast. Of course, he'd clearly spent a long time
in a cast. Muscle atrophy explained some of what was
wrong, but the long scar, as well as his mood, said there
was way more to the story.

She'd mused about how magnificent he must have
looked when whole. The women must have flocked.
Actually, she liked him this way. Otherwise he'd have
that weird curse of being too perfect, too handsome. It

would be like those actors with the perfectly symmetrical features, so handsome that they looked fake, as if no personality could compete with such features.

One thing Steve Mercer didn't lack was personality. She felt battered by the chaos of his emotions: the playboy, the smokie hero, the drone nerd, his desperate need, and his impossible tenderness.

That's what had done it, what had made her weak in the head on the subject of Steve Mercer. She couldn't predict him. With Linc, you always knew the next sentence before he spoke. With Steve, not even close.

Then he'd spotted her looking at his leg as her thoughts wandered. That's when he'd closed down. She hadn't connected the timing this morning, but that was definitely it.

Some part of her had thought that the morning-after sex had been taken as cheap or easy and he'd decided to cast her off.

But for once maybe it wasn't about her.

What if it was about him?

She uncovered her eyes and looked across the cabin at him.

As if sensing her, he turned.

His face quiet. Again that calm moment, making sure she knew the choice was hers. How did he do that? He didn't give her anger or try to dump guilt; he simply waited.

She offered a short nod of acknowledgment, which he returned ever so carefully before facing forward once more.

Once again he'd done the decent thing.

Damn him.

Chapter 22

STEVE KEPT STOPPING IN WONDER AS THEY SET UP camp.

Betsy had led them to a lazy curve high in the headwaters of the Rogue River. A broad rock ledge had forced the river to swing wide to the south before curling back around the other side and continuing on its way. It created a low rock promontory surrounded on three sides by water and by towering trees on the fourth.

The rock also made a perfect perch for the Firehawk, its black-and-fire paint job appearing to actually burn in the last of the sunlight.

In the upstream and downstream curves of the rocky bluff, two broad beaches of sand and small gravel had been built by the spring floods. It didn't take a group of firefighters more than a few minutes to have a good campfire rolling on the upstream beach. There were a few pitched tents, but most were clearly going to opt for an air mattress and a sleeping bag under the stars.

It was past nine o'clock by the time they were set, but another meal seemed in order. You couldn't help but be hungry when surrounded by the cobalt blue sky of dusk, the fresh air, and the noisy chatter of the river working stones downstream toward an ocean two hundred miles away. They could be all alone in the world right here.

Shaved twigs were soon sporting a variety of hot dogs and marshmallows. S'mores were in the making. Steve hated marshmallows, but grabbed a couple of graham crackers and some chocolate to eat while his hot dog got crispy.

Carly sat not quite across from him. Setting the fire directly between them would have been too obvious a snub. But just as clearly, she wasn't ready to trust him after how he'd treated her this morning. Thankfully, people were mixing it up a bit so their mutual avoidance wasn't too obvious.

Betsy had settled between Emily and Margaret to play with the baby, who had discovered the game of alternating flashing smiles and sticking out tongues. Chutes, clearly at a bit of a loss, had landed between Henderson and TJ.

Steve ended up with Henderson on one side, and Akbar and Tori between him and Carly.

"Why Akbar the Great?" Steve asked to appear casual.

"Akbar is my middle name. My first name is actually Johnny."

Tori laughed. She had a good laugh. And talk about the ultimate pickup line. "Hi, want to go on a camping trip in a Firehawk helicopter that I rode into a forest fire just yesterday?" Damn, Steve had never had a line that good.

"Johnny the Great?"

"Akbar means 'great.' So my name is Johnny Great the Great Jepps. Makes me feel all-powerful sometimes… right until a tree smacks you." He nodded over toward TJ, who had downgraded to a cane. "That was good, Steve, what you did." He turned to Tori.

"This guy"—he pointed at Steve—"saved that guy's"—he pointed at TJ—"life last week. Not bad for his first day on the job."

Steve pulled his hot dog out of the fire, blew on it to put out the flames, and put it on a bun he'd been toasting on a flat rock near the coals.

"You'd have done the same, Akbar."

"Sure. But you were the dude there when it counted. I was busy hustling my ass down that cliff."

"Which is the only reason that tree didn't land on your head."

"True, but a tree hits this head, it's gonna bounce off. Warning you, Tori, I'm a hard-headed dude."

"As long as you're hard-bodied as well." Her smile was pure tease.

Steve could feel the heat where he was. He'd bet Akbar the Great's body temperature had just gone fire hot. He was almost surprised the man didn't burst into flames on the spot.

In a matter of minutes, there was no longer anyone sitting in the space between Steve and Carly.

———

By some form of mutual consent and in the same instant, they each shifted one spot toward the other around the fire. Both in motion, too late to stop without making it look stupid.

Carly would have welcomed a remaining gap between them, but she knew they needed to talk. By shifting together, they also shifted away from the others and had at least a feeling of privacy.

"This morning—"

"I'm sor—"

They both stopped.

Rather than play some stupid "you first" game, Carly

just kept her mouth shut. Steve didn't make her wait long. A simple nod, acknowledging he had some explaining to do.

"This morning…" A nod to acknowledge her words. "I'm sorry that I overreacted."

She waited for more.

"I…" He turned to study the fire, his hand absently moving down to massage his thigh.

He didn't appear to be able to continue.

"Does it hurt?"

He jerked his hand from his leg as if it had been burnt, then set it back down slowly with a sad smile.

"More the memory of pain. At least I still have the leg."

"How long out of the cast?"

"Two months. I'm supposed to be in PT still, but I couldn't miss another season." His voice was clear on that point, definite.

Carly didn't know what she'd do if she couldn't fly to fire. She'd lost her father and her fiancé to fire, and still she flew.

"I…" She reached deep, not even knowing why she did. Maybe for a good man in such obvious pain. Pain of heart. "I know what it takes to do that."

"How could you?" His scoff was practically a slap. "You're goddamn perfect. Such a reputation leading wildfire air attack that I heard of the Flame Witch all the way down in Los Angeles. Though no one mentioned that you were a woman who was so beautiful that a man would be an idiot not to die to protect you."

Carly didn't know what to do with the compliments. They were so wrong and so strange that she didn't even know where to begin.

"I don't need a man to die for me. Too many have already done that." The ice ran into her veins, freezing her right to the very core.

Steve's face went blank, then his skin paled to almost white, despite the ruddy light from the fire. His sympathy, no, his empathy went straight to her—

No!

She couldn't let another man in.

Couldn't lose yet another.

Carly rose and strode into the night. Walked blindly until she was past the Firehawk and down the length of the western beach, where the beach ran out and the low, rocky cliff met the fast-running water. She could go no farther.

There she waited in the darkness. She needed an answer. But none ever came, no matter how many times she asked the question.

"Why?"

Her whisper was lost in the sound of the rushing water.

Chapter 23

STEVE'S HANDS WERE INCHES FROM CARLY'S WAIST when she cried out into the night.

How many times had he faced that one unanswerable question? Hundreds? Thousands?

He finished the gesture, slipping his arms around her.

She fought. Without hesitation. Pounded her fists at his arms where they crossed in front of her belly. He heard the sobs, felt them shake her. She redoubled her force then, unleashing one last cry of anguish before she stopped as abruptly as she'd started.

Carly turned in his arms, rested her face against his shoulder, and wept.

He held her close. Rested his own cheek upon her hair. What the hell was he doing? He didn't rescue women, and he especially avoided weeping women.

But a rocking motion came from somewhere inside, like the motion of the living trees in a breeze.

How long they stood, how long she cried, he didn't know. Had no measure. She soaked his shoulder with her tears long before she quieted. At long last, she turned her cheek and rested her head there.

"I..." Her voice cracked. "I made you all wet and snotty."

"It's okay. I'm sure that sooner or later someone will throw me in a river to wash up."

It earned him a sound between a laugh and hiccup.

Again he simply rocked and held her, not that he knew what else to do. Some stupid part of him started picking out the stars of the two bears where they peered at them from over the treetops.

"His name was Linc Hanson. We were engaged."

Steve did his best not to react. Jealousy? Or anger that someone had hurt her this badly?

"Last summer, at the Pedro Creek Fire, he made a mistake. A series of them." Now she'd gone so quiet he almost feared she'd fainted. He held her a little tighter to let her know he was listening.

"He wasn't—" Her voice caught hard. "He wasn't a very good firefighter."

He tried shushing her. "Tell me later. It's okay."

She pushed away. Took a step, perhaps two into the dark, the gravel shifting and crunching beneath her step the only indicator of which direction she'd gone. Her light hair barely a suggestion of reflected starlight.

"No. I've got to get it out. I don't know if I'll be brave enough to face this a second time."

"Okay." He tried to imagine a braver woman, someone who had done more than face the fire after it had taken both her father and her fiancé. He couldn't.

"Linc, ah, got caught with no escape route. Then he snarled his Pulaski in his foil fire shelter and tore the hell out of it in his panic. We found the shreds when we found his body. The fire turned and he wasn't ready. He burned alive screaming for mercy into the radio."

"Did he—" No, Steve couldn't ask the question. It would be too awful to imagine.

"He only fought fire to try and fill the void my father's

death left in my life." Her voice broke with each word. "And I let him."

Total self-disgust dripped from her thickened voice.

"He died begging for me to help him as I watched from six thousand feet in a fixed-wing spotter, the closest retardant a lifetime too far. He burned alive screaming my name. It's why I fly helitack instead of a fixed-wing spotter. So that there's a chance if ever… So I could… In case…"

Steve stepped to the shadow swaying before him.

This time, when he slid his arms around her waist, she didn't fight him. She simply lay back against him, exhausted, and let him hold her.

As if that could ever be enough.

Chapter 24

THE DAWN LIGHT HAD FILLED THE SKY BUT HADN'T reached down to the deeply forested river except for moments here and there when it filtered through the branches, bringing the water to radiant life.

The smoky scent of last night's campfire was gone, fully suppressed as only a wildland firefighter could do. In its place, the air was rich and thick with a morning mist that lay low to the water, and the taste of pine and dreams.

Carly thought she was first up until she reached the river's edge.

A hundred feet upriver, knee-deep in the flowing water, ICA Henderson had his pole out, tip pointed upstream as he nursed his line along with tiny tugs to make it look like a bug dancing on the surface.

What fly would he be using? She chose the Adams. It had always served her well with trout, the only fish up here above the William L. Jess Dam. No fish ladders, so no salmon.

Carly considered shifting downstream around the great rock bend to fish from the downstream beach. There'd be privacy there, but there was a certain social order to fishing. There was companionable separation, and there was downright avoidance. It would be rude to wander so far, unless the other person occupied the only good fishing hole.

She scanned the banks and the stream. There wasn't just one good hole here; there were about a thousand. Carly hadn't really inspected it last night during their sunset arrival, but Betsy had picked an amazing spot. The problem wasn't finding a place to fish, but rather which one to start with. Which would the fish be napping in, dreaming about a morning meal?

After the fly was tied on, she waded out into the cool water. It made her feel fresh and clean, washing away last night. The current cleared away so many things.

She and Steve had been through too much that day for sex. Too many emotional twists and turns. Instead, they had simply lain together and held each other for the longest time. He was good at that. He didn't just follow wherever his libido led. There'd been no question of his body's response, nor her own for that matter, but instead they'd chosen mutual comfort, lying for hours and watching the stars turn. Only deep in the night, after all others slept, did they sate their mutual needs.

Eyeing the river for obstructions, Carly shifted her stance on the rocks and began her cast. Slowly, weaving the pole back and forth, she bled out line until it made a great swirling double arc over her head, just as her father had taught her. Moving the fly through light and shadow, flash and sparkle. Not finding sunlight at this early hour, but finding deeper and lesser shadow, the fly shimmered back and forth above the water.

Were the fish under the surface watching yet? Sensing some motion impossibly out of their reach, but paying attention?

Twice more she flicked the pole, settling the fly closer and closer to an eddy she'd spotted below a big, dry-topped rock that lay nearly midstream. With a last twist, she slid her cast over the rock and dropped the fly at the very edge of the current. It slipped in and washed right into the little curl of quiet water, the place a fish might pause to rest from the constant current.

Perfect! Now that was a good start to a morning. If someone were to bring her a cup of coffee, she'd really be set.

A glance upstream revealed that she'd been observed. Henderson sent her a cheeky two-fingered salute. He already wore the silver Ray-Bans, despite the just-breaking dawn.

She responded with a nod and went back to teasing her line with little midge-like twitches.

Henderson's salute rankled. It was a that's-okay-for-an-amateur salute. Well, she'd show him. Her father had taught her well.

"Don't fret, Carly." Only she could hear her father's voice in the burble of the stream. "Don't even think. The fish will hear you think and they'll swim away, my girl. They can feel you thinking right down that line."

She'd always imagined fishing line like a little fiber-optic cable transmitting her brain waves to the fish.

She could be quiet.

Just her and the stream and the quiet of dawn.

A late bat flitted by, heading into the trees. Too early for even the earliest robin.

And especially too early for Steve Mercer.

Damn the man.

She'd done everything she could think of to drive him away, to not want him. She'd been rude, sprayed him with gravel, proved beyond a doubt that she was indeed the greatest and most complete emotional wreck on the planet.

Still he wouldn't go away.

Her line drifted downstream, the current finally pulling it loose from the eddy.

She reeled it in, barely clearing a snag where a partly fallen tree had draped its branches far out in the stream. Even now, the stream continued to patiently undercut the roots clinging to the far bank's edge.

Again Carly set up her cast. Back and forth. Back and forth. Building momentum. Building arc.

"Until you make a drawing across the sky."

Her cast went wide as she thought of lying on Steve's shoulder and listening to his stories of the stars. Last night the tall forest on the riverbanks had revealed only a narrow slice of the crystalline heavens.

This time he'd told her of Cygnus, the impossibly ugly human who played a harp so beautifully that even the gods had wept. When he'd died, they'd turned him into a beautiful swan and placed his beloved harp nearby as the constellation Lyra.

Again, Steve had played her body ever so gently. Had made soft love to her until all of the pain had simply melted away and flowed downstream, never to be seen again.

At least she hoped not.

How was it possible for a man so strong to touch her that way? As if his hands were made of a brush of silk or a wisp of smoke. He had slowly stoked the heat back into her body, fighting back the chilly darkness.

Even the memory of it heated her all over again, despite the cool water wrapping around her legs.

Unlike any man she'd ever been with, not even Linc, Steve hadn't taken. He'd only given.

He'd brought her such pleasure that her body ached to be once more in his arms. Her body wanted simply to give herself to him.

The chill of the stream ran up her legs then, quenched any fire.

"No," she whispered to the stream.

She couldn't afford to let someone in. Not that far.

Sex, sure, that would be safe enough. Even with Steve. She'd let it be about sex and only sex. After all, it was incredible.

It would hurt to lock up her heart. She could feel the tightness even as she had the thought. But Carly had learned how to survive, how to protect herself.

Close down, pull back, be safe.

It was a familiar feeling, a place she'd lived since her father's death, except for a brief glimmer Linc had offered in the unending night.

But she was having trouble finding that hard place inside her. As if it had gone, scorched away by her tears and Steve's gentleness.

If her place of inner safety was gone, where did that leave her?

She tugged on her line, but it didn't give. Nor was a fish pulling back against her.

Downstream. Her inattentiveness had let the fly drift. It was now hopelessly snarled in the downstream snag.

She tugged once more in vain hope.

No luck.

All tangled up.

Chapter 25

STEVE HAD FELT CARLY RISE AND COULDN'T GO BACK to sleep. Warm, snug between their sleeping bags on the air mattress they'd set out beneath the stars. More sleep had eluded him.

It wasn't the thought of amazing sex that filled his mind, though even thinking that definitely elicited a strong reaction from his body.

He simply wanted to be around her. He considered whether he should be all worried about getting too attached. He always played clean. But Carly was more than a one-inning gal. For now, he'd enter the on-deck circle and just see what happened in the next at bat.

So, he crawled out of the warm cocoon of their sleeping bags into the dawn light and wandered over to the fire pit. There he snagged a mug of coffee that Betsy was brewing on the morning flames. They traded smiles, both pretty damn self-satisfied, if the truth be told. How long had she been waiting for Chutes to notice her? However long, clearly last night had been a good one.

He couldn't miss Carly, a glowing beacon standing in dark water. A tiny stray beam of sunlight had found its way through the trees and lit her hair like that of a fire goddess.

He sat on the rocky bank watching his angel fishing. He watched those fine, long muscles control the pole so perfectly, painting a miracle across the dawn sky. He'd never dreamed of such beauty in such a setting. The world waited breathless for each cast.

The fly soared forever, then drifted on the current. A dozen tiny adjustments. Way more than just tossing a hook in the river, which was all he'd ever done. Her pole was impossibly long and thin; no way it could pull a fish to shore without snapping.

Yet she moved it with the same confidence she fought fire, a step ahead of everything. A focus so total that she made a bubble in the world about her. He could be a thousand miles away, for all he mattered in this moment.

Right now, it was just Carly and the flowing river and her pole.

The tip bent sharply.

He looked downstream to see the fish jump. They always jumped in the movies.

Instead, a tree branch that had fallen in the water wobbled around a bit.

Over the rolling sound of the water he couldn't hear the curse, but he could certainly see it in her stance as she tugged again, wiggling the distant branch.

He rose and waded out to her.

She startled as he came up beside her.

"Oh, hi."

"'Hi'? That's what I get this morning?" Even teasing her was fun. She actually blushed.

"Uh, sorry." She leaned in and kissed him lightly on the mouth, then turned back to face downstream. "I snagged a damned branch."

Well, he clearly wasn't going to receive any further attention until the matter was rectified.

"Here." He handed her his coffee mug and turned

downstream. In the first few steps, he went from calf-deep to knee-deep. By how smoothly the water ahead was flowing, he'd guess it grew deeper toward the snag.

He turned enough to call over his shoulder.

"What is it with you and cold rivers?"

She laughed and sipped from his coffee mug. Clearly it would be empty by the time he got her line unsnarled.

He took another step, except there wasn't one. Unprepared, he plunged into a hole over his head.

He surfaced sputtering as the water drifted him right into the snag. Only quick thinking let him grab a branch that didn't include an insanely sharp fishhook.

A glance upstream showed Carly waving merrily. Beyond her, he could see Henderson almost doubled over with laughter.

Great.

Using one hand to hold himself in place against the current, he found the line with his other hand. It took about a minute to clear it, Carly taking up slack as he freed it.

The nasty-looking little fly, both fluffy and prickly, finally surfaced. Then he spotted the hook and was damn glad he hadn't grabbed that. The little sucker looked nasty. Undoing the last twist, he tossed it clear and Carly reeled it back in. He let go and struck out for shore, finding bottom in another few feet.

Of course she'd snarled the line right over a hole, probably the only one in the entire bend of the river.

Betsy made "Oo-la-la!" noises as he stripped off his freezing, wet clothes.

He made a point of mooning her as he pulled on fresh shorts.

Shorts.

He looked down at himself in surprise. He hadn't worn shorts since the day they'd cut off the cast. The shorts were long, ending just above his knee, but you could still see his bad leg as plain as day, a white stick-pin next to his tanned good one. There was so little meat there that the outline of his bones practically showed against the skin.

No way in hell a woman was going to find that attractive.

But he'd only brought the one pair of jeans, now a sloshy, blue puddle at his feet.

A hand smacked into his ass, causing him to jump forward onto the jeans with a chilly squish that had water running up between his toes.

Betsy leered at him over her shoulder as she headed for the river with her pole. "The cute little blond throws you over, be sure to give me a call." Then with a sashay of her bikini-clad hips and a wave to Carly, she headed downstream. He knew she had twenty years on Carly, but Betsy's body was still incredible. Chutes was a very lucky man.

Defeated, Steve did the only thing he could think of. He wrung out the jeans and laid them on a rock to dry, then retreated to the fire.

Chapter 26

TJ WAS THE NEXT ONE UP, FOLLOWED TO THE CAMPFIRE a couple of minutes later by a very groggy Chutes. Clearly he hadn't had much sleep last night. Akbar the Great and Tori were still nowhere to be seen.

Steve handed around coffee and started setting up to make bacon and eggs.

"Don't like fish?" TJ sat in a little lawn chair, his foot propped up on a handy log, an Ace bandage still in evidence, though no sign of any swelling.

"What, them?" Steve waved his hand toward the stream.

"Ignore him." Chutes slit open a package of bacon and handed it over. Found a bowl somewhere to crack eggs into, handing it over to Steve. Even dug out a spatula. When he handed that over, Steve got the feeling he was being set up. Chutes was being too damn helpful. This wasn't Steve's first season or even his second.

Steve checked his face, but Chutes was looking over at TJ. "You gonna fish today, old man?"

They both carefully avoided Steve's eye. Steve put the eggs back in the carton.

"Maggie said if I was in the water when she woke up, she would be cutting me off."

"Cutting you off where? Another foot?" Steve looked up in time to see TJ's smug smile. It seemed everyone in camp had arrived with one thing on their minds. And had all hit runs.

He glanced toward the stream as Carly's pole lashed downward. He watched a moment to see if she'd caught the snag again. If she had, she could swim after her own damn line.

The pole bent twice as far, impossibly remaining in one piece. She teased the line out, pulled it back in, edged toward the shore, then hurried back into the water. Nursing the line, coaxing it.

Then he saw the fish leap, way better than in the movies. A magnificent splash of sunlight speckled silver and gold, and longer than his forearm. A monster of a trout.

"You're gonna burn your bacon, boy." Chutes's voice pulled Steve's attention back to the fire.

"What?" He hadn't even put the bacon in the pan yet. "What you talking about, Chutes?"

"Me?" Chutes looked dead at him. "Didn't say a thing. Did I, TJ?"

"Didn't hear a word." TJ stretched out his good leg and sipped his coffee.

Again Steve checked the cold pan to see what the hell they were talking about before returning his attention to the stream and the woman fighting the fish.

Someone put a net in his hand.

"Go!" Emily Beale ordered him none too gently. "Take that to her."

He looked over his shoulder to where she had come up behind him cradling her daughter.

Beale kicked him none too lightly in the butt. He stumbled to his feet and headed for the stream.

When he got there, Carly waved him downstream, halfway toward the hole.

"Right there."

He stopped.

"I'll lead him to you, just be ready."

Steve tried to watch the fish but kept turning to watch the woman. Her lower lip caught between her teeth as her brilliant blue eyes tracked the battle. A lip he knew to have the soft taste of heaven. She was as lean as her pole and as strong too, able to bend under impossible loads and still come up true.

This is where she belonged. Fifty miles into the wilderness with nothing but a fishing pole in her hand.

"Now!"

The fish shot nearly across his toes. Only pure reflex let him net the fish. It hit the net with such force that he almost lost it in his surprise.

If the pan had been in his other hand…

He hefted the cast iron in surprise. He'd carried the pan right into the river, not remembering to set it down.

Steve looked back at Carly's radiant smile as she sloshed toward him, winding in the line on her reel.

Burned his bacon?

Hell, Chutes wasn't even close.

Steve was caught and cooked. Hook, line, sinker, and frying pan.

Chapter 27

CARLY SMILED DOWN AT HER BEAUTIFUL TROUT. *LET'S see Henderson top that.*

Then she looked up at Steve. Net in one hand, frying pan in the other. He was so damn cute she couldn't stand it.

She kissed him hard.

For a moment he didn't respond.

Then he wrapped an arm about her so fiercely that he almost knocked the breath out of her.

She pulled back enough to mumble, "You lose that fish and you're a dead man."

With one hand, he pressed his fist wrapped around the handle of the net into her butt.

Then he was devouring her.

The heavy frying pan splashed into the water and clunked down on the rocky riverbed. That freed a magnificently strong arm to wrap around her shoulders. He held her so tightly that she couldn't have escaped if she wanted to.

And she definitely didn't want to.

She didn't care if they were putting on a show. It didn't matter what TJ or anyone else thought. All she wanted was to let the wild current carry her away. His lips and morning stubble were like a fire along her neck until she threw her head back and stared at the sky just to revel in the wonder of it. That unexplained wild man that lived somewhere deep beneath Steve's skin.

She'd shout to the heavens and make a complete fool of herself if his mouth wasn't back on hers, if their tongues weren't warring, caressing, tasting.

He stopped, pulled back sharply as if in sudden awareness of what he'd been doing. Whether it was that he was ravaging her or that he was doing it in front of a guaranteed audience, she didn't know or care.

She trapped his head with her arms wrapped around his neck, the pole slapping against his back.

"I…" he whispered.

"…don't want you to stop," she finished for him.

Those dark eyes inspected her carefully.

She faced him back, let him read the truth in her eyes that he wasn't doing a single thing wrong in her book. In fact, he was doing a whole lot of things right.

He leaned back in and kissed her so gently it hit her heart like a hammer, far harder than if he'd returned to his frenzied and welcome attack. Rather than clamping their bodies painfully together, his hand slipped into her hair to cradle her head.

When at last he stopped, she knew she had never in her life been so thoroughly kissed. Not upright, not horizontal, not in the throes of passion.

No. The best kiss of her life had been standing knee-deep in water so cold that it put goose bumps on her legs, with a netted fish flopping against the back of her ankles.

Steve left her weaving for balance when he stooped to retrieve the pan from underwater.

She tasted her swollen lips, tasted Steve on them.

She did her best to merely smile at him as he stood back up.

It was either smile at him or drag him down into the cold water and rocky-bottomed river right now and see just what he'd do to the rest of her, audience or no.

Chapter 28

CARLY'S AND BETSY'S FISH EACH OUTWEIGHED EITHER of Henderson's.

He looked actively offended when Carly told him she'd used an off-the-shelf Adams. He'd custom-designed and made his fly that morning before anyone was up because the hole below the larch definitely need a streamer, but not a bunny streamer, and he'd...

She'd merely shrugged as his explanations quickly dove into some netherworld. He was one of "those" fisherman, off-the-deep-end passionate about it. She and her father had just fished. He'd taught her that the fun was the important part of the whole process.

Henderson tried to argue that his pair of trout combined at least weighed more than Betsy's, even if not as much as Carly's.

She simply linked her arm through Betsy's and offered Henderson a cocky two-fingered salute, much as he'd offered her this morning.

"All yours, hombre!" She led Betsy off, leaving him with cleaning duty for all four fish.

Akbar finally showed up too late to fish for breakfast, but not too late to fry it up. Tori tried to help, but Aunt Margaret and Betsy pulled her out of the fray. In minutes, every guy in the group was giving Akbar conflicting culinary advice, and the women left them to it.

For some reason Chutes kept harassing Steve about

how he really wanted bacon and eggs instead. Steve was studiously ignoring him.

No one commented on the kiss made on full display before them all. What was there really to say? It melted her bones just thinking about it. They'd fired off enough sparks that it definitely changed how some of the couples were looking at each other. As if she and Steve had heightened their awareness of each other.

What Carly needed, really needed, was—she debated simply dragging Steve off behind the nearest rock or tree but discarded the idea—a little distance. Because, if she didn't get some, her body might spontaneously combust, and even a dousing in the river wouldn't put her out.

She took a fresh mug of coffee and returned to the river. Wading out to midstream, she sat on top of her rock. Right below her dangling feet swirled the eddy current where her beautiful four-pounder had indeed been hiding.

Here, with the current so noisy, she could pretend she was somewhere else. Some time else.

In her peripheral vision she saw someone moving toward her through the water. A quick glance showed she was safe.

"I was afraid you might be Steve. Don't know if I could handle that right now. My nerve endings are still sparking."

Emily smiled. "Can't say that my nerve endings are in much better shape. And I was merely an observer."

Carly scooted to the edge of the rock so that Emily could sit beside her with Tessa in a deep, post-meal sleep in her arms, one tiny hand firmly clamped about a lock of Emily's hair. Together they watched the water flow, tumbling loudly enough over the stones and boulders to conveniently mask the debates among the male chefs. Only TJ's laughter cut through the river's sound clearly, again and again.

"TJ certainly enjoys himself."

"He does," Carly acknowledged. "You should have heard them when he and my dad were together. You needed earplugs. Dad died when I was eighteen, my first official season working hotshot. TJ tried to take over for him. Tried to be an even better man than he already was. He made me finish college and got me training as a spotter so that I'd get out of the fire."

Emily rocked her sleeping daughter.

"Makes my husband crazy that you outfished him with a standard fly. He's rather rabid."

"I'll admit I noticed."

"I didn't realize. There wasn't much in the way of rivers and lakes where we were flying when we met, and none that were sanitary or safe."

"Safe like in bad stuff in the water or safe like, uh, bad guys with guns and stuff?"

"Yes," was all Beale answered.

"Oh. Uh, okay." Carly tried to imagine someone squatting in the woods across the Rogue just waiting for a chance to shoot them all. It sent a shiver up her spine. She tried to imagine a world where death could be behind any tree just a dozen yards away. That in a moment they could all be dead, slaughtered. Even thinking about it seemed to make Carly's world grow dark.

"You and Mark lived with that?"

A shrug was the only response Emily offered and clearly all she had to say on the topic.

"I was a city girl. It wasn't until our honeymoon that I learned I had better get to enjoy fishing, or at least camping along rivers and lakes."

Carly studied the stretch of river. "My dad and I fished a hundred streams like this. All over the Northwest. I'd fly in the spotter plane to every call, just like Tessa does. Every time he got a break from the smoke, we went out. This is where I'm happiest."

"Couldn't help noticing." Emily opened Tessa's blanket to the spangled sunlight filtering down through the trees.

Carly knew that they'd just arrived at the heart of the matter, why the pilot had followed her into the middle of the river.

"You're a real no-nonsense kind of lady, aren't you?"

Emily shrugged and didn't need to look up from cooing at Tessa to make her point.

Carly had never in her life felt as incredible as Steve had made her feel. Ravaged and alive and so desired.

"I know I look pretty good." Men's reactions told her that even if she didn't always agree with them.

Her companion didn't even deign to answer that one.

"Obviously not what Steve is about."

Again, the confirming lack of response.

Right. Sure, he'd been gob-smacked at the beginning. But since then, he'd stood through her anger and her tears. That didn't happen with a guy only interested in her body. Not the way he held her, even when she didn't want to be.

He'd forced her to face Linc's death as she hadn't in a year, simply by being strong and steady and refusing to let her run from herself.

Last night was the first time she'd told the story since the investigation closed the day after Linc's death. Panic, fatal mistake, dead, case closed. A whole life wrapped up in under twenty-four hours and a three-paragraph report. Except the wake and funeral, which had delayed the whole process by only three more days.

The report didn't question Linc's lack of skill. Firefighters were drawn to the battle. Wildfire drew those with a deep connection to the land and trees. Linc would have been happier in an office somewhere, but that wasn't a place where Carly would survive.

So, Linc had learned the techniques of wildland firefighting. But he didn't have that sixth sense of other smokies. That extra sense that always told them their way out, always had them tracking their back door, the fire, the fuel, the winds, and a dozen other interacting factors.

He'd also never learned that sometimes the right thing to do in an emergency was to move slowly. It was the hurried panic that had caused him to shred his shelter.

She didn't want to tell that story ever again. It took too much out of her, filled her head again with Linc's screams. But she no longer wanted to shut down at the merest memory. That was a change.

"He helped. Steve. He helped."

Emily didn't ask about what, or how. She simply nodded and they sat together watching the river flow into ripples around the rocks.

The occasional fish jumped for a fly. A bird circled close to inspect the intruders in the middle of the stream.

After far longer than it should take to cook a couple of fish, a shout from shore announced breakfast was ready.

Emily climbed off the rock and stood upstream of it for a moment.

"The good ones help. That's how you know they're the good ones."

And again Carly sat alone in the middle of the rushing stream.

Chapter 29

IT WAS A LAZY MORNING. AFTER THE FISH FRY, SO CA-
sually that Steve barely noticed the transition, TJ,
Chutes, and Akbar began quizzing the new members of
MHA's Goonies.

Steve was in good as soon as they found out he'd
been the lead jumper out of Sacramento. Everyone knew
California was a hard post for a smokie—the entire
southern half of the state was a tinderbox, and the northern half wasn't all that much better. They also knew that
you had to be crazy and passionate about the wildfire
fight to work all the way up to leading the first stick.

Then it was Henderson who came under scrutiny, as
no one seemed to want to mess with Emily Beale. By
some unspoken agreement, they focused on her husband.

Steve had sat through a hundred sessions like this
one. On one side of the great divide, rookies who'd
signed on for the romance of the wildfire fight. It looked
good in the movies, but it was some of the hardest and
most dangerous work on the planet. Across the divide,
career wildfire fighters felt honor bound to weed out the
chaff, sometimes before they even got their ears wet.

But Henderson understood.

He didn't talk about fire, a common enough trap. He
talked about watching the blooms come after the snow
on his parents' Montana ranch. He painted a picture
of the waving grass and the tall horses his father and

mother had loved almost as much as their only child. And he talked about his favorite trout stream and fighting the cutties to the net.

It soon became clear that his fishing this morning wasn't an affectation, but came from the core of the man.

Steve had kept it to himself, but he wondered at the contrast of the man who loved fishing almost as much as his wife and who flew Special Forces helicopters into the darkest combat.

It was connection to the land that made the wildfire fighter, not whether he carried a Pulaski or a smartphone and tablet. Steve would have to think about that one later.

Again, everyone's attention drifted to Beale and her sleeping child and then drifted right on by.

Perhaps it was her mirrored shades and just the hint of a smile that even seasoned Goonies couldn't get past.

"I remember this time…" TJ started the story as if nothing had happened. It was the clearest acknowledgment that Henderson had been accepted and that Beale had been declared okay as well.

Henderson didn't react or gloat. All he did was lean in a little to refill his coffee mug and get ready for TJ's story.

"Ham, Chutes, and I were out chasing some blaze or other. What was it, Chutes? Black Canyon?"

"Big Polka-Dot Rock-Candy Mountain? How the hell should I know, old man? It's your damn story."

"You're older than I am, old man."

"So I have an excuse for forgetting." The affection between the men couldn't have been clearer.

Steve could imagine Ham sitting just between Carly and Betsy, tossing in a joke of his own.

"Maybe it was the giant campfire of 1835," Steve offered in his absence.

Carly laughed and looked over. She opened her mouth and then closed it, the smile wiped abruptly from her face. Then it returned, a little tentative but there. Maybe he'd struck a little too close to home.

"Hush," TJ went on, not missing a beat. "This is my story. So the three of us were out on this ugly, damned blaze. We stumbled on this little cluster of cabins that was out there, and I mean way the hell out there."

"They were totally cut off from—"

"Shut up, Chutes. You missed your chance to tell it by sassin' me." TJ was clearly just warming up.

"There were about ten guys, about as many women, and a passel of kids. They had a sweet setup—running stream, drying elk meat, the whole shebang. But when we tried to tell them there was a fire coming, we discovered they couldn't speak a single word of English. It wasn't until later we figured out they were Bulgarians who'd emigrated or escaped back before the Berlin Wall went down and had decided that the Oregon wilderness was their idea of heaven."

Chutes took over the story from there anyway. "Problem was, we had no way to tell them to run. When we tried to drag them off, they dug in their heels. Together, we did save their little community. These guys pitched right in. They were naturals. Took a while to catch on, but we'd saved a whole clan of Bulgarian wildfire fighters living fat off the American land."

That got a good laugh.

Steve told the one about the guy who'd been more concerned with his art collection than his family. They'd finally had to get the cops to tow him away just minutes before his house burned. His wife had divorced him very publicly right after, getting the kids and the rights to all of the art he had saved. The film crew hadn't evacuated yet and the TV *News at 5* became the centerpiece of her case.

"There was a little girl," Emily Beale spoke. She looked down at the bundle sleeping in her lap and brushed a finger along its cheek. "Mostly starved and an orphan by the time we picked her up."

Steve wondered about her. These were supposed to be the funny or touching moments.

"We were in the middle of a mountain range dozens of miles from anywhere and filled with hostiles. My crew chief spotted her, hiding on the ground near a hostile target we'd just removed. There were exploding ordnance and burning vehicles not twenty feet from her."

Emily stared down at the coals in the campfire but Steve wondered what she saw.

"We'd thought she was a burden at first, but then she became a sort of company mascot. Two of the best people I know fell in love because of her and adopted her in the bargain."

She turned to look at her husband who'd gone all quiet.

"That's the moment I decided I wanted to have your child. I'm always amazed at what was born from that firefight."

Mark sat up and kissed his wife tenderly.

Carly had rested her hand over her heart.

Steve wanted to feel that. Truly he did. There was a family he'd lost and could never get back. But he wanted to love someone so much that they'd want to have a family of their own.

"What she's not telling you"—Henderson's easy and deep voice was a sharp contrast with his wife's—"is that the young scamp has become a good friend of the President. Yes, that one. Hangs out in Oval Office every chance she gets and teaches him the wisdom according to J.K. Rowling."

<hr />

As the late morning warmed the air, some napped. Some lay out in the broken sunlight with a novel. Akbar and Tori set off on a hike downstream, two insanely fit individuals going exploring for the fun of it.

Steve wished he could do that. His leg hurt too much, though it wasn't necessarily a bad hurt. The shooting pains that had wracked his leg through the winter had been cured by the third surgery. It wasn't even the biting pain of just a week ago.

Now it was a muscle ache. He no longer thought about using his hand to lift the leg when he wanted to move it. He simply climbed out of the car, with only a little help from any handhold he could grab.

It also hadn't folded out from under him since that first night on base. Even if he'd never be whole, maybe he was getting better. But he still couldn't go rambling for rough miles with Akbar and Tori. Easy to picture Carly striding along with them. She belonged out here. He—

"Hey, flyboy." He squinted up at Carly where she stood haloed by the sunlight, as if she needed the help to look magnificent. So not. Hiking boots, cut-off shorts atop those infinitely long legs. A Goonies T-shirt and his San Francisco Giants hat atop her shining hair. You couldn't make up a woman who looked this good.

"Want to go for a walk?"

He glanced downstream where Akbar and Tori had already passed out of sight and shook his head.

"I packed lunch and a blanket. It's not far."

"What isn't?"

"Are you coming or not?" Carly held out a hand.

Well, anything had to be better than where his head was right now. He shrugged and let her help him up.

She didn't let go as she turned perpendicular to the river. In a dozen steps, they'd entered the woods hand in hand. No one watched them leave except maybe Beale, glancing over the top of her book. Beneath the tall pines, they passed through a narrow line of scrub, then walked across the upward-sloping forest floor.

It was darker here, cooler, lush with moss ranging across a hundred colors of green. Small trees stood little chance in the shadowed heart of the mature forest, leaving only obstacles of fallen giants and fern grottoes along their path. They sometimes had to duck and weave around branches, but Carly let him set the pace and he kept it slow.

A walk under the trees with a beautiful woman.

Funny, all of the ladies he'd scored runs with, both on and off the fire line, and he'd never walked in silence through a forest with one. Yet forests, or at least their fires, had been his only dream since he was knee high.

They didn't talk as they moved through the trees. Occasionally one or the other would point. A red-tailed hawk cruising through the branches on silent wings, moving as if he were crossing open sky rather than threading a thousand gaps fifty feet in the air. Squirrels chattering their alarms. A deer and her fawn, stepping silently through the brush with that strange hesitation step of wild animals even when feeling safe.

Carly lifted their clasped hands to rub the back of his hand across her cheek more than once. Steve found it easy to return the gesture.

Perhaps a mile from the river, the forest lightened ahead as they crested a rise. At the verge they had to force a path through the brush. He held several branches aside so that Carly could get through, then turned to the view.

"A burn." The end of the forest was an abrupt shock. Looking back at the face of the forest, it was easy to see where the near sides of trees had been burned off, the damage halted even as it killed the verge. Not a clear cut, definitely a burn.

"We fought this two years ago. I spotted it on the way in. Hadn't realized back then that it was so close to the river."

Steve looked out. A few of the charred giants still remained, but this fire had been hot and hard, nothing for the logging companies to salvage. It had scorched the soil, killing off everything in its path.

"Slow mover?"

"Old forest. Not old growth, but nearing maturity. It had lots of fuel, so it burned hot and long. We kept it ringed in, had it fully contained, but we couldn't break its back. It just burned and burned."

That explained the soil burn-down and the generation of plant life now showing. No trees had survived. This was recovery foliage.

The hot pink carpet of fireweed spread across the rolling slopes. Sumac and low alder saplings had begun to dot the hillsides. And not much else. In five years, the alder would be a couple stories high and shade out the fireweed. Grasses would be next, but none yet.

He followed Carly to a slight rise where she swung down her pack, untied a blanket, and spread it among the flowers.

She sat and he joined her.

"Now, Mr. Mercer. I have an agenda."

He slanted a leering grin her way. "Thought you might, Ms. Thomas. You are a particularly well-organized lady, if I may say so."

"First, lunch."

"Spoilsport." He brushed a hand down her cheek and traced the line of her lovely neck.

Before he could move farther, she captured his hand by the wrist and held it disdainfully to the side, like a wet and vile rag, before letting it drop.

"Second, you and I are going to have a talk."

Why didn't that sound good?

"Third, you and I are going to make love in the sunlight where we can actually see each other."

That sounded very good.

"And"—she leaned in to nip his ear lightly before whispering into it—"if you don't seriously ravage me in the process, I shall be very disappointed."

Out of the park.

Chapter 30

"SO WHAT HAPPENED?"

Steve lazed back on the blanket and watched the soft clouds poking slowly across the blue sky. Lunch of a roast beef sandwich big enough to satisfy a firefighter, graham crackers, and an apple. Dessert of dark chocolate and fresh strawberries, so big they required two or even three bites to eat, had left him feeling very mellow.

They'd actually changed up the agenda a bit with a quick round of sex, a leisurely lunch, and a nap in each other's arms. Now lazy conversation that had moved them right through to late afternoon.

Carly was easy to be around. They'd been sharing memories of their first fires and some of the real characters who fought them.

A Goonie named Ziggy, who was almost as round-faced as the cartoon character, made his off-season living writing science-fiction novels.

A hot chick named Clarice who had set out on a mission to sleep with every man on the entire Sacramento fire team and made it most of the way before a female smokie gave her a new experience. Clarice had married her rather than completing her quest. Steve told Carly that was before Clarice got to him, though it really had been after. They'd had a fun week together before she'd moved on. She and her partner had a couple of kids now, one each, both natural and born the same day.

But with her single question about his accident, a different Carly now sat next to him. This Carly wasn't easy to be with. This one had brought him here so that they'd be alone and asked a hard question. Now he'd have to answer. Steve half wished he'd refused the walk and lunch.

He sighed, knew there was no way out of it, no matter how long he studied the clouds.

"What happened?" He cast his mind back to the prior summer. When he'd been at the top of his game, a place he'd never be again.

"July 19th. The season was barely rolling. Yet another blaze in the hills above LA. I was the lead, first flight, first stick." Carly would know what that meant, could appreciate it. He'd spent six hard years getting there, the power hitter, the guy they banked on to bring the runs home and keep the team alive in the process. Made it easy to buy toys like his cherry Firebird.

"Stupid goddamn accident." He sat up and pulled out a stem of fireweed. He began plucking the brilliant pink petals one by one until they puddled about his feet.

"We got surprised by a wind shift. I was scrambling ahead with my crew. At first we were trying to get ahead of the fire to cut a fresh line. The beast had already jumped four or five firebreaks. Then we were just flat running because that beast was in a plain, old hurry."

Steve could remember the heat. The crazy roar of the fire ripping at the sky, racing treetop to treetop, devouring everything in its path.

"We ran into someone's mountain still. With the smoke so damn thick that he could barely breathe, the guy actually aimed a shotgun at me. I was so pissed that

I smashed it out of his hands with my McLeod rake. Damn thing fired and hit his still tank. It breached down onto his wood fire and the thing went off like a bomb. He was thrown about fifty feet, not a scratch on him."

Steve brushed aside the pile of plucked petals that had scattered on his shorts and, pulling up the pant leg, forced himself to look at his left leg, something he tried not to do. Carly sat close and really looked as well.

"A chunk of the tank got me. I came to lying on my ass. Thought I'd just been bruised and banged up from slamming into a tree or something, maybe cracked some ribs again or something like that. From here"—he brushed his fingertips just above his ankle—"to here." He marked himself mid-thigh.

"Like I'd been through a log peeler. I left a whole layer of meat and a lot of pieces of bone in that idiot's front yard."

He closed his eyes and focused on keeping his voice steady.

"I was still conscious when they medevaced me out barely a hundred feet ahead of the flames."

Carly rested a hand on his arm, but he couldn't reach for it. Couldn't move.

"A lot of times since then I've been pissed that I somehow missed severing any arteries. Then I'd have been done and gone before they could get to me. I wouldn't have to live every day like this."

—∾∾—

Carly moved her hand from his arm to his thigh.

Steve twitched when she touched him. He would have pulled away, but she kept her hand firmly in place until he stopped trying to withdraw. Instead he turned away, his eyes closed and face resigned.

He barely tolerated it, both arms wrapped around his good leg, pulled up with his chin propped on it. Holding it close. Facing away from her into the distance of the recovering burn.

Then she began to stroke her hand lightly up and down his outstretched leg, exactly as she'd seen him do when he thought no one was watching.

The heat of his leg proved it was still human, still real.

She could see it now, feel it now. His leg wasn't merely emaciated from too long in a cast. There was some muscle tone along the top of his thigh. But the outside of his leg didn't extend much past the bone. The outer side of his leg was missing most of its muscle. He was right—it was a miracle he'd survived at all.

He shivered despite the heat of the sun as she traced her cool hand down the hot scar.

"No one has ever touched me there."

His voice was cut off, frozen from her. He spoke about himself clinically, as if it had all happened to someone else.

"Doctors sometimes poked or prodded it, but that was all. I wouldn't let the nurses rub in any salves, always did that myself no matter how goddamn much it hurt. I made them do PT with machines or exercises."

Slowly, ever so slowly, his leg relaxed. His back slowly settled into a less rigid arch as she traced the scar again and again.

"We're two pretty damaged souls, aren't we?" Carly knew for sure she was.

"I guess." Steve still kept his cheek on his knee, facing away from her. "Hard to call you damaged, though."

She stopped stroking his leg. She wanted to yell at him in protest, declare that she was damaged as well. But it sounded stupid next to a man who'd spent a year in and out of hospitals, who had multiple surgeries and endless hours of physical therapy.

"Hurt, for sure." Steve spoke without moving as if she sat on the other side of him. "I can't imagine how bad that radio call must have hurt."

It was the single worst memory of her life. Even worse than her father's death. When he knew he wasn't going to survive, her father had clicked onto the circuit to the radio tower and simply said, "Tell Carly I love her." And never transmitted again. Linc had inhaled fire while drawing breath to scream her name one more time for help she wasn't able to give.

Steve turned to rest his other cheek on his knee so that he now faced her.

With one fingertip, he reached out and traced the line of her cheekbone. Her dry cheekbone.

Carly rubbed at her eyes, but the tears weren't there. They had always leaked out on the rare occasions she talked of Linc's death.

"How did you come through it? How did you find your way?"

Carly's laugh caught in her chest and came out half-strangled. "How did you?"

Steve's smile was sad as he traced her cheek again. "Who says I did?"

Chapter 31

STEVE HAD NO IDEA WHY CARLY WAS HERE WITH HIM. She practically shimmered in the late-afternoon sunlight. Her eyes the color of the sky and as bright as the flower petals still scattered on the blanket and ranging out of sight over the rolling hills ahead of them.

Chamerion angustifolium, a pioneer species of regrowth. Fireweed was one of the first indicators of soil recovery.

She'd chosen the spot well. The surviving forest behind them, the new one, not yet grown, stretched before them. This was the line a firefighter walked every day.

"I fought this fire two years ago," she'd said. Even if she hadn't walked this land as a smokejumper, she'd certainly been in the air when it counted. She was no less important than the smokies or hotshots in turning and killing the fire.

Drones were still cutting-edge technology on forest fires. Maybe Steve did have a place, even if no one except Carly thought so. A part of him wanted to say she was biased because they were sleeping together, but there'd be no such thing as "good enough" for Carly Thomas when it came to fire. If it wasn't stellar, you had to fix it. And if it was stellar, you'd have to make it better.

He looked down at her hand where it stroked once again over his damaged leg. Cool, gentle, caring.

For some idiot reason she cared about him. He didn't know whether to be relieved or terrified, or to bow to the gods in reverent thanks.

He could feel the life flowing back into his leg beneath her gentle attention. He could feel the blood flow beneath the scar, could feel the clean summer air he inhaled trickle down to his very marrow. There was just the faintest hint of floral on the air from the odorless flowers. Somehow she did that. Found something in him that could begin to grow once more and turn him back into a human being.

"My own personal angel." The words came out before he even knew he'd spoken.

She stopped. Her attention shifting from his leg back to his face.

Once again, he traced the impossibly soft skin of her cheek with the back of his fingers. This time, when he ran his fingers along her jaw and coaxed her forward, she flowed into his arms.

Her kiss made him more whole than he'd been since the accident, perhaps even more so than any time in his life. She gave to him without consideration, without hesitation. Her mouth drew the heat from deep inside him.

He struggled to hold back, but each time he did, she growled. The woman actually growled at him, nipped his ear, tickled his ribs, nuzzled his neck until he went nearly mad.

He shoved her down to the blanket. Then he reached out and grabbed the pile of petals he'd been plucking from the fireweed in an attempt to avoid the fire building inside him.

Steve sprinkled them over Carly's hair, scattered a

trail of purple-pink down her black T-shirt and dribbling the last of them over her shorts and along the top of one thigh.

Her eyes fluttered shut as the petals fell upon her cheeks, opened to watch him as he leaned over her.

The landscape of her stretched before him. His hands traced her shape, memorizing what his eyes devoured: the shape of breast, the curve of waist to hip, the velvet smooth of well-muscled thigh.

On his return up her body, he hooked the edge of her T-shirt and slipped it off over her head.

He tried to be gentle when he put his mouth to her breast. But she wrapped her arms around his neck, pulling him hard against her as she arched beneath him.

Between one breath and the next, he'd stripped her naked, except for his hat. Damn she looked good in that hat. He savored her body, softer than the petals still scattered about them, sweeter than the strawberries he could still taste on her lips.

Satin and bright summer sunlight, fair skin and tan lines, and a taste that finally drove him off the deep end. He nibbled, tasted, and teased. Drank her in until she laughed and moaned.

She tried to return the favor, but each time she reached for him, he tucked her reaching hand out of the way. Ravaged she'd asked for, and ravaged he'd deliver. He drove her higher and hotter until he knew the Flame Witch burned. And she burned so damn bright.

When sweat sheened the surface of her skin and the fire of shudders rippled beneath, then he finally took her. She cried out loud enough to fill the forest and soft enough that only he could hear her.

Locking her legs around his hips and her arms around his neck, she completely let herself go to the waves roaring through her body.

For one moment, for a single shining instant, they struck flashover together, and for that perfect moment, Steve was burned clean and made complete.

Chapter 32

A RINGING PHONE PENETRATED CARLY'S STUPOR.

She blinked her eyes open and the fading blue sky spanned above her. Steve lay upon her like a man dead or smugly asleep.

It rang again.

She looked around. Trees, wildflowers, remains of a lunch. She managed to flop her head to face the other way. Success, so at least that much of her body was still working. The rest of her had been slain by multiple orgasms and would clearly never function again.

A scattering of clothes. Her backpack.

On the next ring, Steve grunted back to life.

"Backpack," she whispered, unable to unwrap her arms from around his shoulders. His really, really nice shoulders.

His eyes cleared and he looked down at her. A smile completely pleased with itself came into being.

His move to kiss her again was cut off by another sharp ring.

"Backpack," she managed again.

"Screw it. How can there be cell service out here anyway?"

"Didn't bring my cell. That's the satellite phone." The MHA phone she'd grabbed off the chopper while packing lunch.

He groped for it, reaching far enough to create

several very pleasant sensations along her body as he moved.

"Yeah," he answered like a drunkard, shifting solidly back over her.

Carly did her best to suppress her giggle.

Steve's grimace proved that she'd failed entirely, which struck her as even funnier.

"Uh, mile, maybe mile and a half due north. Right on the edge of an old burn. Right. Okay. Out."

He put down the phone and started to get up.

"No way, flyboy." She tightened her arms and legs around him. "We aren't done by a long shot." She caught his mouth with hers, and after an initial resistance, he sank back upon her.

Though she didn't trust Steve's mouth. There was some joke there he wasn't sharing.

She ignored that and flexed her muscles around him.

His response was predictable and wonderful. One of his hands stroking the side of her breast, the other tangled in her hair. She could feel another response where he still remained inside her. With a little patience, they could...

"They're coming." He nuzzled her ear in a wonderfully delicious way, making her giggle again. She never giggled, but she couldn't stop herself. She'd never felt like such a girl as with Steve sprawled over her. Her own personal man-blanket.

"Who's coming? Besides us, I mean." She started to move back and forth in a way she hoped would make him completely insane.

"Them." He kissed her back hard, and her mind blanked for several long, wonderful moments that promised exactly what she'd been hoping.

"When?"

He pushed up on his elbows and smiled down at her with an evil glint in his half-open eyes.

A low hammering thud made her tip her head back until she could see the tops of the trees, upside down at the edge of the forest.

The splash of a shining black-and-red Mount Hood Aviation Sikorsky Firehawk shot into the blue sky like a dragon of old, roaring low over the tops of the trees, directly over their picnic.

Chapter 33

"WHY DOES IT TAKE TWICE AS LONG TO DRESS WHEN someone is watching?" Carly asked him in a soft voice, barely louder than the pounding rotors of the descending Firehawk.

Steve didn't know, but it was certainly true. "Your T-shirt is on backwards."

"So?" She shot a nasty look at him. She was still naked below the waist and maybe thought him overly picky.

He traced a line connecting the tips of her breasts, appreciating how they responded to his lightest touch.

"It makes them labeled as 'Goonies.' Just thought you'd want to know."

She stared down at her labeled chest for several moments and then did one of those female armhole things and got it turned around without taking it off.

He scrambled to pin down the last of the lunch fixings and one of Carly's socks, which was about to be blown away by the downblast of the helicopter's descent. He only had one foot in his shorts. Hadn't worn underwear because the only pair he'd brought had been soaked in the river this morning.

"Can't say why it takes so long, but you're a damn fine sight in any state, Ms. Thomas." About time he used the name she'd insisted on the first time they met.

"Go to hell, Mr. Mercer." But her grin was game and the quick kiss that followed wasn't too quick. It lingered long enough to burn down to places in him that really would be better not heating up at the moment. Definitely not until he finished pulling his shorts back on, at least.

They zipped and tucked, and stuffed laces into boot tops. They were on their feet by the time the Hawk was fully settled a hundred yards away.

As they climbed the slope to the waiting chopper, Steve couldn't help but notice the way Carly moved. Loose-hipped, but still ready to walk over the back of any fire that dared get in her way.

She was the embodiment of the perfect woman, with an amazing body that responded in ways even his fantasies had never imagined, a heart so sweet it put strawberries and fresh flowers to shame, and a determination of spirit that he'd never met in his life.

He managed to catch up with her despite how fast she was moving. As they ducked their heads to stay well below the sweep of the rotors, he leaned in close to be sure he'd be heard.

"Love you, Angel."

He hadn't meant to say that.

Not at all.

He shocked himself to a standstill.

He'd only wanted to thank her for the best afternoon of his life. But once it was said, he knew it was true.

He really did love her. He'd never told a woman that, not since his junior prom when he'd still been young enough to think it was a lightweight word to be tossed about casually. Julie Ann had corrected that assumption damn fast, and he'd worn the hand-shaped outline on his cheek for several days to drive the lesson home.

Carly made it three more steps before stumbling to a

halt and turning to face him with denial forming across
her features.

The rotors spun overhead and everybody aboard
watched them.

Slowly, her head began to shake back and forth.

Steve shrugged, at a bit of a loss.

"I'm afraid it's true."

He had to shout it to be heard.

Steve had to bodily turn her and push her toward the
chopper. Carly's brain was in full spin and she couldn't
get her bearings.

He caressed her ass shamelessly as he helped her aboard.

And it felt great.

But, her mind shouted, what about the being-in-
love-with-her part? That definitely wouldn't do. Shit!
It was goddamn impossible! *No way in hell, mister*.
Great sex, sure, but she hadn't signed up for love. No
way. Never again.

Carly tried to meet Steve's eyes, but failed in the
hustle of getting aboard and secured.

Steve strapped in beside her among the coolers and
other gear hastily stowed aboard. They perched on a
half-deflated air mattress.

They pulled on headsets as Henderson, again at the
controls, lifted them skyward.

"Welcome aboard, campers."

Carly's eyes focused. Everyone was aboard. They
were the last. Oh crap! Her cheeks felt as if she'd just
walked through a raging fire.

"First," Henderson announced as he pointed the

chopper north and put her nose down into it, "I think we need a round of applause for a fine, fine show."

Everyone turned and started laughing and applauding. Chutes and Betsy. Oh God, Uncle TJ and Aunt Margaret.

Carly's cheeks went from hot to flaming, but when she went to raise her hands to them, she discovered that Steve held one tightly, their fingers interlaced.

She checked his face. He might be grinning, but at least there was a blush under his tan. Wasn't there? At least a little?

Chapter 34

"SECOND," HENDERSON CONTINUED, HIS VOICE DROPping and alerting Steve that here was the real reason they were on the move with so little notice. He glanced out the door at the sun, down in half an hour. As far as Steve could tell they were arrowing back to base, and by the sound of it and the tilt of the chopper's nose, they weren't moseying along as they had on the outbound journey.

"Who here can tell me what the Tillamook Burn is?"

He felt Carly's grip convulse in his. Her face, such a splendidly brilliant pink a moment before, was now ghost-white. A glance forward showed all of the locals in a similar state. TJ and Margaret had also clutched hands, and Chutes and Betsy looked grim. Akbar was leaning out the door as if he could see the couple hundred miles to the northwest. Steve knew Tillamook was on the coast somewhere, but that was it.

Only Steve himself and Tori appeared not to be in the know.

Carly's voice was thin when she spoke. "It was the worst disaster in Oregon fire history, 1933 to 1951. Four fires in the Tillamook State Forest, every six years like clockwork. It kept burning and reburning, and they could never control it. A third of a million acres, about five hundred square miles of old-growth forest. If you take out the overlapping burns in different years, it was over seven hundred thousand acres. Over a thousand square miles."

The silence was deafening.

Henderson had to clear his throat, not once, but twice.

"Well, according to the first alert report, the Tillamook Burn is, ah, burning."

Chapter 35

THE FIREHAWK HIT HOODIE ONE CAMP RIGHT ABOUT full dark. The alert had come in too late in the day for even the smokies to get onto the fire. You didn't jump in the dark, no matter what was happening.

They cooked up a game plan while they flew, and Merks hit the ground running. With Carly's help, they had a drone up at full dark. An achievement celebrated with a high five and a kiss that curled Steve's toes.

Steve Mercer was in love. Wasn't that a news flash? About as unlikely an occurrence as batting a thousand.

They'd only known each other for a single week, but he could see the vista of what lay before them. As clearly as he'd seen the rolling hills covered in blooming fireweed. A vista of lazy mornings waking together and lively nights without enough sleep. A vista that he knew to keep to himself for the moment.

He fired up the console in the back of the truck and had the bird circling above the helibase fifteen minutes after they hit the ground. Carly sat so close beside him that he could feel her body heat in the cooling evening. He grabbed his sweatshirt that he'd left on workbench and wrapped it around her. His own body was still running plenty hot to keep him warm.

Somehow, Henderson wrangled an emergency clearance for unmanned flight. The flight plan from the FAA got Steve's drone to the Tillamook State Forest in under two hours, without traveling anywhere near Portland airport's traffic patterns.

At eleven at night, he finally flew the drone over the fire. He and Carly sat in the back of the truck and traced size, wind speed, and terrain.

Henderson hovered close enough behind them that he kept bumping Steve's elbow as he tried to control the aircraft.

Steve ran his heat trace app.

"Shit! It's already a high end of Class F in size, Class G in another hour or two. We're headed into another Type I fire, and at this rate, it will be an ugly one. The second Type I in as many weeks. This can't be happening."

"Anything bigger in area than G?" Henderson was clearly searching the copious training he'd received.

Steve knew he wouldn't come up with anything. Because there wasn't. At least not in the books.

Steve and Carly spoke in near unison. "H is for Hell."

―――――

"There." Carly pointed and Henderson leaned in.

Steve flipped to infrared and overlaid the roads. The synchronicity between them was almost like sex. She barely had to think something and Steve was there.

"Fly the smokies to Skyport Airport in Cornelius. Get them in Jeeps, and run them in on Route 6. They should be able to get alongside the burn here on…"

Steve zoomed in on the obvious road until she could see the name.

"Cedar Butte Road."

Henderson pulled out a walkie-talkie. "TJ. Launch

the smokies, land them in Skyport, and have off-road transport ready."

"Roger that. Out."

As she spun to face him, the jump-plane engines roared to life.

"You didn't put TJ back on active duty?" She phrased it as a question but loaded it with enough venom to kill a lesser man than ICA Henderson.

"Active *radio* duty."

"Oh." Carly swallowed her anger as hard as she could. "Okay."

"I was thinking with his experience and at the rate we're growing, it might be a good permanent spot for him. Mike's been training him and signed him off yesterday."

Carly closed her eyes and rocked back in her seat as the wave of relief hit her.

"Really?" She barely dared voice the hope. After the last accident, she couldn't stand the thought of her uncle getting in harm's way again.

"I think he'll take a little convincing, but he knows it's the right choice. Akbar is more than ready to step up to Ground One."

She couldn't help herself. Carly threw her arms around Henderson's neck and kissed him quickly. He patted her back in a fatherly gesture that had her sitting back and feeling awkward.

TJ out of the fire was worth far more than a bit of embarrassment.

She could hear the planes taking off. How did they get airborne so fast?

Henderson must have seen the question on her face. "The crews loaded an hour ago and have been napping on the planes. Everyone except the heli-crews are already on the road in support vehicles. The choppers are prepped and waiting for first light."

"Oh." He'd reassigned TJ and did his job well despite her doubts. And he'd done a nice job cleaning her fish. Maybe she could unbend a little.

"Uh… Well done, I guess."

He grinned down at her. "Coming from you, that's a high compliment indeed. I need a tape recorder. Steve, you got one handy that I—"

"What the hell?" Steve's curse had them both spinning back to the console.

The screens were blank.

"I had a good signal. I was flying her high up so that I could keep a good signal, since we're out near my range limits. I had it good, five-by-five, and then suddenly it's gone." He tapped some keys. "Not responding on the backup frequency either."

"Is it the bird or…"

Steve was scrolling back through the recording on the right-hand screen to when he'd lost the feed. All he had was a black screen, even though Carly could see the time counter scrolling backwards. Suddenly the screen was filled with data and the bright infrared image of the fire.

He found the last few seconds of image and rolled it back and forth across the loss of the feed from the drone.

"Where are you?" His voice was harsh, angry.

Carly read the coordinates. "You're way ahead of the blaze."

Steve nodded. "I was circling out. Figured if it was lightning strikes, there might be other fires. I wanted to make sure that we only had the one blaze that we were fighting."

"Good idea." She rubbed his shoulder, knew he'd be stressed about losing the signal on the bird.

"The real problem is if it's still flying." Steve brought up the last high overview of the fire. "I started on the edge here, then I set the autopilot into an expanding circle." He traced a growing spiral around the fire. "With eighteen more hours of fuel, it could cause all sorts of trouble. Shit, it's got to be here somewhere."

He returned to the last few seconds of video and rolled it back and forth again and again. One moment there was the fire image with an overlay of airspeed, humidity, altitude, position, and who knew what all. Carly didn't recognize half of the numbers. The only ones changing were the clock and its position in the air. Then nothing. All of the data ended at once.

"Shit!" Steve pounded a fist down against his thigh, then gasped in pain.

She reached for him, but he pulled away.

"Sorry," he muttered before she even had time to get really hurt. "I'm going to be in a foul mood until I find that bird."

He scrolled back further and let the feed run again in real time.

Once.

Twice.

A third time.

"There!" Henderson pointed at the screen, but Carly didn't see anything.

"Scroll back."

They watched the recording again.

"Right there."

Steve slapped Stop.

"Roll back a couple of frames."

"There. Can you enhance that?"

Carly looked at the tiny slash of red on the screen. How had he even noticed that? And why would he care?

Steve fussed with it for a bit, bigger, blurrier, orange then green, then back to red. His movements on the console were as concise as they'd been on her flesh. Carly shoved the thought aside. They had bigger issues, not even counting the fire.

"Uh, that's about the best I can do."

"Okay, keep those settings, just that segment of the field of view and roll forward slowly."

"Two seconds to signal loss." The infrared showed the streak for about half a second and then a slow fade. The rolling greenery of the unburned forest just a ghost in the background. Then nothing.

"Roll back." Carly had seen something. Her eye had recorded it, but she couldn't quite pin it down. "Just a couple frames before the signal loss."

Steve finally pinned down the final four frames. He spread them across the screen.

It wasn't what she was seeing; it's what she wasn't.

"There. What's missing?"

Neither Steve nor Henderson answered.

She arced a finger across the lower quadrant of the screen. "No forest, no rolling hills. Something is blocking the image."

"Shit!" Henderson pulled out his radio but didn't key it. "How high were you?"

"Three thousand feet above ground."

"That would make it just under a thousand meters in two seconds." He keyed the radio. "Hey, Em?"

"Here," Emily's voice came back.

"Check my memory on the speed of a nine-kay-thirty-four."

Carly looked at Steve, but he just shrugged.

"About four hundred and seventy meters per second sustained. As high as four ninety if the air's thinner."

They both turned to watch Henderson's response to his wife's information, but he was staring blank-eyed straight ahead at the wall of the truck. His posture held frozen for several seconds.

Carly noted that Emily didn't ask why. Simply waited while her husband pieced that information together with whatever else he had. Was that how they flew? Nothing extra. Just precisely what was needed with a perfect trust that the other would do the same. Was that why they spoke so rarely but were inseparably close? Maybe they could think each other's thoughts or some such.

Henderson rekeyed the radio, his voice perfectly calm and cool. "Could you call around? See if maybe Kee or Connie wants a little R and R."

"Why," Carly asked, "are you talking about rest and relaxation when there's a fire to fight?"

Henderson ignored her.

"How soon?" Emily's only response to a situation that must make no sense to her. A seriously action-oriented couple.

"Daylight would be good. Tomorrow sunset at the latest. We'll be leaving for Skyport Airport in thirty."

"Roger out."

"Out."

"And that's it?" Carly asked on Emily's behalf. "Not even going to tell her why you're asking?" He didn't strike her as a dictatorial jerk, but maybe her initial assessment had actually been the right one.

"That's it." He clipped the radio back on his belt as if nothing were out of the ordinary. "I'm not going to transmit sensitive information on an unencrypted circuit and she knows that."

Then his eyes refocused. He'd taken off his ever-present shades to see the screens better, his gray-blue eyes reminded Carly of hard steel.

"And neither will either of you. This information is classified. You are not to discuss it with anyone without my prior authorization. Absolutely no radio traffic on this."

"I'm not." Carly stood up in the truck so that she didn't have to crick her neck back so far to look up at him. "I'm not taking orders from you. We're firefighters, not your precious SOAR."

"Carly." Steve rested a hand on her arm but she shook him off.

"Well, Mr. Mercer." Henderson's voice was easy, belying his hard-eyed gaze still fixed on her. "You'll be moving your trailer again, so get it wrapped up tight." He reached out a hand and tapped the two black cases on top of the racks beside him.

Steve flinched.

Carly hadn't seen Steve touch those cases before so she hadn't noticed them herself, but there was clearly something going on here.

Henderson stepped off the tail of the truck and slid his glasses into place, despite it being the dead of night.

The effect was surreal. His eyes hidden behind mirrors, he looked almost mechanical, as dangerous-looking as the fluid guy in *The Terminator* movies.

He aimed the twinned reflection of her and Steve into the back of the dimly lit truck.

"You may want to recall the agreements you signed with Mount Hood Aviation when you officially joined." They'd given her a bunch of paperwork, and she hadn't paid much attention to why they wanted to know so much. They promised her the Fire Behavior Analyst's slot, and that was all that mattered.

Henderson turned to leave.

"Wait!" Steve stopped him. "What happened to my bird?"

Now Steve was pinioned in Henderson's gaze.

"Your bird, Mr. Mercer, was just shot down by a Russian-made Strela-3 surface-to-air missile. Now get your ass moving."

Then he was gone into the night.

Chapter 36

"Hey there, Major. My, how the mighty have fallen."

Steve wiped a hand across his face, trying to wake himself up. He lay facedown on a picnic table, one of the few amenities of this tiny, western Oregon airport. Skyport. Yeah, right. A rusting hanger and an office that was half garden shed. In the hangar crouched a pair of 1970s vintage Air Tractor 300 crop dusters, and in a dilapidated barn, a Cessna 150 that would never again see the skies rusted quietly away.

Now Skyport airfield sported the Firehawk, the two empty jump planes, three trucks of retardant, a fuel truck, and his trailer parked along the grass and gravel runway. A little after sunrise, the other choppers would start arriving.

On the table, the garishly red-and-white remains of last night's buckets of chicken glared at him. When he sat up and managed to focus, he saw a short woman saluting ICA Henderson. She was about as opposite of Carly as possible. Seriously built, and clearly had no problem sharing. Her tight shirt and its open buttons did a lot to fire the imagination, even if he was too exhausted for anything else to fire off.

Henderson saluted back smartly. Right, military. Steve rubbed his eyes again. Hard to forget that after the way Henderson had driven everyone last night.

Steve figured they'd had three hours of sleep, and he was betting that Henderson had even less. Yet he looked as sharp and together as the woman facing him in matching mirrored shades.

Steve tried to pull some semblance of order back into his clothes before looking around. First thing he spotted was Carly. She'd at least stretched out on the ground before passing out. Someone had tossed a blanket over her. Might have even been him, but he wasn't sure.

Light, sunrise. Well, kind of. The stars were fading into the pink horizon. Dawn in half an hour, flight in an hour. They'd had their three hours of sleep.

He just wanted to curl up under the blanket with Carly and tease her awake to make love as the sun rose. She looked so comfortable.

He kicked the sole of her boot.

She rolled to her feet without so much as a pause. How did she do that, asleep to awake between one moment and the next? Steve needed coffee, preferably intravenously, before anything else happened today.

Then he noticed that Carly hadn't actually moved yet. She stood there weaving and blinking her eyes against the predawn light. It made him feel a little better.

"Planet Earth," he told her. "In a mythical land called Cornelius. The only Cornelius I ever heard of managed the Philly Athletics for almost fifty years. Weird to name an Oregon town after a Philadelphia ballplayer."

"Hero of *Planet of the Apes*," Carly mumbled at him and dropped onto the opposite bench just as he managed to stand.

Henderson was bringing over the woman with the chest.

Slightly more conscious, Steve also noted black hair with a gold streak and skin the color of a really exceptional tan. Big smile, way too much energy.

Steve dropped back to the bench.

"These two live wires are the core of the fire control team. Steve Mercer, Carly Thomas, Kee Stevenson."

Steve tried to wave. Carly simply groaned and laid her head on the table as his had been.

Beale wandered up without her kid.

The salute that this Kee Stevenson gave Beale was a whole different story than the cocky one Beale had aimed at Henderson, even though they were both majors. Even though they were both retired. Suddenly the woman went all stiff and rigid, the salute was picture perfect and held tight until Beale nodded back.

"You really landed us in bumfuck nowhere, Major."

It was true. The Skyport was a mowed strip between two fields of shoulder-high corn. Five miles west of where the outer parts of Portland's suburbia petered out. Five more miles to the Coast Range and the Tillamook State Forest. But here at Cornelius, there was nothing.

"We're about to break out of Class G into your Class H," Beale announced, ignoring Kee's comment. "Rick is flying in to take overall command as this is definitely a Type I incident already."

Carly sat up like someone had injected her with adrenaline.

"How soon can we get a bird in the air?" Carly shot at Henderson. Then she turned west. Even in the faint light, Steve could discern the brown and black cloud of smoke rising from beyond the horizon.

"Gray bird is up and circling from last night." They'd

launched the drone an hour after landing at Skyport, but he'd kept it well clear of where he'd lost the first one. He and Carly headed for the Firehawk.

Henderson stopped them. "First thing, I want the black-box bird aloft."

"Ten minutes." Steve broke into a run.

"Then I want you to show Kee last night's recording," Henderson called after him.

"Then get her ass over here." Steve didn't look back to see if she followed.

―――――∿∿∿―――――

Steve had the black-box drone on the rail in three minutes.

"This looks way different." Carly stroked a hand down the fuselage, all angles and strange curves that felt slick rather than hard like the metal of the other drones. And the gray-box ones had been black with MHA's fire red. This was odd, dark gray above and painted a pale blue below.

He handed the checklist to Carly. She tried to read it but couldn't quite get her eyes to focus yet.

"You didn't see this bird," Steve said. "I'm not even supposed to launch it in daylight if I can help it."

"You aren't, yet. Sun is still fifteen minutes off. I think." But his comment only made it all the more intriguing.

"The paint job is designed to be very hard to see against the land from above or against the sky from below. The surfaces are all curved for stealth, anti-radar. If someone out there is still watching, they really shouldn't see this one as it flies over. It's also much faster, carries more payload, but it can only stay up for four hours instead of twenty."

She read off the details of the wing-attachment section of the checklist, but Steve had them on even before she finished. She started on payload mounts.

"Shit! Where's Henderson? Find him. What gear does he want rigged?"

Steve didn't even look up to see the ICA standing behind him.

"Radiometer and biohazard sensors," Henderson answered before she could ask. "And put on a target-lock tracker. I'd like to know more about who's shooting at you."

Carly saw Steve shiver for a moment before reaching back into the case and pulling out three objects, two the size of a calculator, the third as big as her two fists.

Kee breezed right up. "Sweet. Even we don't have these yet."

"That's because they don't exist, Sergeant. Clear?"

Carly watched Kee slant a look at the Major, but her reply had none of the bravado of a moment earlier. "Crystal, sir."

Carly looked back down at her checklist and did her best to read off the instructions for Steve, but she couldn't.

"Radiometric," the list informed her, was for detecting trace radioactivity. A small table listed distance, reading strength variations along flight path, and cross-referenced possible relevant bomb types and yields.

She swallowed hard against a dry throat and skipped that section to start reading out the electrical hookups, taking comfort from Steve's steady and precise hands as he inserted the detectors behind the cameras.

Chapter 37

AFTER THE BLACK-BOX BIRD LAUNCHED, STEVE LET the shakes run through him. It took him three tries just to get the screwdriver back into the goddamn toolbox.

He'd read and signed all of the crazy paperwork MHA insisted on but not really thought about it until he'd seen Carly's face go sheet white while reading the instructions.

Nuclear bomb detection. She hadn't read the table aloud, but he could tell the instant she reached it. Her eyes were normally wide and welcoming—except when she was pissed at him, which was often enough. But now they had shot huge. The thought that there might be a nuclear bomb twenty miles to the west was freaking him out.

Were they inside or outside the blast radius? How about fallout?

How the hell was he supposed to know? He sure wasn't going to ask. Better not to know.

He reached for the console controls but couldn't make his fingers work. So he sat on his hands in the back of the parked Firehawk, hoping that would steady them down.

Now all of those clearances and background checks made sense. There'd been rumors about Mount Hood Aviation, the kind you laughed off as being silly. The rumors had been around as long as

MHA. Sure they'd always been firefighters, flying choppers since the sixties.

But rumor said they'd purchased the old Air America fleet from CIA operations in Laos and Cambodia during the Vietnam War. Other rumors said they still flew on-call CIA black ops.

Stupid. It was all stupid.

He felt the Firehawk shift and glanced over his shoulder. Carly climbed aboard and rested her hands on his good right thigh as she sat on the cargo-bay deck. Kee moved up close and squatted so that her eyes were level with his. Henderson and Emily climbed in and sat in the seats in the middle of the bay.

Two retired Army majors. No, two retired SOAR majors, a much more serious proposition. And this new lady, Kee of the crisp salute.

One thing was damn sure. He should have read those papers a lot more carefully when he was signing them.

—∿∿—

Steve shut down the replay of last night's loss of his drone. The five occupants of the Firehawk remained silent. The two console screens now just dark eyes staring at him.

He looked down and brushed his hand over Carly's hair where she sat cross-legged on the deck beside him. He did it as much to reassure himself as her.

Kee had changed while watching the video. The wry humor she'd aimed at Henderson was simply gone. Now her focus was complete and she was actually as scary as Beale. She'd had Steve run it a half-dozen times in normal light and then in infrared. She'd asked about wind speeds and air pressures. He gave her what he could.

"Definitely a Strela-3. A little too slow to be the 2M and way too slow to be any of ours. Even the old Redeye was faster than that. They've got the Igla now, don't know why they even make these damn things anymore." She still squatted close beside Carly as if she could stay that way for hours without moving.

"Russians wouldn't waste time with those, but they still sell them to a couple of dozen other countries. These things are a real pain, especially because any damn fool can buy and operate one. They practically give them out like candy."

"But"—Carly's voice was impressively steady— "what are they doing in our Oregon forest?"

Kee looked out the door for half a minute, and neither of the Majors interrupted. This was the woman they'd called within minutes of determining his drone had been shot down. Steve kept his mouth shut as well.

"Do you have a current image?"

Steve flipped over to the surviving gray-box drone that he'd launched last night after arriving here.

"I've been keeping this one circling over the fire all night, but every time I get to the north end, I take an IR capture of the same coordinates. Keeping my damn distance."

"Strela-3 is only good to four kilometers, so two and a half miles should keep you clean."

"I'm closer to five miles out, but the resolution is pretty good." He ran the series of images.

"No infrared movement. No people or vehicles moving about."

"Not that show through the trees."

"They're either under cover or dug in."

"How far is the fire?" Carly was keeping tabs on it all.

"Nine miles, almost ten. Right now at least. The way it's moving, if we can't stop it, the fire will pass well west of that site."

Henderson glanced out the door, and Steve followed his gaze across the empty airstrip. Predawn dusk.

"These are the worst visual conditions. How soon can you do an overflight with the black-box drone?"

Steve turned back to the console and flipped over to the second bird's control frequency. "How high?"

"Five hundred meters, but don't slow down to admire the scenery."

Steve set up the run and programmed it in.

"Two minutes out." He'd brought it in close while they were looking at the other images. Creepy to think that whoever had shot him down was close enough that he could fly the drone there in under fifteen minutes.

He slipped his fingers into Carly's where they still rested on his thigh. It was kind of cool to do that. He'd never been much of a hand holder, but being with Carly was making him a convert.

Except Carly's hand was freezing. He cupped it between his hand and his thigh to warm it. Maybe this wasn't so cool. Maybe this was also scary as all hell. What kind of crazy back in the hills didn't like drones and shot one down with an old Russian surface-to-air missile?

"This doesn't sound like a moonshiner." At first, Steve hoped that it wasn't a moonshiner. He'd had enough of them. Of course, what if it were something worse?

"Nor a survivalist," Carly added.

And she was right, it didn't.

The actual overflight happened so fast that he could barely see it.

Once it was done, Steve rolled back and scrolled through the data more slowly. "Negative on radioactive and negative on biohazard. At least that's what this stuff says. There's some reading here I'm not sure of, but not biological." He felt the relief sigh through his body, a tension he hadn't realized that he was holding.

"K-band," Kee said, sounding disgusted as she read the data on the screen. "They've got a damned cop's radar speed trap aimed at the sky."

"Okay, Steve, bring that bird home, long way round. Then you and Carly get focused on the fire."

Henderson made it sound like an order, and Steve wasn't about to complain. No real chance of K-band radar spotting a black-box drone, even if he came back the same way. The gray-box one would have stood out just fine, though.

"So," Carly said, looking up at him and squeezing his thigh. "Maybe it is just some crazy survivalist."

"Yeah, I guess so." He glanced up at the other three over Carly's head. But they were looking at each other in some kind of silent conversation.

Kee casually turned back to the monitor.

"Think I'll go for a walk." She tapped a short fingernail about four miles south of where the drone had been shot down. "You can drop me right here on your first pass at the fire."

Steve looked back at the Majors and decided he didn't

like the sudden itch between his shoulder blades. It felt as if a target were painted there.

He stroked Carly's hair again to keep her distracted from seeing their grim expressions.

Chapter 38

THE FIRE WAS UGLY.

Carly sat in the back of the Firehawk studying the overnight images of the fire and trying to stuff down an egg sandwich and plasticized hash browns someone had rustled up in town. Thankfully, they'd also brought back some wonderfully huge cups of really bad coffee. At least it was strong, which was all she really cared about.

She tried another view on the console but didn't have a real feel for the controls yet. Steve had showed her which menus she could use before going out to pack up the returned black-box drone.

He made it look so easy, a click here, a roll of the mouse there. But what she had was shit.

By the time he climbed back aboard, she almost cried out with relief.

"You make it look so damned easy."

She started to climb out of the chair, but he leaned in and trapped her with a kiss. For half a moment, irritation rippled along her skin. She needed to see the fire. The next half of the moment, she was leaning into the kiss and reveling in its confidence and reassurance.

Then she pushed back enough to speak. "Damn it, Mercer. The fire."

"Yeah, I can feel it." He aimed one of his saucy grins her way but eased her out of the chair. He slid in front of the controls, his fingertips trailing deliciously over her hip as they finished trading places.

"Love you, Ms. Thomas."

Her knees let go. She did her best to mask that as she knelt on the cargo-bay deck.

"Don't say that!" She hissed it at him even though no one else was around.

He shrugged. "New for me, too. But I'm kinda enjoying it." Then his smile proved that she hadn't hidden her complete discomfiture from him for a single second.

Well, her body was now more awake than her brain was. Before she even had her breath back, he had set up a time lapse of the changes through the night.

She watched the fire's perimeter change and shift. Saw the center die out, then reignite to burn anew.

"It's like someone is breathing straight down on the center of it. The damn thing is spreading in like five different directions."

"Fuel."

He had a point. The Tillamook Forest was supposed to have undergone a controlled burn a dozen times in the last twenty years. But the environmentalists wouldn't let it out of court. At first it had been the crowd that was against the controlled burn. The ones who didn't yet understand that burning up all the crap on the forest floor let the forest live longer.

By the time they were convinced, about a decade ago, the watershed people kicked into gear, and then the endangered-species set. Finally, there was just too damned much tinder on the forest floor and no one dared light it off. You didn't do a prescribed burn in the middle of a box of kindling.

Now someone or something had, and a half-dozen square miles had become fully involved in the first day.

"The smokies who drove in last night are here, cutting this line along the northeastern flank."

Carly leaned in close over his shoulder. Close enough that she could feel his warmth and the strong, male scent of him. The safe, warm feel of him so close. Those crazies back in the woods had scared her half to death.

Now, only the fire mattered. She could deal with that, but she didn't pull back from the comfort of being close to Steve.

"Run the time loop again and include the footage from the first drone as well." This time she let herself watch the fire and feel what it had done. Watched it spreading along valley lines, eating fuel wherever it could be found when the winds were calm at sunset. Then legging west in the evening with the land breeze.

"Again."

The very end of the loop showed the beginning of the southeast push that would normally be traveling down the coast this time of year. So it wasn't actually growing in all directions simultaneously, but the winds were working it that way.

"Zoom in here. More, more. Put a marker here." She tapped the screen, and Steve clicked in an orange flag.

"Really? How in the hell do you figure that?"

"Point of origin. Bet I'm within a hundred yards."

"No bet."

Carly had an evil thought, one that just might distract Steve from his "being in love" nonsense. She bit his ear lightly.

"You sure you don't want in? I'll bet an hour of time

as a sex slave that I'm within a hundred feet. But it will cost you double if I'm within fifty." She wasn't that positive, but she figured it was a no-loser bet.

He groaned. "How can I pass up a chance like that?"

"Good, you lose. Tell the investigators to start right there." It was a valley, not a ridge. Probably not a lightning strike. A couple of hiking trails crossed the wilderness right there, the end of a fire road close by. Sloppy camper or hunter most likely. "Have them check the end of this fire road for recent usage."

Steve kicked out the message while she watched the tape loop again. "Damn, it really is growing in every direction."

"There. That's your helispot." Steve zoomed in to show her.

Beale climbed aboard and began preflight on the chopper. Henderson stuck his head in.

"You two gonna make me proud?"

Carly grinned at him. "If you start by moving the retardant tankers up to this pullout across from Elk Creek Campground on Highway 6. Trees are too tight for us to be dipping a snorkel in the river."

Henderson pulled out a radio and got them moving. She could hear the diesel trucks start up and leave the airfield. They'd obviously been in position awaiting instructions.

"Rick Dobson is on-site in another twenty minutes from Crater Lake. He has two more teams of smokies en route. Missoula and Sacramento each gave him one. He says they're here in two hours."

"Here and here." Carly drew two lines along the fire's northwest side. "See if we can pinch off at least one direction."

"Tankers will start flying in about half an hour. Rick is setting up Incident Command at Hillsboro Airport five miles east of here. That's where the tankers are running from as well, so they'll have a fast turnaround time."

"Why are we here instead of there? Five miles doesn't make any difference, and they've got to have better coffee."

Henderson simply pointed at the black case locked up on the trailer.

"Oh." Far fewer eyes in the middle of this mowed farmer's field. "We're going to need everything we can get, and no bad winds."

"Yeah, about that. By midday tomorrow, we've got some bad news rolling in from the southwest."

Carly bit back a curse. That was too soon. No matter what they did, they couldn't make any real headway on a blaze of this size in just two days.

Don't think. Just fight what's in front of you. That's all you can do.

She clambered out, giving Steve's shoulder a squeeze as she did so. The simple gesture made her feel better, far better than it should if he really were just a lover. The girl in the mirror was smiling smugly at her about something.

As Carly climbed down, Kee came up and sat on the edge of the cargo deck. She didn't climb aboard, just sat there as if that's where she was going to ride, feet dangling out into the wind.

Except, it wasn't Kee. Before, she'd been a sassy civilian in shades and a shirt so tight and unbuttoned so low that Steve hadn't been able to drag his attention away from her serious chest. Carly knew she herself was lean and no competition for that kind of a build.

Then she thought of Steve's kiss and knew his eyes might travel, but it wasn't Kee that he was really watching. And he did say he loved her, which was still freaking her out.

But now Kee was in heavy camouflage. Bits of grass and rope that looked tattered like weeds were draped over most of her body. A substantial backpack was strapped to her back and a gun, almost as long as she was tall, hung slantwise across her chest.

"Holy shit."

Kee flashed her a grin through the green-and-black makeup. Her helmet as masked as the rest of her.

"Just going for a walk in the woods."

"Uh, sure." Carly thought back to yesterday—was it just yesterday?—when she and Steve had worn boots, shorts, and T-shirts for their walk in the woods. The most dangerous thing in their lunch-sized backpack was a pocketknife.

All of the creeped-out nerves that had faded away as she worked to understand the fire slammed back in.

"I thought this was no big deal. Aren't there like, I don't know, cops or something to send?"

"Nearest fire roads are half a mile in any direction. Not even any hiking trails through there, at least no official ones. They chose their place very carefully. Bet they have alarms on the roads. I know I would. And they fired a Russian SAM, granted one that's a decade or two out of date, at a poor little drone. Specifically at a surveillance drone, which means they knew enough to distinguish that from Joe and Martha flying their Piper out to the coast."

Carly swallowed. "Uh, makes sense." Made her head hurt. "Why you?"

"Because she's the best." Emily leaned over between the seats. "Now climb up front if you're coming."

Carly glanced up at the rotors starting to spin overhead.

When she looked back down, Kee was staring transfixed at Emily who had turned away to finish a chat with her husband.

"Doesn't give compliments much?" Carly asked Kee softly.

The woman just shook her head slowly. "Not ever." Her voice was barely a whisper.

Chapter 39

AS THEY FLEW TO THE FIRE, BEALE STARTED CHATTING with Kee Stevenson like old friends. It was one of the strangest conversations Steve had ever listened to.

Beale was flying a Firehawk toward some crazy survivalist with a surface-to-air missile. Kee was sitting idly on the edge of the cargo bay as if her feet weren't dangling three thousand feet over the ground.

"How is Dilya?" Beale could have been serving up tea with that voice.

"Sprouting. I swear she grows an inch a day. Passed me by last month some time. She could end up tall as Archie."

"Pretty unusual for an Uzbekistani."

"Pretty unusual for an Uzbekistani to be eating five decent meals a day. And she's still as thin as you, Major."

Steve checked Kee's coloring again. Green-and-black camo paint. Okay. But he'd seen her clearly this morning. She was pretty much a white chick with Asian eyes and dusky skin.

"She and Archie are hanging out with Peter and Calledbetty this week," Kee continued, ignoring the spiraling descent of the chopper.

"Spending a lot of time at it. You okay with still being in?"

"Sure. This is what I do."

Steve saw her pat her rifle like an old friend.

"But I like Archie being in DC more than if he's in the field. Better for Dilya."

"Drop zone in ten."

"Roger, Major. You keeping your kid in the air?"

"She stays up with Mark in a spotter fixed-wing plane most of the time. He knows I will murder him if he actually flies her over the fire, so she's as safe there as anywhere. Carly's dad did the same and it seemed to work out pretty well for her. We'll have to see."

Steve could feel Carly's silence on the intercom. Emily Beale was using Carly as an example for how to raise her own child.

Beale had been easing down closer and closer to the treetops as they approached where they were dropping Kee.

Steve had become so intrigued with trying to unravel the conversation that he'd forgotten to watch out the door. When he did, he'd have reeled back in shock if he weren't strapped in.

They were slowing and sinking the last few feet.

Kee lifted her feet to clear a treetop that slapped the Firehawk's wheel.

Beale held the chopper with the wheels between the trees.

"See ya later." Kee handed the headset to Steve, winked at him, and tossed the descending rope out the door.

Steve had expected low profile as soon as he saw Kee's rig, but this was freaky. He could reach out and touch the treetops right outside the door.

Kee didn't even use a rappelling rig, just heavy gloves,

the length of rope trapped between her boots, and she was gone. The rope went slack impossibly fast.

He heard a simple squawk over the radio, "Clear." And then nothing.

He retrieved the line as Beale scooted several hundred meters south before rising out of the trees.

"Who the hell is she?" he asked over the intercom.

"She's married," Beale answered.

"I got that and it isn't what I was asking."

To that he got no response.

"Peter," Carly said over the intercom as if everything now made sense.

And suddenly it did. Beale and Henderson had told the story of a young orphan they'd rescued who now was friends with the President. And Kee's kid was in DC. Peter must be President Peter Matthews.

Steve looked down at the trees to see if he could catch another glimpse of the woman who was both a sniper and an adoptive mother to a friend of the President. They'd already started to climb and head for the fire, which left Kee somewhere lost behind them. Something about her made him feel almost sorry for the crazies with the Russian SAM. They had no idea what was coming for them.

Chapter 40

OVER THE NEXT HOUR, THE FULL FORCE OF THE Goonies were pulled in and focused on this latest version of the Tillamook Burn.

Carly kept Steve hopping, trying to have his drone be everywhere at once. All other craft, each at their designated altitude, circled above the fire in a clockwise pattern. Air Attack, the actual runs of retardant or foam, was the lowest layer. Above them in a stack were helicopters, then the air tankers, and finally the Incident Commander—Air in his spotter plane.

Occasionally Rick, as Incident Commander, flew up at Henderson's level. But he spent most of his time on the ground in Hillsboro where a crisis center had been driven in and set up. Dozens of screens fed him everything from Steve's imagery to satellite feeds and weather channels. He'd also have a massive screen showing a terrain map. A half-dozen techs would keep updates on the fire's perimeter and every engine and ground member.

Above them all, Steve had been given a flight space to manipulate his drone as he wished. With the zoom on the cameras, the elevation was of little consequence. At a thousand feet, he was closer than he'd been when he took the image of Carly's face gazing up into the sky in wonder.

Beale starting making trips to the pullout near Elk

Creek. Two trucks of retardant were on-site by the time they arrived. To speed loading, they set up a pair of pumpkins. The five-thousand-gallon flex tanks, like oversized pop-up kiddie swimming pools, allowed them to avoid landing the helicopter. They simply flew up, dipped in their snorkel, and forty seconds later they were gone again, a thousand gallons heavier. While they were gone, the tankers refilled the pumpkins.

The smaller choppers had joined in. The 212s dipping their Bambi Buckets to capacity and the MD500 also snorkeling full its belly tank. In a matter of seconds, the fleet had a full load and was turned back toward the fire.

Henderson, in the Beech Baron with his daughter flying copilot, led the two fixed-wing air tankers on tracks called out by Carly. Steve noticed that he flew higher than most guide planes typically would and studiously went nowhere near the flames.

Steve's coffee had long gone cold, and he still couldn't find a moment to get a swallow.

Carly kept the tankers beating against the north edge of the fire. And he couldn't blame her. The Oregon Department of Transportation had already closed Highway 6 due to smoke. If the fire crossed the road, it could be closed for a long time due to melted asphalt and burned-out signs and guardrails.

Steve had pulled up the winds' forecast. They were coming—and coming hard. Tomorrow noon at the latest, they'd be hitting the coast.

"Carly?"

She completed a call to Henderson on the next line to attack, flipped frequencies to the bucket brigade of littl' choppers, and sent both Huey 212s after some spot fi that Akbar reported through TJ as taking too much time away from the smokies on the ground. Rick shifted one of the ground teams and let her know.

"Go, Steve."

"Uh, there's a pinch here. I can't figure it out, but there is one."

Carly didn't ask him what kind of pinch. Didn't need to. It was something to do with the attack plan; he just couldn't find it.

"God damn it!" Steve punched the side of the chopper for lack of anything better to hit. "Shit! Ow!"

"Hard pinch?" was Beale's wry comment on his punching her helicopter.

"Yeah." He shoved the mike on his headset aside to suck on his bloody knuckles. Tried to keep the hiss of pain to himself. Whatever he was feeling, he knew it was bad and it made him crazy that he couldn't pin it down.

The bucket brigade called in for new instructions.

"Uh." Carly hesitated barely a heartbeat. "Keep hitting the spot stuff for the ground team at the moment."

Carly brushed off Henderson as well. "Keep following the same line and give me a minute."

"Roger."

"Emily, could you get me some height on this monster, but not up in the smoke?"

As per usual, Beale didn't ask why, but the chopper climbed on long, ground-eating clockwise spirals. Steve could hear her on the radio with her husband getting clearance as she crossed upward through air-tanker space, lead-plane altitude, and finally up past his own drone space above the level of Incident Command—Air, six thousand feet above the fire. With the number of the people now on the fire, Henderson had climbed up and mostly directed the other lead airplanes rather than flying the routes himself to guide the big tankers.

Steve leaned out the side door of the cargo bay, the side he knew Carly would also be looking out because it gave her the best view from her seat. He stuck his head right into the wind to feel the heat and smoke, to taste the burn of conifer so different from the oak he knew so well.

It looked horrible. As bad as the 2009 Station fire in the California hills above Los Angeles or the 2012 Waldo Canyon in Colorado.

Fast little surface fires had swept the browned grasses from all of the clearings. But the deeper, duller orange of ground fire had caught in the dead branches and fallen trees. Those fires were lingering, traveling slowly behind the forefront of the racing surface fires. Settling in for a deep, tree-killing burn. They'd be back to fireweed if they couldn't kill off those fires—and kill them quickly—but they were everywhere. They were so hot that they ignited anything nearby. The burn was even crawling back down from ridges against the slope.

And they were getting some broad sections of crown fire developing now—the fire racing from treetop to treetop, casting embers in the wind. Any remaining crown fires were going to become a disaster when the winds hit tomorrow.

Carly looked down and felt numb.

Steve was right. Something was wrong with her attack

plan. She'd tried shrugging it off as nerves because of the survivalists. Then she'd tried attributing it to the chills that followed the warmth of Steve's words. She'd only ever loved two men, and she'd lost both to the fire. She wasn't going to risk that again.

But that wasn't it.

The problem lay somewhere below. Something she could see, if she only knew how to look.

The Tillamook Burn hadn't been the biggest in Oregon's history, but it had certainly ranked as the most devastating. Only the Biscuit Fire in the Siskiyou Mountains in 2002 even came close. But during the Tillamook Burns, six hundred thousand acres burned in the two fires that happened during the Great Depression. Money the state lost in lumber sales. It was cash they didn't have but spent on the firefight. Money they wouldn't raise until the late 1940s to start the reforestation. Those two blazes had almost bankrupted Oregon out of existence, and the two that followed hadn't helped much either.

She'd trained her whole life for such a fire, and nothing had prepared her for this. A couple years back she'd flown the Long Draw Fire, a sprawling monster of three-quarters of a million acres. But she hadn't been lead commander. She'd made some of her reputation on that fire, but old Charlie Schmitz had led that one for MHA. Then he'd retired right after. He'd told her he was leaving the fight in good hands.

Yeah, right.

That had been a fast surface fire over rolling grasslands. This was hundred-foot fir trees, tight massed together on steep-walled valleys between thousand-foot ridges. The fuel, heat, and oxygen metrics of the Fire Triangle for this fire were completely different and a hundred times more complex than the Long Draw.

There weren't open spans like Long Draw where you could lay down a wet line, do a backburn in front of it, and hope to God the fire couldn't jump the gap this time.

Even the Coast Range rivers weren't much more than glorified creeks in the heart of the Tillamook State Forest, the branches often touching from each side. A crown fire strode across them as if they weren't even there, though at least it broke the surface fires for a while. Stopped them until the crown fire collapsed onto the forest floor and the whole cycle started over.

Beale circled them around to the south, miles and miles of timber stretched almost to the horizon before the fire would reach anything other than more fuel. The occasional homestead could be defended individually. If the fire burned all the way down to Highway 18, they'd have truly lost the battle. She couldn't think about that right now.

The fire wasn't moving west, so the coast towns were probably safe, but she had to watch that. They couldn't exactly retreat out to sea if an evacuation was needed. They'd only have the winding two lanes of Highway 101 as an evacuation route if it came down to that.

She'd been fighting the north, trying to hold Highway 6 as a line for no particular reason other than it was there. A line in the sand, where she could say "this far and no further." If the fire jumped the road, which wouldn't even make this monster blink, it would find another five hundred square miles of the same open forest. Except for a few nutsoid survivalists and hermits, nobody lived out there either.

The crews attacking the northeast and northwest flanks, as much as there were flanks, had narrowed the area of attack from five miles wide to about three on the north edge, but they were a long way from closing that gap.

She could glance over at Steve's tablet if she wanted and see the crews, but they were clear in her mind's eye. Three crews of twelve smokies each, almost a tenth of the nation's total smokejumpers, split across the flanks.

Three hotshot crews, totaling sixty guys and a few women, had marched in from as close as their Box could get them. She'd ridden in the MHA Box for only one season but could feel sympathy for them. It looked like a long ambulance with side windows and was used for just that far too often. All the gear you needed to fight a fire for weeks at a time, except for somewhere soft to sleep or a shower to clean up in.

Then continuing her clockwise rotation around the site, Emily showed the east of the fire.

From their altitude, Carly could see from the edge of the fire over the steep hills and abrupt valleys slowly rippling out to eventually flatten out into the sprawling Willamette Valley. The population pretty much ended after Cornelius and Forest Grove, turning into a spatter of farms snuggled up against the foothills.

They had to stop the fire above that, on this side of Henry Hagg Lake at the very worst.

From here, Carly could see what she hadn't when they'd overflown it in the post-dawn light this morning.

"Clear-cuts," she whispered over the headset.

"Clear-cuts," Steve agreed. He'd felt the same pinch and seen the problem and solution almost as fast as she had. Damn, but she could really learn to appreciate him in ways other than wrapped together in a blanket beneath the stars.

"Henderson," she practically shouted into the mike. "Where are you?"

"Ouch! Right here. A thousand feet below and a half mile back."

"Look west. That's where the wind is going to drive us."

"Okay, so what am I looking at?"

"Clear-cuts." Carly couldn't help but feel smug.

"I see them, but what good do they do us? They're so far east that it can't matter."

"Trust me. If that front comes in as predicted tomorrow, we could have our backs against it by afternoon."

"No way…" She had to give him credit. He wasn't arguing; he just didn't believe her.

"On the Long Draw, we lost a hundred thousand acres in one night of high winds."

"That was grasslands."

"This is cracking-dry conifer," Carly shot back. "It's a repeat of the first Tillamook Burn. That's what I was missing. Oh damn. That's what this is. It's a bloody replay."

Carly tried not to be ill right on top of the Firehawk's console. She knew that Beale wouldn't appreciate it, for one thing.

"In 1933, they lost three hundred thousand acres in twenty hours."

"That's, what, almost five hundred square miles? You have got to be kidding me. Please tell me you are."

Carly let silence be her answer.

"Shit!"

It was the first time she'd ever heard Henderson curse. She glanced at Emily at the controls. The eyebrows raised above the line of her mirrored shades confirmed how unusual an event that might be.

She could hear Henderson take a deep breath.

"Look, we need more aviation fuel and a new plan. Let's meet back at Cornelius. I'll have some food waiting."

Chapter 41

Steve looked down at the map spread across the picnic table at the Cornelius Skyport. The corners were pinned down by bags of burgers and fries. Sweating paper cups of soda sat forgotten as Carly attacked the plastic-covered map with markers.

Beale was over nursing her daughter and making the maintenance crew nervous. They were using the break to perform some quick service on the Firehawk, changing air filters and whatever else it was they did. One of the 212s came in for fuel, but it didn't stay long.

Besides Steve and Carly, all three incident commanders were there. Henderson for air, TJ for ground, and Rick Dobson, the overall commander. Steve hadn't really met him yet. He'd expected the IC to be older, but he was maybe early thirties, a handsome guy with black hair and blue eyes that radiated a quiet confidence.

Carly tossed a black and a red marker at Steve. "Draw the black and the fire perimeters."

An orange marker almost hit Henderson in the chest before he caught it. "Air attack lines."

Totally in her element, she shone like the Flame Witch that she was. She had the fire on the run, even though it was less than ten percent contained. He could feel her confidence radiating out into those around her.

Somehow, the heat in his own direction had turned

up as well. He didn't know what she saw in him, but he sure as hell wasn't complaining.

Henderson sat down across the picnic table from Steve and began drawing.

They took turns checking the drone's feed on the tablet. Steve re-aimed it a couple of times to double-check the line and had the outline of the black drawn fairly quickly. The fire took a bit longer because it was on the move in so many directions. Forty-five square miles, thirty thousand acres and growing.

She tossed a green marker at TJ, who'd come over for the conference. Chutes, TJ, and Betsy were supporting the smokies and the jump planes that were dropping supply loads out of Hillsboro Airport. That meant the tanker crews were at least getting Betsy's good food, small consolation there.

"TJ, show me the crews."

He sketched quickly. "Smokies here and here. Hotshots along these lines. Wildland engines are working to hold the southern edge along these fire roads. The local districts have mobilized a half-dozen quints."

Only the first three of a quint fire truck's five capacities really applied to wildfire, but the pump, hose, and built-in tanker combination was essential. If the ground ladders and extensible multistory ladder were not called for, neither were they in the way.

TJ referred to his smartphone display as he drew. "The locals we're keeping along the west here and along this line. They'll be even more motivated than usual since they're defending their own turf. I've embedded MHA supervisors into each local."

Locals were fine, but wildfire wasn't their specialty.

It was one thing to beat down backyard brushfire or a small wildfire that you could contain with a half-dozen crews, some cut and slash, and a backburn.

It was a whole other art to fight a fire that could leap crowns at twenty miles per hour or roar over a prairie at twice that with the right motivation. TJ knew that and had given each team someone who could help them. That thinned MHA's resources, making it look like a bad idea at first, but it would ease communications and increase safety for the overall fire teams.

"Rick, what's our total count?"

The Incident Commander looked up at the sky for a moment.

Steve followed his gaze. It was gray with ash. Ash that was being thrown so high by the roaring fire that it was spilling in every direction. Portland and Salem, as well as the coast towns, were already dusted. If this continued, they'd be grayed over in the next day or so.

"We've got about three hundred folks on this fire."

"You need to find me another two hundred." She phrased it as an order, completely ignoring the fact that Rick, as the Incident Commander, was her boss.

That drew Steve's attention from the dirty skies back to Carly. They already had all of MHA's smokies and their two hotshot crews in the field. They'd even scrounged up two more flights of smokies and another hotshot crew. Add to that the locals and all of the fire dozers in this part of the state.

Dobson wasn't looking surprised. He was past that and merely gazing down at her speculatively. "And where do you be suggesting I get them? We're already mobbed across state lines." He'd added an Irish

accent that, based on his looks, he could well have
come by naturally.

"Don't care where they're mobilized from. They
won't be anywhere near the fire, so they don't have to
be firefighters. Loggers, power-line guys, tree trimmers,
dozer operators, that's what you need now."

Rick squinted those blue eyes at Carly, then at the
map, then back at her. "And what the hell are they supposed to do?"

"This." Carly took a blue marker and slashed it down
the eastern edge of the Coast Range.

—⁓—

Carly waited for them to see it.

Steve was first, of course. He knew what she was going
to draw on the map almost as soon as she did herself.

While Steve and TJ had been making their markups
about fire and crews, she'd drawn little boxes of each of
the recent clear-cuts where the trees hadn't grown back
yet. They followed a broken line right along the edge of
the state forest.

Rick was nodding his head. Clearly thinking about it
and liking it more with each moment.

"Connect the dots." Steve's comment turned on the
lightbulb for TJ and Henderson.

Then everybody started talking over each other.

She didn't need to participate in what came next. The
three Incident Commanders could take it from here. Carly
rose and grabbed a bag of food and one of the big sodas.

Henderson dropped his tablet computer on the corner
before it curled up, and began making notes.

She snagged Steve's hand and headed down the

runway. It felt so damn good to stretch her legs. For a hundred feet or so, he didn't say a thing. She just tipped her head back and felt the relatively cool air of a midsummer field, one that wasn't on fire and burning the air.

A laugh bubbled up inside her.

Before it could escape, Steve spun her into his arms and his kiss crushed down on her mouth. With those strong arms, he wrapped her so hard against his chest that she couldn't breathe. She couldn't think, couldn't do anything but feel.

It wasn't just a toe-curler.

All on its own, one of her legs wrapped around his hips, pulling him even tighter to her body.

When at last he moved his attention from her bruised lips to her throat, she breathed out on a sigh of the heat that had scorched up her body from the moment she'd touched his hand.

"You know it won't be that easy."

He nuzzled her neck. "Never is." His voice a thrum direct from his chest to hers, his hands exploring down her back and up her sides.

For a moment she hoped that he understood she'd been talking about the fire.

The way he was making her feel, she knew the fire wasn't the only thing that was getting out of hand.

Steve lowered her to the grass runway.

"No. Hold it, Mercer. You are not making love to me in broad daylight right in front of everybody." Then she remembered the two of them lying naked in an old burn with a helicopter hovering overhead. "Okay, you're not going to do it again."

His kiss said otherwise, but he didn't start stripping off her clothes.

Instead, he traced his fingertips down her arm to the paper bag she'd somehow retained through his dizzying kiss.

With a slight pull, he tugged it away and opened it. After looking down at the contents, he offered her another of his smiles that didn't make her feel naked, but rather made her wish that she was.

"So, Ms. Thomas. What are you going to have?" And he folded the bag closed and held it possessively against his chest.

She leaned forward, brushed her lips on his, and idly leaned a hand on his thigh above his injury so that her fingertips slipped along the front of his pants and all the hard heat straining against the denim.

"I'm"—she teased his lips with her tongue—"going to"—she deepened the kiss until she almost lost her direction again, but managed to recover enough to lean back by a whisper—"have this."

She slid the bag from his nerveless fingers.

Carly was halfway through the first burger before Steve recovered enough to pull another one out of the bag.

Chapter 42

CARLY CHECKED THE PLAN THAT THE THREE ICS HAD cooked up. They stood in silence around the picnic table while she inspected their additional markings.

"Tell me."

"If the fire comes this far east"—Rick pointed at Carly's blue line—"they'll have a good chance of stopping it. We'll cut fire lines, as wide as possible, from one clear-cut to the next. As soon as they cut the full line, they'll go back and cut it deeper."

A two-hundred-foot-wide swath along a half-dozen miles. It was a task of impossible scale under any other conditions. But by connecting the old clear-cuts, two-thirds of the way was already cleared. The cleanup and salvage of such a massive amount of cutting could take months, but a hundred percent of the timber would be recoverable instead of the typical ten or twenty percent that might be salvaged from what remained inside the black. In the Tillamook Burn, they'd salvaged almost half of the old growth, just because the trees were so damn big that the core was still usable.

Henderson pointed at the markings he and TJ had added to her blue line.

"We're going to work it in waves from the center out. That way, we can respond more quickly to either the north or south if the fire shifts."

"It sounds solid."

"Good, because we already have the first teams en route. We'll have the crews out and switch in the fire teams if the fire even gets close."

"Based on the forecast"—Carly had brought over her own laptop and checked the latest reports—"the center of the high pressure is going to pass south. That means that the winds will be hammering straight in from the coast. Maybe even a little from the south. Rare for it to come up the coast this time of year, so I'm betting it will be pretty violent. They call the pattern the 'Pineapple Express' as the winds are coming off Hawaii."

"What fun." Dobson found some cold french fries. "By the way, just got a report from the inspection team. You nailed the ignition point. Twenty thousand acres were burned before we even arrived, and you nailed it dead-on."

Carly arched a look at Steve, who merely grinned. When she considered their last midfield kiss, having him as a sex slave might be a more dangerous bet than she'd intended.

"Two vehicles were parked at the end of that fire road." Rick scrounged up a burger somewhere and took a bite. "Down the trail they found a campfire and some tents, crisped up nice. Found a bunch of spent shotgun shells and some personal effects. Source wasn't the fire, but about fifty feet away."

"Firing their shotguns into the woods for the fun of it." Steve felt disgusted.

Henderson nodded. "Fire took off so fast they lost one of the vehicles. The plates had melted, but the VIN on the engine block was still readable. We were able to find the owner. He and his buddies were out for a drunken guys' weekend. That's exactly what they said happened. Even dumb enough to admit they saw the 'No discharge of firearms' warning on the red-alert fire-hazard sign going in."

"It's going to cost them."

Rick's smile was grim but righteous. "Gonna cost them over ten million so far, and we're a long way from done here."

"Damn straight!" TJ looked ready to beat the money out of the idiots.

Carly checked Steve's grin again. He didn't look at all upset at what their bet was going to cost him. She really needed to get her head on straight and figure out what she thought about that.

"Want to go double or nothing?" She wasn't sure what the bet would be, but it might get her either out of or deeper into trouble.

"What's the bet?" Steve smiled down at her in a way that was sparking heat that just might cause her bodily damage before it was done.

"Will you two cut it out?" Henderson was grinning, though. Clearly he'd guessed what they'd bet. "Let's say we get back to it before it costs them twenty million that the Forest Service will never see."

"Let's do it." Steve's voice was enough of a caress that TJ turned to see Carly's reaction, but she couldn't look away from her lover's dark eyes. She couldn't even raise her hands to her burning cheeks.

In minutes they were aloft and back in the maelstrom.

Chapter 43

"MAYDAY! MAYDAY! MAYDAY! HOODIE LITTLE FOUR is hit. Repeat, I'm hit. Going down."

Steve's brain had gone fuzzy. It was late afternoon in a very long day, but the adrenaline of the call snapped him wide awake. The interior of the Firehawk was unchanged. Five more hours of ferrying retardant had done nothing but add some energy-bar wrappers to the trash.

Shaking his head to clear it, he looked at the position of the MD500 on his feed from Beale and saw the drone was close.

He swung the drone north. North. Shit! All he could think was another surface-to-air missile.

Beale called, "Nature of hit?" Her voice was far steadier than his would have been. Obviously she had the same thought.

"Damn tree!" The pilot cursed. Female. Pissed, not scared. "Fire shot a chunk of tree over a hundred feet up when it blew. Damn! And I was having such a good day."

Steve had the chopper on screen, spinning, but not wildly yet. It was in a controlled autorotation, also known as going down fast. She'd flown past the fire and was spinning in the air well over the black. A small, black-and-red four-seat helicopter in the midst of the nightmare world of charred hundred-foot spikes. She needed a—

"Clearing," he called out, then remembered to key his mike. "There's a clearing a couple hundred yards due west."

"What? Where?"

But he could see on the drone's camera feed that the trend line for the tiny helicopter slewed in the right direction even if it kept spinning around. Sometimes backward, sometimes sideways, but still moving toward the only opening among the burned trees that was anywhere close.

"You're coming up on it in," he estimated wildly, "about ten seconds."

"I'm gonna be down in ten."

"You'll do it."

She'd better or she was in trouble. On every side were trees still smoking from the recent passage of the fire. Massive limbless trunks stretched forth, seeking to take out her rotors. Then she'd free-fall the last hundred feet of her life.

It was more of a ledge with a small flat spot above a steeply descending slope, but there just weren't any other options.

"Glad you think so."

"Pretty damn cool operator" was all Steve could think.

Then the tiny chopper flared sharply and fell the last twenty feet hard. Hard, but right onto the center of the ledge. It tipped sideways, downslope, but the steep hillside at the clearing's edge kept the spinning rotor from catching the ground.

After a precarious moment, with the chopper balanced on one skid tottering toward an ugly fate of rolling down the hill with flailing rotors that would ruin the chopper and probably do worse to the pilot, it flopped back onto its skids and remained upright.

"Hoodie Little Four is down safe," the pilot reported. Steve could see the rotors already spinning down. Her voice was impossibly steady, as if she hadn't just had a brush with death. He'd bet she had the shakes pretty good now that she was on the ground.

"Roger. Hawk Zero-one en route."

"Uh, thanks. And thank whoever found that hole. Saved this girl's ass."

"All part of the service," Steve answered, trying to mimic her steadiness of voice. Then he sat back in his chair and stared at the drone's camera screens as Emily flew to the crash site. He rolled back the drone's camera to the moment that the "Mayday" had gone out. While he hadn't caught the hit that damaged the helicopter on tape, he did have a clear view of the camp beneath the trees from that same time stamp.

Nothing. The camp appeared to be completely quiet. So it was just a bad-luck hit by some chunk of tree thrown aloft by the roaring whirlwinds of fire. Steve reported his finding to Beale and Carly over the intercom, then set the drone back to auto-flight.

He'd just saved someone—and saved them in a way he couldn't have done from the ground.

He blinked, trying to make sense of what he was feeling.

One part of him was pretty damned pleased that he'd helped save a life. That's what he was out here to do—douse fires and keep people safe.

But another part of him remembered the guy in the hospital earlier this year. Steve recalled the cripple in the mirror, haggard, leaning heavily on a walker, his emaciated leg dead to his requests to move. He, too, had teetered on an edge, one with a desperately steep fall and a bad ending. But somehow he hadn't gone there.

Instead he'd dug in. Found some inner reserve or determination or something that let him land safe, if not intact.

Despite several attempts, Steve had never been able to trace where that motivation had come from, but it had been somewhere deep. The motivation that had turned him into a model patient. Need stronger arms? He'd worked the Nautilus until he sweat and ached. One leg as good as gone? The other would have to make up for it. Pretty soon he'd shed walker, then crutches, and finally the cane.

He looked down in surprise. He hadn't even thought of his leg in the last forty-eight hours.

"Too damned busy," one part of him said.

"Didn't need to," another part argued. He flexed it tentatively. Sore, but sore from use. Since he'd ditched the cane, it had improved quietly over the last weeks. Because he was using it, or because he'd stopped paying so much attention to it? Perhaps more of the latter. And Carly hadn't appeared to care either, which certainly helped keep his attention on other things.

What he did know was that he'd finally found the thing that had turned him from being a cripple in the mirror to being in the right place to save the chopper pilot a world of hurt. He liked saving people. Way back to when he'd watched a firefighter save Vincent's life when his fellow first grader's house had burned. They'd grown up together as brothers, because neither of Vincent's parents had made it out alive.

So, that's how the change happened. He hadn't seen himself in that hospital mirror. He'd seen a cripple who needed to be saved and set about doing so.

Maybe he'd finally succeeded.

~~~

"Ready to do it again?" Beale asked over the headset.

"Huh? What? Do what?" Steve looked around the back of the Firehawk, but nothing had changed. Except on the screen.

In the drone's eye he could see the Firehawk hovering a hundred and fifty feet above the downed MD500 chopper.

"Uh, you can lift that?"

"Little Four. Tank status?" Beale asked over the radio.

"Dumped on the fire already. I'm light on fuel besides."

"I can lift about six of them with this bird," Beale responded over the intercom.

"Oh, okay." Steve was glad yet again that he'd signed on with MHA. Firehawks were just too damned cool.

"I've got the lifting harness in the back with you, behind the cargo net. You okay going down a few feet on a rope to hook me up, or do I need to go find a clearing?"

"Rope is fine." Steve got moving. First he kicked out the descending line that Kee had used this morning. He checked his watch, she'd been gone over ten hours. He hoped she was okay.

Mindful of Beale's earlier threat, he slapped on a hard hat. They were well inside the black and far from any flames, so he didn't suit up in the full Nomex gear. He wasn't going to the ground anyway. However, not being crazy like Kee, he pulled on the harness with the rappelling brake. After he fished out the head of the lifting harness, he sat on the edge of the cargo-bay deck in the open side door. A deep breath and he eased his line down.

And almost hung himself.

With a curse, he pulled off his helmet, undid the headset still wired into the helicopter, and tossed it back into the cargo bay on his seat before reattaching the helmet's chin strap.

Sliding a little lower, he got to where he could reach the harness hook in the middle of the retardant tank and got it snapped in.

That's when he realized his mistake. Again he hadn't attached himself to the winch. Getting back into the cargo bay was going to be supremely difficult. The rope was too thin to climb barehanded, and once again he'd forgotten to pull on gloves first.

He looked back up at the lip of the cargo deck so irritatingly close.

Carly, headset still in place, stuck her head out the door and looked down at him. He could see that she couldn't think of how to help him either.

Down below, the line had plenty of length.

When he saluted Carly, he could see her roll her eyes as if saying, "Not again."

Then Steve slid down to the MD500. The ground was all red. Retardant. It hadn't stopped the crown fire from ripping through here, but by the lack of char he could tell it had minimized the surface burn. These trees, at least, would recover. But, his clothes were still clean, relatively, so he sure wasn't going to touch the ground and get them all sticky red again.

As soon as his boots hit dirt and he freed the

rappelling brake, Carly began pulling up the rope. He stuck his head in the open door of the helicopter.

The pilot still wore her headset. She'd somehow squished herself around in the tiny cockpit so that she slouched deep in the pilot's chair and her boots were up on the windscreen, heels resting on the top of the center console.

"Hi. Need a lift?"

She laughed and held out a hand which he shook, strong grip in black fingerless gloves. "Dude, that was sweet. How the hell did you see this little clearing in all… Wait, you're the drone guy. Merks." She grabbed a handhold and leaned over backward out her side of the cockpit, looking up into the roaring downdraft of the Firehawk hovering a hundred feet above. She dangled practically upside down with her booted feet still atop the console.

Good legs in tight-fitted jeans. Nice butt. And an oversized Goonies T-shirt, hacked off at the waist, that had slid up far enough to reveal a well-muscled midriff and the lower curve of generous and braless breasts.

Then she popped back up and grinned at him. A face like an elf, narrow and laughing. Bright red hair.

"Hi, I'm Jeannie. Jeannie of the bright-blue hair."

"Uh, your hair's red." She made him feel a beat slow. He'd just walked into some setup and hadn't even seen it coming.

Her grin emphasized it was her point won and she knew it. "But it *was* bright blue. That's the point. So how high is your drone?" She didn't even leave breaks between her words. She leaned back out to inspect the sky again and he did his best to ignore the view.

"Six thousand feet up." That popped her back up to a seated position.

"A mile up and you can see shit. That's frickin' awesome. Saved my sorry behind."

Steve heard a clunk on the outside of the bird. He pulled his head back outside and looked up. Between Carly and Beale, they'd gotten the harness lowered. He checked the lie of it, then began snapping the clips onto the little helicopter's lift points.

Jeannie of the bright-blue hair had climbed out and was trying to hook up the other side, but she was having problems.

Steve came around to see if he could help, careful of the steep drop-off mere feet from her side of the chopper.

"Damned fingers aren't working." She wasn't able to open the gates on the lifting clips. It was the first sign that he'd seen she had nerves. Miss Cool and Collected had been shaken right down to the core. Staring down that slope as her broken helicopter teetered over the brink would have unnerved him too.

He snapped them in for her.

"Uh, thanks."

He circled back around and was just about to climb aboard when the forest floor at his feet moved and rose up before him. Steve wasn't sure if he cried out as he fell over backward. His butt landed in a puddle of not quite dry retardant.

Kee Stevenson stood above him in her carefully tattered camouflage, looking down at him as if inspecting an ant.

Jeannie crawled across seats and stuck her head out the passenger side of the cockpit to also look down at him. One cute redhead, one shocking soldier dressed like a green-and-brown alien and still carrying that long, long gun mostly shrouded in ragged burlap cloth. Both stared down at him where he lay on the forest floor, the retardant now squishing through his pants and soaking his butt.

"He's cute." Jeannie's observation.

"Not my type, but yeah."

———

Back at the Skyport base camp, Beale lowered the chopper carefully. Jeannie called the distance to ground. "Twenty, ten, five, slow, contact. Down."

Kee jumped out of the chopper almost before they were down and headed over to the stack of pizza boxes someone had set on the table.

Steve helped Jeannie free the harnesses, though her nerves had recovered during the flight back to the Skyport. By the time they had it clear and the Firehawk was settled beside them, the shadows spilled sideways across the airfield. Last flights of the day. Whatever happened for the next nine or ten hours was up to the crews on the ground.

Jeannie was taller than she'd looked slouched in the pilot's seat. Her legs were longer and her waist slimmer. She'd ripped off the lower third of the T-shirt so it left a few inches of that trim waist showing above her jeans, which only emphasized the power of her curves.

Then she shattered the illusion. She pulled off her headset and pulled a baseball hat out of her back pocket. A blah-blue hat with the white "LA" logo of the Los Angeles Dodgers on it.

"I have to despise you now."

Jeannie stood grinning at him, hipshot, hands in her back pockets definitely emphasizing her fine form.

"Any particular reason?"

He tapped his temple and she looked up at the bill of her own hat, then grinned back at him.

"Giants fan, huh? Then where the hell are your colors, man?" She flicked an idle finger against the brim of her hat.

Steve turned just in time to see Carly slide up beside him and wrap an arm around his waist, hat in place.

Then she jerked back—"Eww!"—and looked down at her red-stained arm. "What is it with you and retardant, Mercer?"

"Can't get enough of the stuff." He did manage a quick kiss before she scooted back.

Jeannie was looking at the black-and-orange hat on Carly's head. Steve couldn't stop the smile. Double whammy on Jeannie's low-life Dodgers. Steve's girl was wearing his team's hat. "His girl." He liked the sound of that a whole lot. Even if she wouldn't touch him at the moment.

Jeannie aimed a cocky grin at Carly. "Damn, girl. You snatched up a good one before I even saw him." She made an elaborate pout before moving to inspect her helicopter.

Beale was already there.

Steve could see that the rear rotor had its blades snapped off and the lower fin of the tail section had crumpled up at a strange angle. Something had hit it good and hard from the bottom up. Not a missile. Still it was a miracle she'd landed the thing at all.

Beale and Jeannie settled in and started talking. Henderson delivered Tessa to Emily, and the three—four, counting the sleeping child—stood there bonding over their helicopters.

Steve turned for the pizza, but Carly waved him off.

"Shower truck is over that way, Mercer. I'll get you some clean clothes from your kit."

"Gonna scrub my back?"

"In your dreams, Mercer. In your dreams. And definitely not your butt."

He watched Carly head toward the barn where they'd all tossed their gear. A quick glance back at Jeannie, competent, confident, sexy enough to light a room on fire. Jeannie would definitely have been his type just a short while ago.

But his eyes returned to Carly. Quiet, forthright, and driven as all hell. And Steve knew one thing for sure.

Henderson was right. There was no way he was going to let Carly get away.

Chapter 44

STEVE DIDN'T MANAGE TO ENTICE CARLY INTO THE shower. Which was actually just a nozzle on a water truck backed up against the woods. The water hadn't warmed up in the least since they'd pumped it from some subglacial stream, so he was done the instant that he stopped flowing red.

"You missed a spot."

He spun to see Carly leaning against a tree a half-dozen paces off. "What are you doing there?"

"These." She waved a handful of clean clothes at him. "And admiring the view. You missed a spot here." She slapped her right backside.

"Come on over and clean it for me."

She smiled at the tease, but not much. So Steve turned the freezing hose back on, palmed some soap, and scrubbed the last of the retardant off.

He took a towel from the top of the stack on the truck's bumper, not big enough to cover anything, but at least he wouldn't soak his clothes when he pulled them on. When he was as dry as the little piece of cloth was going to get him, he moseyed over to Carly. Considered pinning her against the tree and seeing just what they could do, but she was holding out his underwear. The look on her face was quiet and a little distant.

He took his clean underwear.

—◦◦◦—

Carly was definitely feeling short of breath as Steve pulled on his clothes.

His naked body did things to her blood pressure that Linc's had never prepared her for. It wasn't just the fine muscle tone, nor the innate maleness of everything Steve did, every move, every gesture. Even in the little time she'd known him, looking at his body filled her mind with a thousand images.

The goofy expression as he, all unsuspecting, stepped off into the deep hole in the Rogue River to free her line. Or the look of desperate need when she thought she'd be dunked deep into the waters of the Payette and had instead landed deep in one of the best kisses of her life.

Steve casually dropped chaos into her neatly ordered routines. From spewed gravel to sex in the sunlight. She'd bent or broken every relationship rule she'd created to protect herself. Steve was a wild card and everything about him was fast. Mercury "Merks" Mercer, indeed. It did fit him.

He made a show of taking his clothes from her hands one piece at a time, demonstrating reluctance as he stepped into a clean pair of jeans. Flopping his shirt over one shoulder, rather than pulling it on, so that she could see the little remaining drops of water that outlined his chest and arm muscles.

She met his eyes, dark with the shadows.

And he had said he loved her.

Carly had seen how he looked at Jeannie, but something inside her didn't turn that into doubt, despite the woman's undeniable sex appeal. How could she doubt the way Steve looked at her, the way he made her feel? Even now, he was so in tune with her mood that he stood unmoving. So close she could feel the heat from his bare chest, but far enough away that she could easily step clear if she wanted.

How many women had he swept off their feet with that perfectly balanced sensitivity to mood? That ability to hold what she knew must be raging desire, as she felt it herself, in such perfect control?

She was in terrible danger here and couldn't move a single muscle.

Steve reached out to brush his hand down her cheek, and she knew she'd be in his arms a single heartbeat later. If only she knew whether that was the smartest or the dumbest thing she'd—

"Unless you two want an audience, you need to move deeper into the woods." Kee stood by the hose, most of her camouflage gear stripped off. Now she wore just panties and a tight tank top, both army green, that hid absolutely nothing. Her face, neck, and hands were still green-and-black painted. She had a piece of half-eaten pizza in one hand and a bag of fresh clothes in the other.

"'Course"—she turned her back on them and peeled off her tank top—"I never cared much one way or the other who was watching. Makes my husband, Archie, a little crazy, but he's loosening up."

Carly dragged Steve away before Kee got her underwear off. Sure, he'd followed her instead of Jeannie, but there was no point in needlessly tempting the man.

Chapter 45

THE DINNER CONVERSATION AROUND THE PICNIC TABLE stayed focused on the fire. As sunset progressed, a Coleman lantern was fired up at either end of the table. The plastic-coated map from the afternoon now sported many more notations, an expanded fire except on either flank of the northern leg, and several pizza-grease spots.

That north front was worrying. Their chances of stopping it from crossing and closing Highway 6 were decreasing hourly. At this point, it would be only two miles wide when it crossed rather than the original five-mile swath it had threatened to cut. But it wouldn't be good either way.

Steve had tried a couple of times to ask Kee what she'd seen, but after she ignored him the first time and Henderson cut him off the second, he shut up.

Damn it! It had been his drone they shot down. He had a right to know what she'd found. It took him a while to overcome his grumpy mood. Once he finally did, he began to see what was happening.

Kee faded into the background, settling into one of the small lawn chairs at the edge of the light. Her interest in firefighting tactics was clearly somewhere below cleaning the last of the camo paint from under her fingernails. That she used the tip of an alarmingly long knife to do so made him give her all the space she might want.

Rick doodled down one edge of the map while offering thoughts aloud that Carly and the two ICs pushed back or modified. Finally, TJ made a dozen radio calls back and forth with Akbar the Great and a couple of the hotshot crews. They shifted some of the attacks a bit. But, until the winds hit tomorrow, they were mostly guessing.

Evans showed up with a report of how many gallons of retardant they'd dumped from both the helispot across from Elk Creek campground and the air tankers out of Hillsboro. Any normal fire would be showing some sign of forgiveness for all this work, but the New Tillamook Burn, as this fire had been inevitably dubbed, showed no signs of abating.

Steve had landed the gray-box drone, given it a full systems check, refueled it, and gotten it back aloft before the night closed in. He wished he could change out the bird, but the other gray-box drone was scattered in a thousand little pieces over the northern Tillamook Forest and the black-box one didn't have the endurance to fly through the night. SkyHi promised a replacement delivery by tomorrow.

Kee still hadn't drifted away, despite the strategizing, and now sat in total darkness. She remained just slightly faded into the background, exactly as she'd been two hours earlier. Except with cleaner fingernails.

Still waiting. Motionless.

Steve looked around the table. Most people had drifted off, some hoping for sleep. Rick said his good-byes and dragged TJ back to Hillsboro Airport. He was still limping, but no cane. Henderson had his daughter asleep in his arms.

Steve hadn't ever thought about having kids, but the

idea of a little Carly curled up in his own arms wasn't as repellent as it would have been just a year ago, hell, just a week ago.

He'd said he loved her. He'd actually said the word, not one he'd used for anyone other than his mom.

Did that mean that the word "marriage" wasn't far behind? It hadn't worked for his mom, but it was clearly working for Henderson and Beale. They sat hip to hip on the bench. Jeannie was parked close beside Beale. It was like she, too, was in love. When he focused on their conversation, he could hear them going back and forth about angles of attack, velocity-based dispersion rates, and cyclic back pressures. He was wrong. Jeannie didn't love Beale, though there might be some worship there. It was that they both loved flying helicopters.

When Evans wandered off to make sure he had enough retardant inbound for the next day, Steve understood that he, Carly, and Jeannie were the outsiders here. Henderson, Beale, and Kee weren't going to talk until the three of them were alone.

As much as he hated not being in the know, he started to rise. He tried to pull Carly along, but she resisted. She too clearly felt the need to know what Kee had found in the north woods, if anything.

Henderson waved them back to sitting. Steve started to feel relieved, right until Henderson shifted into that serious mode of his.

He pointed at the three of them one by one—Jeannie, then Carly, then Steve. He felt as if he'd been stabbed in the chest when Henderson's attention reached him.

"You three are civilians. Do I need to lecture you about what's going on here?"

Steve started to shake his head but decided he'd better just listen for once.

Carly slipped a hand onto his thigh and held on as she leaned forward. "I don't think so, but why don't you give us the short version anyway?"

Steve noticed that Kee was moving back to the table. He scooted down so that there was space beyond Carly. Carly kept her hand on his thigh as she moved with him, and he covered her slender fingers with his own hand.

Now there were just the six of them, some empty pizza boxes, and a lot of half-empty bottles of water.

"Okay. You know that Mount Hood Aviation flies under two contracts. We contract with the U.S. Forest Service in a firefighting capacity and have done so for almost fifty years. You were also told, when hired, that another arm of MHA flies transport flights for the CIA, an operational holdover from the purchase of the Air America assets after the Vietnam War. This is all public knowledge. Or close enough. Right?"

Steve found himself nodding with the others. But he knew there was another shoe to drop. Carly's fingers tightening on his thigh, only confirmed the conclusion.

Kee made a point of poking through the pizza boxes until she found one with several slices of Hawaiian. She took one casually and then turned to set the empties on the lawn chair she'd previously vacated. It was only as she turned back that Steve caught what she was doing, surveillance of the immediate area to make sure they weren't being overheard. When done, she nodded to the Major who just barely acknowledged the gesture.

"Everyone welcomes firefighters. U.S. wildland firefighting forces have served in well over fifty countries.

Our big air tankers have entered almost a hundred countries to fight wildfires."

"We know all this," Carly cut in. Of course she
would. She'd been around MHA since she'd been
born, so she knew all these nuances that Steve was
just discovering. The paperwork he'd signed had been
about security clearances, not about mission profiles.
Transport for the CIA. He'd heard the rumors but never
really credited them.

"There's a third contract. One under which Emily and
I were brought aboard."

That stopped Carly. Something she didn't know
about MHA. Steve paid closer attention.

"There are conditions," Henderson resumed when he
was sure of everyone's absolute attention. "Conditions
where insertion of operational assets into a political en-
vironment can be very difficult. We, however, can arrive
under the firefighting umbrella and, ah, pursue another
agenda as needed."

"But that's..." Carly started but went silent.

Steve knew what she was going to say. Crazy. Crazy
and dangerous.

"Up there"—Henderson pointed to the northwest—
"someone is sitting on U.S. soil with a Russian-made
missile. While this wasn't anticipated, this is well within
the purview of MHA's new third contract. So..." He
reached down the table and snagged a piece of pizza
without disturbing the baby asleep in his arms.

"The question is, are you ready to cross over?"

Chapter 46

"CROSS OVER TO WHAT?" STEVE STILL DIDN'T GET IT.

Carly saw it but didn't know if she liked it. She'd trained to fight fires. It's what she did. She didn't want to get wrapped up in politics or any other nonsense.

"Slow on the uptake there, Giants boy." Jeannie answered Steve's question. "I knew the Giants sucked, but I didn't know their fans were as stupid as their teams."

"Like you LA freaks could hit a ball if we slow-pitched it to you."

"Talk, Giants boy. Nothing but talk."

Steve grabbed the bill of the hat that Carly was still wearing and pulled it down, dragging her head forward in the process. She could feel him tapping the silvery signatures on the brim.

"See here."

"Sure, looks like a bird pooped there." Jeannie was laughing at him.

"World Series 2012. Zito, Bumgarner, Vogelsong, and Casilla. Winning pitchers in four straight. They'd have whupped your sorry asses, but, wait, you weren't there. So we had to whup on Detroit instead." Steve was practically crowing, and Jeannie was looking bummed.

Carly liked her. She flaunted but didn't play the field more than any other cute girl. She'd hooked up with Evans for much of last season, been flying solo for most of this one, which had depressed Evans no end.

That gave her an idea. Carly pulled the hat free from Steve's grip, letting her sit up straight again, and slid it off her head to study the signatures.

She winked quickly at Jeannie, then asked Steve, "So, I got from the SF that this is San Francisco. But is this is a baseball team… Or maybe basketball?"

Steve and Henderson both groaned in pain as Jeannie crowed with triumph.

"I'd been meaning to ask," Carly added, driving another nail in Steve's coffin. She'd thought to hand the hat back to him, holding it like a dead mouse, but he looked so distressed that she pulled it back on and dragged her ponytail through the back hole.

Then she hooked a hand behind his neck and kissed him solidly on the mouth. She could feel his smile returning before she pulled back.

The kiss won them a little round of applause, and a smile and wink from Jeannie. But Kee had remained dead silent. Unmoving beside Carly. She could feel the woman's stillness.

"Okay." She cleared her throat. "Okay. So if we 'cross over' as you say, what does that mean?"

"See the people at this table?"

"Duh," Jeannie said, saving Carly from making a similar observation.

"Around this table is the circle of knowledge. If you cross over, you can never talk about it with anyone who isn't sitting here. In SOAR we call it black-in-black. Some fire marshal shows up with questions, you know nothing. An Army general tries breathing down your neck, no dice. Someone appears with a photo of you at the scene, you swear under oath in a court of law that it was Photoshopped. Want to impress a new boyfriend? You better not be talking about any third-contract action. Or even the existence of a third contract."

Henderson inspected each of them again. "This is your moment. Walk away and take some of this damn pizza with you, or stay and cross over."

Carly stared not at Henderson's steel-gray eyes, but at the brilliant blues of Major Emily Beale, retired. A woman who had clearly loved what she did and left it to bear her daughter. This was a woman who flew into danger because someone had to and she was qualified to do so, perhaps one of the most qualified on the planet.

And Carly was being asked to choose whether she wanted to fly with someone who was the very best.

Beale didn't respond. She didn't offer any answer, neither encouragement or "go away, little girl." She met Carly's inspection with an absolutely neutral expression.

Steve squeezed her hand where it rested on his thigh. He'd made his decision. He was in if she was, out if she wasn't. She didn't want to be responsible for both of them. It wasn't her decision to affect two lives rather than just her own. Yet who would she want to fight fire with more than Steve Mercer? He'd faced down his own injuries to return to the fire. He hadn't hesitated in saving TJ's life. He'd been out of the chopper before she'd even thought about the idea, breaking the first firefighter's rule of safety to save another.

Carly looked at Jeannie.

"Oh." Jeannie waved a negligent hand. "I'm so there." Dragged her fingers across closed lips, tossed aside the key, made a crisscross over heart, spit in her palm, and held it up for someone to high-five. No one took her up on her offer as she actually had spit. It glistened in the light of the camping lanterns.

Carly turned back to Emily Beale. This was the woman she wanted to fly with, wherever it led. She understood why Kee had saluted Emily differently, why she'd been in such awe of receiving the compliment this morning.

Carly's slight nod of agreement was returned by just as small a gesture.

She felt as if she'd just stepped off a very high cliff.

And as if she'd never earned such high approval before in her life.

Chapter 47

"ALARMS, HERE, HERE, AND HERE." KEE'S FINGER INDI-cated points along the three fire roads nearest the olive slice she'd let fall on the map, at exactly the point where the attack on Steve's drone had originated.

Carly noted that Kee made no notations on the map. Nothing written, nothing where others would see it. Maybe Kee remembered the shape for fortifications the way Carly could remember the shape of a fire. She tried thinking of it that way and found it easier. Burn lines, here and here.

"Trip alarms on deer trails." She ticked off six more places. "I expect the same pattern around the north, but I didn't waste the time checking."

Henderson nodded.

"MRUD line starts at two hundred meters out."

That snapped Henderson's attention from the map to Kee's face. "MRUDs?"

"Well laid, too. Not just the trip wire. They laid pres-sure antipersonnel mines beneath the trip wire so that you'd blow yourself up while trying to back-trace it to the main weapon."

"Ah…" Steve held up a hand like an uncertain boy in class.

"M-R-U-D," Henderson spelled it out, "is a directed-fragmentation mine, like our M-18 Claymore. You know, in the movie *Predator* when Schwarzenegger sets those bent green mines in a circle around their camp. Like those. They'll kill or disable thirty percent of your force at fifty meters, about a hundred and fifty feet. The fact that they also put mines beneath the trip wire means that we're probably dealing with professionals, not just some jokers with a still."

"Oh. Ah. Thanks." Steve lowered his hand.

Carly sat there trying to swallow and not succeeding.

"Don't worry. We're not going to send you walking in there."

Steve made a sound between a cough and a laugh. "Good. I appreciate that."

"Me, too." Jeannie looked far more subdued than she had a moment before.

Henderson turned back to Kee. "Is this what I think it is?"

Kee shrugged. "I called Archie. He said hi, by the way, and he had a chat with Frank, Peter's buddy."

Carly had figured out that when they said Peter, they were talking about the President of the United States. So, Kee had called her husband who'd had a "chat" with one of the President's advisors. What the hell had she stepped in?

"This camp isn't on his list," Kee continued. "But it's definitely a terrorist training camp. I saw nineteen individuals in full camo. AK-47s, M-16s, handguns, lots of ammo and targets. Didn't see any SAMs, but I'm sure they're your source."

"Terrorist camps on U.S. soil?" Carly found her voice finally. "In Oregon?"

Kee just shrugged. "Couple dozen that Frank knows about, most of them back East and in the South, couple in California. Protected by the Constitution as long as they don't hurt anybody. Of course, what they're doing is training to hurt people. Makes you kinda love and hate our country at the same time, doesn't it?"

"What I don't understand"—Emily spoke for the first time—"is why did they fire at the drone? Without that, we'd never have known they were there."

Henderson nodded in agreement. "That's the only thing that I can't make sense of."

Carly was still back on the white-hot fear of a camp of legally sanctioned terrorists in the depths of her forest. She'd studied the Tillamook Burn. Knew the first word and last on what had worked and failed in the four historical firefights: crown fires that blew over firebreak after firebreak, ground fires that reignited behind the crews, and embers so hot that they refired the black.

It was a wonder that only one person had died. The only thing that had beaten the first Tillamook Burn back in 1933 had been a fogbank followed by the September rains, putting it out three weeks after a logging crew started it by accident. Five hundred square miles had burned in the first fire alone.

How many times had she flown over those woods and pored over the maps, studying the terrain so that she'd be ready if this happened?

"I'm sorry to say, I can probably answer that." Kee put down her pizza and studied her hands for a moment. When she spoke, her voice was soft.

"In the center of their compound is a single body staked out on display. He may have still been alive, but I don't think so. Something had been eating him, feral dogs perhaps. I don't think the folks running the camp were happy with him. I considered putting a round in him as a mercy, but knew you wouldn't want to risk spooking them. I expect he was your shooter, firing without orders." She reached for her half-finished pizza, then appeared to think better of it. "It, ah, wasn't pretty."

Wasn't pretty. Carly was going to have nightmares from even that concise description.

"They didn't appear to be on the move. High alert, yes, but no signs of packing up."

"Steve." Henderson didn't sound surprised, just rock steady.

Carly tried to draw strength from that and the viselike grip Steve had on her hand.

"I need a black-box flight again. This time I want thermal and radar imaging. Everything inside the circle Kee just mapped out. Anything as warm as a mouse, I want its exact location. Radar to show me every bit of metal bigger than a toothpick. Use a band they can't see. And I need to keep an eye up there. The very moment they move, I need to know."

Chapter 48

CARLY WAS ASLEEP UNDER A BLANKET, LYING IN THE back of the Firehawk cargo bay. She'd been exhausted by orchestrating the firefight all day and the intensity of the crossover meeting. Still, she'd managed to stay up with Steve until he'd completed the first passes over the terrorist camp.

Now Henderson and Kee were sitting with Steve in the Firehawk. Beale and Jeannie were asleep somewhere, probably in the barn. They had to pilot tomorrow, at least Beale did. A crew had shown up to look at the little MD. If Steve leaned out of the Firehawk, he'd be able to see their work lights as they removed broken pieces and inspected the rear rotor's drive system for other damage. Jeannie would be going nuts if they didn't have it fixed by morning.

He had the best overlay image he'd been able to build up on the main screen.

"Here's their alarm line." Kee traced it on the tablet and Steve captured the line as an image overlay. "Here's the line of antipersonnel mines." An inner ring.

"My overlook was twenty meters up a tree here, probably one of these."

Well inside the circle of mines. Steve looked at her again. You wouldn't look twice at her on the street, except to admire her. She was his age, short, built. "Pretty" is all any male would register. Not "trained sniper able to penetrate enemy camps wholly undetected."

"There were four guards in well-camouflaged hides inside the mine perimeter."

They'd been so well shielded that he'd had to fly the drone barely two hundred feet above them to pick them out. He'd sent the drone flying a near-silent crisscrossing pattern to map everything.

He'd had to struggle; he hadn't used this part of the software before except for that one day of training. Once he had someone located, he was able to place a follow tag on them. That was normal enough to make it easy to track the whereabouts of fire crews. But the software could also do a trace-and-follow. If someone moved between drone readings, the program would see who had moved and conjecture as to the path of each individual. Anyone in motion left a light trail behind them that faded slowly.

"Twenty-six total," Steve announced.

"A lot of metal in this area." Henderson pointed.

"Kitchen," Kee answered. "Residual heat from the stove or fire."

The area did glow hotter than the other areas.

"More metal here."

"Weapons cache." Kee leaned in, then back as Steve zoomed in on it. "A lot of little stuff, rifles and the like. Enough stacks of ammo boxes, if that's what those are, to shoot up a small city. Looks like they have a couple more SAMs over here along the side. But what's that big guy there? Or is it two of them?"

"If it's radioactive or biohazard, the sniffers couldn't taste it last night." Henderson didn't sound happy.

"Chemical or explosive?"

Steve pulled the readings back up from the prior night

and studied them. He looked at the help menu. Instead of an entry, there was a phone number.

He looked at Henderson.

"Call it."

"It's three in the morning."

"Call it."

Steve had wondered why a phone and headset were built into his control console, and now he knew. Leaving the phone on speaker, he clicked on the number and it was answered on the first ring. Rather than a greeting, he received a recording, "Control-shift-click the reading packet. Enter your pass code and click Submit."

He did so. Within seconds the auto-voice announced, "Packet received. Hold, please."

How civilized that someone had programmed in a "please." It was about the only thing that kept Steve's nerves steady enough to work the keyboard.

"Is thermal image available?" The recording again.

"Uh, yes." That odd delay while voice recognition software waited to see if he'd finished speaking.

"Control-shift-click the image file. Enter your pass code and click Submit." And a few moments after he sent it, "Packet received. Hold, please."

"Hi, mate." An Aussie voice sounded so loud that it echoed in the cargo bay of the silent Firehawk. "Aw, that's a beaut. I haven't seen a FAB-250 in just an age."

"Who..." Henderson wagged a finger at him and Steve stopped. He tried again. "Uh, what can you tell me about it?"

He cranked the volume down, hoping not to wake Carly, but saw that it was too late. Her eyes had opened, though she didn't move from under her blanket.

"This is Russian made. Actually these. Looks like you got a stack of two-by-two here. A kiloton if used all together, figure a quarter of that is casing and such, still make a bloody big bang. Can't tell the era, but I'm guessing old. Love to get up close with this beauty. You see the wedge tail…" Steve didn't but would take the guy's word for it. "Rather than a circular one. Chances are it was dug up rather than purchased new. You see, in 194—"

"Could you"—Henderson cut him off—"give us some idea of the damage radius?"

"Nothing much, each one on its own is just a little girl. Take out your average city block. Useful on a high-rise, too. Used together, if you could get these old ladies to trigger together, pressure wave and fires could take out a small city core."

"Right, thanks."

"Pleasure, mate." And the line went dead.

Steve looked over at Carly and saw her staring back at him. He really wished she'd slept through that.

Chapter 49

"Okay, Steve. Need you to keep sharp today."

Henderson. He couldn't have slept any more than Steve, so how could he sound so damn cheerful? Steve hunched against the cool dawn at the picnic table. His eyes were open, but that's all he could lay claim to.

"We're into the fire Day Three. Winds are coming, and I want you to tell me the very instant anything moves up there in the north."

"Uh." He tried to shift into smokie mode. When jumping a fire, or before that when working hotshot, you got used to sleep deprivation. Sometimes three, even four days between breaks for any shut-eye. Get right into hallucinations and you could still work the line if you knew how. But now he'd be flying two drones and keeping close lookout on the fire and a terrorist camp. That was a different tale.

"Sure," he managed and clambered to his feet. Henderson slapped his shoulder hard enough that Steve almost face-planted in the cold pizza he'd been considering for breakfast. But it looked like a squirrel or something had snuck up on the picnic table last night and stripped off the crusts. Apparently the local squirrel wasn't a fan of cheese or pineapple.

Steve scrubbed his face again, wishing to find some coffee by the time he stopped.

"Here."

He opened his eyes and there it was, Carly's hand holding out a giant cup of coffee.

"Oh God." He took a sip, scalding his mouth. "Oh God, you have to marry me now."

"You better be joking, Mercer."

Steve managed to focus his eyes on her face. Scowl and squint. Didn't scare him anymore, not the way it had those first couple dozen times. It meant she cared.

"Don't know." He took another hit of coffee and almost wept with relief. "We'll just have to wait and see if I'm joking." Actually, he didn't know himself, not for sure.

"Damn you!" But it was a soft curse, mostly under her breath. Then she clearly reset her face with a subject change, gentle smile, normal gorgeous eyes. "Did you get any sleep last night?"

He shoved a hand through his hair, then shook his head sadly.

"You got about three hours," he informed her, and she looked as fresh and beautiful as ever. "Wish you'd had more. Sorry about that. Wind is coming today."

She stood beside him and leaned lightly into his shoulder. They just stood there, waiting for the sun to climb into the sky.

"This one's going to be hard."

That he knew without looking at the ash-filled skies.

Chapter 50

CARLY STUDIED THE PROGRESS AS THEY FLEW TOWARD the fire.

The ground crews had run right through the night.

The northern crews still hadn't managed to close the gap. Every time they squeezed the fire's flanks closer together, the fire shot out to the north, east, and west, squirting a half mile at a time in fantastic leaps that were both beautiful and horrifying.

The west and south crews had kicked some serious ass. They'd somehow played the fire right, firebreaks across where the night's land breezes tended to gather and drive the fire hard, and simple ground work where the winds didn't rip flame from one tree to the next faster than a man could run.

Carly got the air tankers laying beautiful long strips of red retardant on the west and south side in support of the ground work. It took dozens and dozens of runs with the air tankers to back up the magnificent ground effort. The air tankers could lay down a half mile per load a hundred feet wide. They had to cover ten miles of the west edge of the fire and four more across the south. Overlapping passes from both directions, three runs wide.

As the western and southern heads of the fire finished consuming the black, the fire ran head on into a firebreak backed up by trees soaked in retardant. And it died. It fought and struggled, spit and sparked, shot embers into the superheated air hoping for a good little spot fire, for just one spark to catch beyond the human defenses. Then it could roll unimpeded to the sea, not caring about the five thousand souls cowering in Tillamook with the sea at their backs. The Firehawk, 212s, and Jeannie, back aloft in her MD500, tackled the few fires that did flare up in unburned forest.

A pair of Canadair tankers that could scoop water on the run showed up midmorning. Carly got them dowsing the fire directly on the south and west, fifteen hundred gallons every ten minutes. They'd hit the fire, working to knock it out of the crown and back to the ground so that it couldn't jump the firebreak. A few miles' flight to Tillamook Bay, twelve seconds on the water, and they were full and on their way back with another seven tons of water.

With the south and west reasonably secure, Carly turned her attention north and east. Everything that had gone right on two sides of the fire had gone wrong on the other two.

The fire had jumped firebreaks, overrun fire roads, ignored terrain, and generated its own winds so strong that it wasn't toppling trees, it was just ripping them straight out of the ground.

Debris, like that first chunk that had hit Jeannie, flew hundreds of feet into the air.

Air tankers and choppers had to fly high enough to stay out of the chaotic microbursts. When they did spill retardant at that high an elevation, it was almost impossible to predict where it would land, and it definitely landed without the tight patterns and high effectiveness of the western runs.

One local engine company had gotten cut off, their beautiful new quad fire engine on the wrong end of the fire road when the fire crossed it. With Steve providing guidance from the drone's eye view, they managed to find a safe line to hike out. Steve had showed her the footage of the engine going up in flames and finally exploding in a ball of flame when the fuel tanks were breached. Add another seven hundred thousand to the cost of the fire, pretty trivial as they were on the verge of crossing over the hundred million mark on this firefight, not counting lost lumber revenue.

Hotshot crews had held and lost, held and lost along the east. They'd spent more time in retreat last night than in actually fighting the fire. It had played with them, first slicing south, then cutting back north. They'd make a stand and the fire would skip that ridge entirely only to climb and meet on the back side of the next one.

Even the smokies were hitting their limits. Four of them got trapped, with no helicopters or tankers nearby. They had to pull out their foil shelters and hide in a balloon of silvered material the size of their bodies with their faces planted in the dirt as a thunderclap of flame rolled over them.

Carly had to ride out a burnover once in a much smaller fire. Her boots hooked in one end of the elastic, her gloved hands and helmeted head in the other, arms and knees pinning down the sides, trying to make the best seal possible with the ground. The air in the tiny shelter had gone from summer dry to superheated between one heartbeat and the next. She'd dug a hole a foot deep in the dirt and planted her face in it, the only thing that kept the air cool enough not to scorch her lungs.

The hardest part had been staying there. Every instinct was screaming at her to run. The two other firefighters trapped with her had joined in her yelled encouragement from their own shelters until the air became too hot and the fire's roar so loud she'd wondered if she'd ever hear again. Then it was gone. They'd answered her shouts. Then they'd all lain still, giving the land time to cool back to safety before emerging unscathed.

Now, the Firehawk raced toward the scene in silence for three impossibly long minutes before they had a radio contact from the team.

Her chest hurt as if she had just remembered how to breathe again herself when TJ called in the "all okay."

Jeannie ducked her MD500 into some impossibly small clearing and heli-evaced one of them to the hospital for smoke inhalation, but he was okay. He was breathing oxygen from a tank, between telling Jeannie he was just fine, and that he could go back to the fire right now. She knew better than to give in to his pleas. She knew enough not to even let him appeal to the ICs.

The winds slammed in while they were refueling at Cornelius, both the chopper and themselves with sandwiches and soda someone had scared up. The tone of the reports on the radio altered abruptly. They'd scrambled back aloft, half-eaten meals tossed aside and scattered in the rotor wash.

The winds were here.

The squall line hit out of the southwest. It had everything a squall always did—roaring winds, chaotic direction changes, violent microbursts, and wind shears forcing all aircraft out of the zone until it had passed.

It had everything except what they needed most. It didn't have any moisture.

The front had passed south as predicted, but farther south than anticipated. It then curled north up the Willamette Valley. They'd hoped it would gather moisture from the summer ocean, moisture that it could dump on the fire as rain or even fog. Instead, it left its rain in the Rogue River watershed. Then the dynamic low had sent strong winds to gather the achingly dry air of the prairie and high deserts of eastern Oregon, only to swing them over the Tillamook. The relative humidity plummeted, and a dry fire was now struck by a parched wind.

The squall swept upon them like a blowtorch.

Carly closed her eyes so as not to watch for a moment, just one moment while they hovered clear of yet another snarl of wind-driven fire vortices. They'd spent the last two hours doing nothing but helping get crews to safety. The Firehawk spent a half-dozen retardant runs just to open a path for a hotshot crew to a clearing that then let Beale descend and fly them to safety.

The locals were practically drag-racing their fire engines down narrow logging roads to escape. One rolled his command vehicle when a section of the old fire road slid into a creek right in the middle of a curve. At least it hadn't been an engine. One of the 212s did medevac this time, the injured firemen climbing right into the Bambi Bucket dangling a hundred feet below the chopper to be dumped unceremoniously at an ER ambulance apron while the chopper hovered above.

It was a mess and Carly just need a moment's break.

A hundred and twenty thousand acres were already lost. Two hundred square miles of timber burned despite the amassed air and man power. Even if her eastern line held, the minimum loss would be another fifty thousand acres. And there was no question that this wind was about to test her "connect the dots" plan to its limit.

"Carly?" Steve's voice was soft, so soft she almost didn't hear it over the intercom.

"Yeah?" Her voice sounded beaten, even to herself.

"I think you need to see this."

She forced her eyes open and looked down at Steve's tablet now mounted beside her laptop.

"The fire just jumped Highway 6 to the north."

Chapter 51

THEY HELD THE EAST. IT HAD TAKEN EVERYTHING they had, but the line had held. Loggers and housing contractors had refused to leave, even when the exhausted fire crews came to take over. They had ridden their dozers right against the foot of the flames. Two machines had been lost when the crews abandoned the bulldozers before the fire overran them. Over a hundred thousand gallons of retardant and water had been dumped all along the line, beating the fire out of the crown and forcing it to the ground where the engine crews could hit it and hit it hard.

The night was going to be brutal, but they had the Burn contained on three sides.

Steve had the added satisfaction of knowing he'd saved a whole section. He'd spotted a freak gap in the wind with the drone. Carly and Beale had put together some extremely quick work with the Firehawk, a hotshot crew, and the local engine company that had been hiking out. Between them, they'd saved twenty thousand acres that Carly had already written off.

At least saved it for now.

He knew the fire's caprice was not to be underestimated, but for now, a million and a half trees had been saved.

When they landed back at Cornelius, no one had the energy to move. Long after the rotors on the Firehawk had spun to a stop back at the Skyport, Steve simply slouched in his seat.

One last check showed that the fire had slowed after jumping Highway 6. With the squall gone, the winds had died. It was still a couple miles from the terrorist camp, would probably pass to the west of it. And still no sign of change at the camp, though they had to be aware of the fire if only from the ash that was painting the land gray as far as the Canadian border.

He dragged himself to his feet and stepped down. His back ached even more than his leg, and he was too damn tired to stretch either one out.

Through the window of the left-side cockpit door, he could see Carly still slumped in her seat, her eyes closed.

Steve opened the door, freed her harness, and managed to lift her out and set her feet on the ground. She simply wrapped her arms around his neck and slumped against him, her head on his shoulder. He leaned back against the side of the chopper, kissed her on top of the head, and held her close.

"You did good, Carly. No one could have done better. Not even Will Spyrison who was IC on the Station Fire."

He could feel tears running into his shirt.

"It's just exhaustion, honey. It's okay."

She nodded against his shirt but made no other motion. He kissed away her tears as they continued to seep from her closed eyes and relished her warmth spread against him. Of course, his body responded.

"What is it with men?" Carly asked quietly, but didn't move away.

"Warm body, doesn't matter who," he teased her.

"Who or what." A little humor. That was a good sign.

"If it's warm and cuddly, our bodies react."

"So that's all I am, warm and cuddly?" She snuggled more tightly against his chest as if just trying to prove her point.

"You." He rubbed his cheek across the top of her head. "You are Steve Mercer's personal dictionary definition of warm and cuddly."

She turned her face up to his, and the kiss was everything their prior ones hadn't been. It wasn't hunger or need or sex that coursed through Steve's veins. All he could think was how proud he felt to fly with this woman. She'd achieved magic, Flame Witch indeed. She'd broken the back of the New Tillamook Burn. No one else he'd ever fought fire with could have done better.

That she'd turned to him when exhausted to the point of tears, that she kissed him with a tenderness born not of fire but of safety, that's what made him feel so damn strong. If he could protect this woman, if he could be her safe place, he could protect the world. He'd never felt so powerful. Not first out of the plane nor first on the line, none of it. Nothing came close to holding her in his arms.

As she responded, slow and languid, the fire in him didn't flash to life. It burned slowly and deeply.

Steve knew for certain that Henderson had been wrong.

It wasn't that he couldn't risk letting her go, it was that he had to stay with her for all time. He could no longer imagine a life that didn't have Carly Thomas in his arms. His life simply wouldn't make sense without her.

Just last night, he'd been wondering if marriage

to Carly might be on his to-do list someday. A mere twenty-four hours later, he understood. Without her, there was no point in having a list. Without her, all of his struggles to get back to the fire, all those endless hours learning to fly the drones, the thousand or more hours of physical therapy... Without her in his life, it would all be meaningless.

She slid out of the kiss, returning her head to his shoulder and resting there.

He searched the sunset sky for some way to express what he was feeling. To capture it with something as lame as words.

"Go ahead." Her voice was a whisper against his neck. "Go ahead and say it."

"I love you, Carly."

A soft sigh escaped her. He could feel it through his hands upon her back, through her chest against his, as the slightest brush of heat from her breath on his skin.

She didn't answer, but she was willing to hear it.

Chapter 52

THIS TIME, THE SIX OF THEM WERE ALL CRAMMED IN the back of the Firehawk, behind the cargo doors closed to keep out the increasing crew numbers at the Cornelius Skyport. Carly knelt beside Steve where he sat in his control seat. Henderson, Beale, and Jeannie all crowded close, watching the monitors. Kee Stevenson was again in the background, sitting on her pack.

TJ and Chutes had shifted operations over from Hillsboro. Betsy had dragged in a kitchen on a trailer and served them a fiery chili that almost managed to keep them conscious. Smokie and hotshot crews had started rotating out to sleep like the dead for six or eight hours before plunging back in, their first break in days.

Carly had helped Steve get the new gray-box bird aloft, and even now its feed ran on his monitors in the cargo bay.

The south and west were holding strong. The east was good, not strong, but her "connect the dots" plan was holding so far. And Steve was right. Without her doing that, the towns to the west would be gone and the Cornelius Skyport would be burning right now. All she had to do was look west, and she could see the bright light of the fire enraged for being held at bay on the face of the foothills above the town of Forest Grove. But the crews held the line.

Carly did her best not to look at the screens when Steve's drone showed the north.

The only one who didn't look exhausted was Kee. She'd slept through the day while they fought the fire.

Carly could begrudge her that, except she'd had three hours more sleep than Steve last night. It would feel selfish to hold Kee's rest against her and expect Steve not to do the same of her.

"Carly?"

"Huh?" She had to blink several times before she realized that Henderson was talking to her and that she didn't remember a single word. "Huh?" she managed to repeat.

"Steve," Henderson said, eliciting an equally incoherent noise from him, which made Carly feel a little better.

"Bring up the north view."

Steve made a few adjustments, and both screens went blank, then painfully white. A color-test pattern flashed at them. He cursed quietly, scrubbed at his face, then tried again and the image came on screen.

"Here's a live feed of the fire. This is Highway 6." Steve traced a line buried deep in the flames. The fire had slowed now that the squall had passed, burning almost lazily as it devoured its way into a new stretch of forest. They'd had no time or resources to lay in any preparation beyond the highway. The forest here was untouched. And for the next several hours, the crews they needed were passed out around the camp, unable to keep their bodies moving any longer.

"These lines are the flanking ground teams." Carly traced the images on Steve's monitor. "Here's the blackout zone around the terrorist camp. A one-mile radius so that no one walks into it by accident, but you can see we're going to remain well clear of the circle so no firemen will be getting near any mines."

Steve practically snarled at the monitor, "Isn't there anything that we can do about them?"

———◦ω◦———

Steve glared at the circle on his screen. Two miles across, three square miles of booby traps, old Russian ordnance, and a bunch of terrorist crazies.

"The Constitution says they have a right to be there." Kee's voice sounded uncaring. He could almost see her shrug in the darkness.

It pissed him off. But before he could voice it, she continued.

"Besides, if we send in cops or even an armed unit, then we're going to end up shooting a whole bunch of people and they're going to be shooting back. They're dug in pretty hard. I don't mind going in for a peek, but I wouldn't want to take them on without some serious hardware and a couple of platoons of trained troops."

That set him back on his heels a bit.

"They scare me to death." Carly rested her elbow on his leg and propped her head up on her fist. "Every time I think of them squatting out there, I'm afraid of the woods. I don't like being afraid to enter the trees."

"She's right." Jeannie spoke for the first time. "Serious creepitude."

Beale and Henderson remained quiet.

Steve could see they were thinking and not liking the answers they were coming up with. He tried to picture it. A fleet of helicopters raining judgment and death down on people who hadn't technically done anything wrong yet. Worse, they'd be mounting the attack in the heart of a tinder dry forest. They could start a whole second burn. And if someone like Beale or Henderson or Kee was shot down, would the price be worth it?

"Shit." Steve faced Henderson. "You guys really face these decisions every day, don't you?"

"Not every day, and usually they're much easier. Good guy, bad guy is more often clear. They shot down the drone, but that's just a machine. Do we take lives for such an action? Sounds like someone already has been punished for that task. That might scare up a murder charge, if you could prove anything."

Carly had laid her head on his thigh. Steve brushed the hair off her cheek and tucked it behind her ear. She was too tired to have to face this. The fire should be enough.

The fire.

"What?" Henderson must have seen the change in his face.

The answer was in the fire.

"What would happen if they weren't in their camp?"

Henderson shrugged. "We'd sweep them up pretty easy. Question or deport them. Bet the CIA would be glad to take them off our hands. We could also see if we can't hang the murder charge on at least the ringleader so we can lock him up forever and a lifetime. What are you thinking?"

"Carly?" Steve brushed a hand along her cheek.

"Hmm…"

"Carly!"

"Yeah, what?"

"Can we stop the fire before it passes the terrorist camp?"

She blinked herself back from the edge of sleep. Raising her head, she checked his eyes for a long moment, then turned to the monitor.

"Run the last six hours in time lapse."

Steve set it up and they could see the fire jump Highway 6 and roar off into the northern part of the Tillamook forest. The head slowing but growing a bit wider as it burned northward.

"No, there's no way we can stop it that fast. Even if the winds remain favorable, the fire will run a couple miles past the camp along this ridge to the west or the one beyond it."

Steve kissed her on top of the head, then smiled at the others before he asked the question he already knew the answer to. The answer was, not much.

The question was, "How much harder is it to turn a forest fire than to stop it?"

Chapter 53

"Jeannie." Henderson had been handing out orders like candy.

Steve had been sidelined the moment that Carly had answered his question. "Just a matter of fighting one side to a standstill before tackling the other side, especially if the winds continue from the south. Probably what we'd have to do anyway. I was just going to suggest running against the other side first to steer it away."

"Yeah, boss?" Jeannie looked pretty bright-eyed for a woman who'd just flown fourteen straight hours against fire.

"Your bird is rigged for nighttime flight?"

"Sure. But not for night fire. And I'm at my limit for the day, little over actually."

"Fine. Log Kee as the pilot. She's just been sitting on her ass all day anyway."

"Hey," the woman protested in mock anger, but Henderson rolled right over her.

"Kee. Jeannie's going to run you up to Fort Lewis. Tacoma's only about an hour's flight north of here. Make sure this girl gets bedded down somewhere. Then see if you can scare up some folks at the Fifth Battalion. Need a Hawk, preferably a DAP, and a 47. Also bring back two more for your ground team. This is on the QT, real quiet. Try to keep it to folks we know well."

"Nonlethal?"

That brought Steve up short, but thankfully it wasn't up to him to answer.

"Riot gear. Tear gas, rubber bullets, sonics if you can scare them up. But don't come unprepared."

Kee slapped her sidearm. "You won't find this girl bringing a stick to a knife fight."

"I, uh…" Jeannie raised her hand, which slowed Henderson down enough to aim a smile at her.

"I don't have clearance to fly into Fort Lewis. They'll shoot my ass. It would be far less cute with the extra hole in it."

Henderson's smile indicated that he had some thoughts on that. He grinned at his wife, who clearly sent him a warning look to keep his damn mouth shut.

Steve would bet there was a good story there. He was getting to know Henderson well enough that he might find a way to get the rest of that tale some other time.

Henderson cleared his throat and turned back to face Jeannie.

"Kee can deal with the tower from the air, and they wouldn't 'shoot your cute ass' until you were on the ground."

Then Jeannie got a wicked smile. "Can I take the Firehawk?"

"You aren't checked out in it." Henderson's statement brooked no challenge.

"No time like the present." Jeannie had more guts than he would have.

"Forget it."

Jeannie pouted for a moment, until she caught Beale's bland expression. Then she straightened up. After Jeannie looked away, he saw the shift in Beale.

He'd bet good money that Beale would be training her at the first opportunity.

"And what's the Fifth? Who are they?"

"The Fifth Battalion," Henderson ground out, nearing the edge of his patience, which Jeannie blithely ignored. "Belongs to the 160th SOAR, the Special Operations Aviation Regiment, Airborne. It's our old unit."

"Hey," Kee protested.

"She's still there. Doesn't think what we're doing is interesting enough."

"Fire isn't my thing." She shrugged as if she hadn't a care in the world.

"Okay, I'm calling this Operation Pure Heat. Carly, how long do we have until the fire hits this line?" He pointed at the screen.

Only as Henderson started orchestrating the pieces, did Steve see what he was doing.

It was perfect, if the both the fire and the terrorists cooperated.

Chances of that? Even with Carly at the helm, he wouldn't be betting good money just yet.

Chapter 54

THE SMOKIES AND HOTSHOTS HIT THE WESTERN LINE of the fire's northern head at sunrise. To keep out of sight from the terrorist camp, the Firehawk and the 212s delivered all the crews by helitack rather than parachute. They began cutting off the fire's angle of attack foot by foot.

As soon as possible, Carly began bleeding teams off the south and west of the main fire. From her perch in the Firehawk, she directed whole sections of the attack. She set them to clearing a firebreak along a ridgeline two miles north of the camp. It was probably the line she'd have chosen anyway, far enough ahead of the fire to give the ground teams time to cut it deep and paint it wide with retardant.

Henderson kept all air traffic to the north of the ridge, just in case any other trigger-happy maniacs got big ideas. He didn't explain why; he just told the pilots that anyone who disobeyed him was going to get their asses kicked. He said it in that tone that ensured no one asked why they couldn't fly south of the ridgeline.

Jeannie had returned, but she was busy to the north. Henderson was coordinating that part of the battle, though Carly kept him in the loop while she concentrated on the main fire. The battle on the three contained sides was far from over, and there were still half-a-hundred different blazes in different places throughout the black.

Steve had a gray-box drone circling over the main body of the Burn. Carly gave him the 212s to order about, focusing on the south and west spot fires. The 212s hit the spot fires and anything else that his thermal imager turned up as critical.

Carly concentrated on the still-spitting east side and turning the northern head. The Canadair water scoopers kept punching long strips out of the fire's hide, and the east was holding strong.

Several fires threatened to erupt in the black, still plenty of fuel and heat there, but the drone's ability to see the buildup in infrared before it flashed over had to be one of the best new firefighting tools Carly had seen in years.

Her attention kept drifting to his tablet. It wasn't that she didn't trust him. It was that she liked watching him work. You could see his personality in his attack patterns. He didn't fix things; he attacked them. Her own methods were about precision and control — just enough, then move on.

Steve hammered spot fires called in by TJ for the ground teams or Rick. He dumped on them so hard that they never knew what hit them. Then he'd pound them one more time, partly to make sure they didn't even think of coming back and partly, Carly was sure, out of pure former smokejumper spite.

She brushed the edge of the tablet with her fingers, as close as she could come to brushing his cheek at the moment.

Beale looked over at her. She hadn't missed Carly's gesture or its meaning.

"Busted," Carly mouthed. Steve was on the open intercom so she didn't speak aloud.

Beale just smiled at her. A long, slow smile that had nothing to do with fighting fires and everything to do with two women sitting side by side above the fire's heat.

Carly could feel that heat. But rather than rising to her cheeks, it warmed the area around her heart.

Beale looked away, out her side door window, and then, responding to a call from her husband, swung them back for another load of retardant. A hotshot team was embattled on the west side of the northern head.

Carly didn't need to see Beale's face to know that it looked as goofy as her own, thinking about their men who fought fire.

Chapter 55

FOR THE FIRST TIME IN THIS WHOLE ORDEAL, THE WIND and fire cooperated. Once again the sun was setting, the sky turning blood red with smoke and ash.

The fire wouldn't live to see the sunrise. They'd have it fully contained by then. Mop-up could take weeks, but they'd have it trapped but good. There'd be plenty of dousing, monitoring, and cleanup, but when it hit the massive bulwark of their northern barrier, it should be stopped.

Carly checked the full view one last time before the final attack. The locals and Steve had held the west and south clean at yesterday's limits. The east had one bad spot-fire burn, but it only ate a couple dozen acres before they'd killed it. The whole rest of her connected line of clear-cuts had held.

The black was a long way from being fully black, but it was contained. Fires burned here and there, but nothing that could do any real damage, as long as it didn't get away from them again. Where the fire had jumped ridge to ridge, the occasional oasis of green shaded the valley floors. Steve had even shown her a live feed of a herd of elk spared by the fire, nosing out into the edge of the black around their temporary haven.

The New Tillamook Burn was at rest.

Except for the northern head.

There, the last mile-wide head was roaring ahead.

She was impressed they'd managed to narrow it that much. Everything was in place for the final showdown.

With the Firehawk they'd made a couple of strategic hits of retardant at the center of the fire's head directly in line with the camp, about a mile out. They'd flown down in the treetops, only after Steve had validated that the area was clear. Not the best dispersal at that altitude, but it had worked.

The fire had slowed in the center. Not stopped, but slowed. It would come up the sides first, scaring the camp's residents and funneling them straight into the waiting arms of the military's elite helicopter forces. On the run, they hopefully wouldn't have their wits about them enough to bear firearms. Then they could be easily—and relatively safely—scooped up.

Kee and several of her teammates were on the ground to the north of the fire, about halfway to the firebreak to watch for strays and direct the military's actions.

The daytime sea breeze had helped turn the fire toward the camp. Tonight's land breeze would drag the remains of the fire against the western line they'd been cutting and dousing all day. No weather was predicted, so the fire would die against the north and west firebreaks.

After it had overrun the camp.

MHA's only job now was to fly the outer line and wait. The Firehawk and Jeannie's MD500 would pick up Kee's team if something went wrong. Otherwise they'd mount the choppers they'd brought down from Fort Lewis, along with the captives.

Chapter 56

STEVE WATCHED AS THE FIRE APPROACHED.

He needed to remember never to piss off ICA Mark Henderson. The terrorists must be crapping in their pants right about now.

A mile-wide wall of fire was marching down three sides of the ridgeline to sweep right into the camp's valley. Flames rolled a hundred or more feet into the darkening sky.

Sap exploded, shattering trees like a cheap bat whacked on the trademark. He'd stood in the face of a big fire on a rampage any number of times. It was a moment that defined a smokie. Did you face the devil and beat it back? Did you turn tail and run? Or were you so damned sure of yourself that you stood fast until the beast was upon you?

He'd been trained in how to read the fire, and every single thing he could see about this one sent a single message.

Run!

But they didn't.

He had to keep repositioning the black-box bird to see what was happening in the camp, rather than the fire. There was no way they'd be firing at his drone. They had far more important things to think about, even if they could spot him. So he made a couple of high-resolution runs and then sent the drone climbing steeply to get well clear of the abrupt wind shears and fire-driven whirlwinds.

The fire didn't know it was dead. It still burned with a fierce, tree-eating heat. It wasn't being driven ahead by the wind, but rather by the availability of fuel and fresh, oxygen-laden air. It moved slowly enough that it had the chance to thoroughly burn everything it touched. This was a strip of the black that would be a long time recovering.

"They should be moving now." Henderson on the radio. He'd said they'd be using some encrypted signal, so it was okay to talk.

"Nothing." Steve looked at his traces that should show the snarl of people moving about the camp and then turn into long streaks sprinting to the north. They weren't.

The fire was close enough that he couldn't retain consistent tracking of the figures on the ground, especially from his increased altitude.

"They're clustering in the center of the camp." But the software couldn't count them, they were overshadowed by the approaching fire's heat.

"Leaving it to the last minute, don't you think?" Kee from the ground. "Am I supposed to go in and give those gun-happy idiots a red carpet before they singe their asses?"

Steve kept watching. They were too close together to distinguish now, bodies massed in the center of the camp. A cluster of them started for the area where the weapons were stored.

At that same moment, one of the leading tongues of flame reached the perimeter line. Whether the mine burned and fired or a flaming branch dropped on a trip wire made no difference. There was a bright flash as first one mine fired off, then another, then two more.

"Mines are going off along the east edges. They're still milling in the central area. Three, maybe four are going for the weapons store."

"Idiots!" Kee again. She kept swearing for several seconds before regaining control. "Team Three, pull back. I repeat, Team Three, pull back. Re-form in the open clearing a hundred meters from the Chinook chopper. Remain in the clear. Do not stand behind a tree."

Steve couldn't look away as the fire hit the western perimeter, and finally the temporarily slowed central portion of the fire stormed in from the south.

The flashes of the exploding antipersonnel mines was quickly overshadowed by the driving fire.

The figures headed for the weapons store were driven back by the heat.

One, then another, figure broke and ran.

Then, as a mass, they began moving north.

"Hang on, everybody." Steve had been told to warn everyone the moment the fire hit the weapons store.

It took ten long seconds.

Enough time for most of the people to get clear the camp, but even the first runner had barely a hundred yards' lead when the bombs went off.

Chapter 57

FOR DAYS CARLY TRIED TO REMEMBER WHAT THE FIRE-ball had looked like, but she couldn't. The flash had been too bright, the sight too shocking. One moment fire and runners on Steve's tablet and a wall of fire marching across the landscape. The next? Nothing but white.

In that instant, the sky outside the Firehawk's wind-shield had lit like daylight. The evening dark was blasted away for a moment by an impossible brightness.

Beale had them hovering well north of the ridge, placing them two miles from the blast center, and they'd pulled back all of the ground crews as well. For a long moment, the clouds of ash and smoke above the ridge had been brilliantly lit from within, shining like an evil beacon in the falling night.

Then the darkness had returned.

The shock wave arrived seconds later and battered them, despite their distance.

Once it too had passed, Beale had flown the Firehawk to just above the ridge. The SOAR choppers were al-ready sweeping forward. By the time the fire ground crews would arrive, nothing of the camp would remain except for a strange area where all the trees would be blown outward from an unlikely crater over a dozen meters across and a half dozen deep.

The Army's Special Forces teams cleared the few remaining perimeter mines. What little remained of the camp was gathered up, and a long line of body bags was loaded into the big Chinook helicopter Kee had brought down from Fort Lewis.

Oddly, the blast had blown out a whole section of the fire. The thin remaining finger of the New Tillamook Burn had died with little more than a whimper against the northern firebreak.

—◆◆◆—

It had taken eight more long days of mop-up to finally kill the Burn enough to hand it off to the Type II crew. Spot fires, hot spots, and new flare-ups had left the sleep-deprived crew on the run, or rather on the stagger, for a full week before they had it killed. The size of the fire and the roughness of the terrain had made it a back-breaking task to mop up.

The blast had been explained away as an abandoned propane tank, which at least satisfied the newsies who'd seen the light as far away as Portland and Salem.

Carly found Steve where he'd been most of the last two days, when he wasn't asleep in her bed or lying in her arms.

She'd placed two wooden Adirondack chairs on the back deck of her cabin. From here, there was nothing to see except green forest. Doug fir. Hemlock. Larch. They towered above the cabin, sprawling uncut for a hundred years over all of her twenty acres except where the cabin and garden sat.

Squirrels played here. Deer wandered up to the verge to stare at the humans before returning silently into the woods.

Steve pulled her into his lap with that easy strength of

his that made her feel so safe. Carly slid willing into his arms and let herself melt into one of his luscious kisses before resting her head in her favorite spot on his shoulder.

She stroked a hand over the T-shirt that matched hers. The word "Tillamook" flamed diagonally across his chest. "I fought the Burn!" crossed over his heart in blue letters. Water dripped off them and had extinguished the *M* and *O*, leaving them black. It was one of the cooler fire shirts she'd seen. This one she'd keep for a long time.

"Back to it tomorrow." Carly could feel his voice vibrating through his chest. She nuzzled against it as if she could burrow right in like a hibernating bear, all warm and cozy.

He was searching the towering trees. She could tell that he was once again seeking for words to express all of the wonderful things inside him.

"Go ahead," she whispered, leaving a kiss on his neck. "Go ahead and say it."

He huffed out a sad sigh as if sorry that he couldn't offer more.

"I love you, Carly."

The words just melted her every time. She'd never tire of hearing them. And she finally knew what she wanted to say in response.

"I love you, Steve."

There. That was it. Those were the words she hadn't been able to say. Perhaps the problem had been that they weren't her words.

The words were theirs together.

They loved each other. What more could she possibly need?

She lay against his shoulder and let her eyes drift closed. She allowed herself to become lost in the smell of the pine forest, near enough crushed by the strong arms of the man who belonged there with her.

End Notes

The Tillamook Burn was a series of four forest fires. They arrived at six-year intervals as if they could read a calendar: 1933 (caused by a logging operation), 1939 (another logging operation), 1945 (possibly ignited by a Japanese fire balloon launched into the jet stream to drift to America and start forest fires as a last ditch attack during WWII, which joined a second blaze caused by a discarded cigarette), and 1951 (logging again). Three quarters of a million acres burned, which is about 1,000 square miles (just a little smaller than the state of Rhode Island). Due to overlapping areas of the four burns, the ultimate damage covered 550 square miles (almost twice the size of New York City, including all five boroughs, sixteen times Manhattan alone).

A few factors make this fire, or rather series of fires, unique.

In 1933 the Tillamook was the largest standing continuous grove of old-growth forest left in the country. Disastrous burns, some over a million acres such as the Silverton Fire in 1865, had scorched across the Oregon landscape. However, by pure chance, the steep hills and valleys of the Tillamook Burn had remained untouched by fire for almost five hundred years.

The first fire started on August 14, 1933. It was nearly contained in ten days at 40,000 acres. Then a dry, gale-force wind slammed into the 250-foot-tall old-growth forest and the fire spread at three acres a second, burning twenty-one square miles an hour along a fifteen-mile front. To this day, it remains one of the fastest-moving forest fires in U.S. history.

Ultimately 311,000 acres were burned in that first fire, most of that in just twenty hours before the winds died and a fogbank rolled in. Early arrival of September rains finished off the fire on September 5. It had been fought to a standstill by the efforts of more than 3,000 people during nineteen days, surprisingly with only one fatality. The loss from just this first fire of the four has been estimated at 700 million dollars in 2012 currency.

After being turned down for funds by the U.S. Forest Service and other federal agencies due to the project being too big or even impossible, the state and citizens of Oregon took on the reforestation of the Burn in 1948. It was a twenty-five-year effort, but the Tillamook Burn, officially designated the Tillamook State Forest on August 14, 1973 (the fortieth anniversary of the first fire), once again stands tall and filled with wildlife.

And the men and women of the U.S. Forest Service and their contracted firefighters stand ready to protect the trees the next time the fire comes.

For it will come.

Take Over at Midnight

The Night Stalkers

by M.L. Buchman

—∾∾—

NAME: Lola LaRue

RANK: Chief Warrant Officer 3

MISSION: Copilot deadly choppers on the world's most dangerous missions

NAME: Tim Maloney

RANK: Sergeant

MISSION: Man the guns and charm the ladies

The past doesn't matter, when their future is doomed

Nothing sticks to "Crazy" Tim Maloney, until he falls hard for a tall Creole beauty with a haunted past and a penchant for reckless flying. Lola LaRue never thought she'd be susceptible to a man's desire, but even with Tim igniting her deepest passions, it may be too late now…With the nation under an imminent threat of biological warfare, Tim and Lola are the only ones who can stop the madness—and to do that, they're going to have to trust each other way beyond their limits…

—∾∾—

"Quite simply a great read. Once again Buchman takes the military romance to a new standard of excellence."—*Booklist*

"Buchman continues to serve up nonstop action that will keep readers on the edge of their seats."—*Library Journal Xpress*

For more M.L. Buchman, visit:

www.sourcebooks.com

Wait Until Dark

The Night Stalkers

by M.L. Buchman

—⁓—

NAME: Big John Wallace

RANK: Staff Sergeant, chief mechanic and gunner

MISSION: To serve and protect his crew and country

NAME: Connie Davis

RANK: Sergeant, flight engineer, mechanical wizard

MISSION: To be the best… and survive

Two crack mechanics, one impossible mission

Being in the Night Stalkers is Connie Davis's way of facing her demons head-on, but mountain-strong Big John Wallace is a threat on all fronts. Their passion is explosive but their conflicts are insurmountable. When duty calls them to a mission no one else could survive, they'll fly into the night together—ready or not.

—⁓—

Praise for M.L. Buchman:

"Filled with action, adventure, and danger…
Buchman's novels will appeal to readers who like
romances as well as fans of military fiction." —
Booklist Starred Review of *I Own the Dawn*

For more M.L. Buchman, visit:

www.sourcebooks.com